Lasso the Stars

Lasso the Stars

a novel

L.L. Nielsen

TATE PUBLISHING
AND ENTERPRISES, LLC

Published by Tate Publishing & Enterprises, LLC
127 E. Trade Center Terrace | Mustang, Oklahoma 73064 USA
1.888.361.9473 | www.tatepublishing.com

Tate Publishing is committed to excellence in the publishing industry. The company reflects the philosophy established by the founders, based on Psalm 68:11,
"The Lord gave the word and great was the company of those who published it."

Book design copyright © 2011 by Tate Publishing, LLC. All rights reserved.
Cover design by Blake Brasor
Interior design by April Marciszewski

Published in the United States of America

ISBN: 978-1-61346-854-8
1. Fiction / Romance / General
2. Fiction / General
11.10.27

Dedication

For Lillian and Helen, Joan and Penny,
Corral Del Ciello, and the Pastures of Heaven

Prologue

It was a delicate spring day just before the white blossoms would burst from the trees. Five-year-old Dina was sitting in the old apple grove with her friend. She knew when the flower's perfume scented the warm air, the bees would fill the orchard, and she and her friend would have to find another place to play.

Jillian, Dina's older sister, had told her that she was just a baby, even more of a baby than their little sister, for actually thinking she had a make-believe buddy, but Dina knew better. Her friend had never had a name, yet they'd known each other forever.

The little boy was different today. His scruffy overalls were pressed, and his curly hair had been combed into submission. She felt uncomfortable with his new neatness and began to talk too fast.

"Oh boy. This is the year I get to start kindergarten. Mom said I go in the fall. But baby Rachel can't go. She's too little, really too little. Will you go with me? Please?"

"Nope. I can't go with you there." He pushed his legs out in front of himself and rocked back on his hands.

"How come?" Dina sensed a woeful feeling surrounding him.

He glanced at her and muttered, "'Cause I'm moving."

"Where to?"

He smiled. "You're going to meet lots of kids now, and you'll forget about me." In between the green leaves, the sun danced around his head, leaving a halo of brilliant sequins.

Dina had seen this before and remained unimpressed. She sulked. "You can't go till I say it's okay. That's the rule. Remember, we made that rule?"

The little boy looked forlorn as he nodded his head. "I'm really sorry, Dina. I didn't know we couldn't always be together like this, but I'll be around, looking out for you."

Dina crossed her chubby arms across her chest. "That's not fair. You're making me mad."

From behind his back, the boy picked up a shiny red apple. "This is for you." He pushed the apple into Dina's hand. The wind swayed through the old apple tree, and the boy listened intently. "My brother's calling me. I've got to go now. I have a lot to learn too. Just like you, Dina."

Both children stood up, Dina holding the apple and her friend immersed within his shimmering halo. They clasped hands and left the shade of the tree. Then he was gone, and Dina was alone.

Chapter 1

Oaks grew in the gentle creases along the dry country lane. I walked slowly, savoring the gold-leafed days of autumn. I headed toward the old, wooden fence that bordered the edge of our property and wondered how many times I had passed the timeworn gate without a thought of its countryside charm, yet I'd always been aware of its existence. It was clearly visible from the top of our drive and had played a part in my life on numerous occasions. The gate led to the old ranch where Jillian would take Rachel and me to feed the horses when we were little girls. I'd also sorted out teenage dilemmas on the front porch, even after the owners had moved and the property was boarded up. *Well, that's life for you*, I mused. *Nothing lasts forever.* Best I could do was tell myself that the gate now led to a rented pasture where cattle, or maybe horses, still grazed in pure contentment. Yes, I liked that.

Honestly, I thought, throughout my life, I must have just coasted, involved in my own private world. So many events had gobbled up my attention that I hadn't time to think about the fate of that old ranch. My mind paused in mid-thought. It was funny that it now seemed important. I tossed the notion away as if it were a residue of an idea, left over from too much medication still swirling around in my brain.

The empty road stretched ahead of me, and I thought that somehow a sliver of my essence would always remain after I was gone, charged with the responsibility to sort out my life's fate.

A deep breath and a fragment of a smile crossed my face. I refused to be sullen while the sun was beaming in a perfect sky and I was still able to walk. I rounded the bend in the road, and a sudden movement drew my eyes toward the old, wooden gate, where a man sat, his long legs angled comfortably over the weathered fencing. I felt myself embraced by a quick flutter of the future, and even though I couldn't put it into words, I no longer felt so alone.

The man was watching a cat gracefully pick its way across the old boards, slowly meandering toward him. Drumming his fingers, he indicated it should come closer; but being a cat, it stopped where it was, sat down, and looked at him. I smiled, thinking of the many barn cats that had filled my childhood with just such antics. A slight breeze pushed past my face, and I glanced toward the man. It was strange that I hadn't noticed him earlier because I could see the gate from the top of the hill and on a couple of the turns in the road. *Oh, look here!* my inner voice sounded off. *I do believe you also missed the horse. That's the animal behind the man.* I couldn't help but think that maybe Rachel was right—if I wasn't paying attention to what I was doing, I shouldn't be out walking alone.

I shook my head. *Well, the man and horse didn't just vaporize out of moist air, and neither did the cat.* I must have overdosed on the pain meds that morning, so I was still foggy. Yet I felt fine; a bit tired from my walk and certainly dusty from the dirt road, but overall I was okay. As long as the man and his companions were there, I'd better say hello.

A cowboy hat pulled low across his forehead revealed nothing of his features as he turned to speak softly to the horse at his side. The sounds of the day became muted when I realized I was listening intently to the tone of his voice. Without warning, fanciful thoughts swept through my mind, and I realized I was smiling to myself. What was the matter with me, having romantic notions about a handsome stranger and knowing full well that I had limited time to pursue any type of relationship? How dare I permit such foolish ideas to enter my head! My main concern rested with my sisters and my responsibilities to them and to myself. I clearly had no time to spare for anything else. *There,* I said out loud in my mind, as if I'd put an end to my feelings.

But instead of using good judgment, I stopped abruptly. Bending down, I fumbled with the ties on my old sneakers. Without reason, a flush of happiness swept across my face, turning into a full blush. *One quick glance at him,* I told myself, *and then I finish my walk.*

"Hey, how y'all doing?" His voice was low and carried a slight drawl.

I kept my head down, hoping the blush would pass before I had to face him with an answer. But the cat would have none of that. Leaping from the fence into a pile of crunchy leaves, he created enough activity that I forgot my blush and lifted my head.

Tossing autumn foliage in all directions, the feline picked himself up with great dignity. As he strolled past me, his sun-warmed fur brushed against my hand, and for a moment, his green eyes held mine. Happy memories circled around me.

"Dang cat." I sensed a note of humor in the man's words. "Butch, mind your manners some," he continued in a pleasant tone. "Don't go jumpin' around and causin' a ruckus, now. You hear?"

The cat ignored the man, blinked at me, then scampered off. I watched as he disappeared into the tall grass, intent on his next destination.

I brushed off my baggy sweatshirt and inhaled deeply as I stood up.

The stranger waved at me. "Hey."

My response blew out unexpectedly with a rush of air. "Hi." Immediately, I chastised myself for sounding silly but managed to hold my hand up in what I hoped would pass for a greeting.

"Don't you go payin' no never mind to Butch there. He's just playin' some, tryin' to show you what an agile fella he is."

The man had an easy-going smile. A pair of aviator sunglasses rested on his nose. His dusty Levi's covered long legs that ended in well-worn cowboy boots. For the first time in weeks, I thought of something other than my illness.

He stepped down off the gate and held his hand out. "Gil." I immediately noticed how tall he was. I reached toward him, feeling his firm clasp and calloused fingers. He released my hand, nodding toward the country lane. "I've seen you walkin' here and figured it would be neighborly to say howdy-do."

"Right." I hadn't heard of any new folks moving in, and he clearly was a person I would have remembered. "Are you new to the neighborhood?"

He tipped his head toward the gate. "Been settlin' the horses for a while. Bunkin' at the old ranch."

"The old ranch is nice. Been awhile since anyone's lived there." Not knowing what else to say, I nodded. "Well, welcome to the neighborhood." I began to look for the cat. I was pointing toward the side of the road where Butch had disappeared. "I've had cats, and they're, well…" I expressed my amusement with a sheepish grin. "Well, I like them." My hand still felt faintly warm where Butch had nudged against me. "They're funny and…" I tried another deep breath and let it go. Suddenly, I couldn't help myself from smiling. "Butch is a nice name for a cat." I realized that long hours of being scared and sick had slowed my social skills, which were never that great with strangers anyhow. I felt slightly tongue-tied, but somehow it didn't matter.

I paused and looked at the familiar scenery around me, wondering what to do next. Then he asked, "You live around here?"

"Yup, sure do." I waved my hand in a vague movement. "Top of the hill. End drive. With my sister Rachel. Oh, and I'm Dina."

His face, caught in the glow of the late afternoon sun, was tanned and appeared weathered by too many days spent outdoors. His friendly smile showed white teeth that slightly overlapped, giving him a boyish charm. "Ya like to ride?" he asked.

"Huh?" I felt foolish, caught off guard. "Ride what?"

His laugh was deep, full of a richness that warmed my soul. Reaching out, he stroked the brown nose of the horse at his side. "Name's Joe. He's a beauty. His mate is even gentler. I think you'd like her."

"Yeah. A horse, huh?"

"Yes indeed." He leaned against the gate. "A fine horse, Dina."

"Well, truth of the matter is ... ah, I've never been riding."

"That so?" Grinning, he nodded at me. "Then I'd have to say it's high time you gave it a shot. What do y'all think?"

"Actually, horses are ..." I wished I'd put on lipstick, not that it would have made a big difference. "Well ..." I cleared my throat. "Horses are big. You know?"

A perplexed look settled across his forehead as he considered what I'd said.

I should have let Rachel talk me into wearing a wig. The chemotherapy had thinned my brown hair. Being of average height, average looks, and until recently a bit overweight, I realized I wasn't looking my best. I brushed the toe of my sneaker into a swirl of fallen leaves. Looking down, I added, "I'm not exactly athletically inclined right now."

"Come on. I'm no athlete myself." He waved me toward the gate. "My mare's gentle as a kitten. You meet her and then decide."

A voice inside told me it was a fair request. After all, I didn't dislike horses. I'd always been around them, but I'd never paid much attention to them. Gil smiled, and I realized this wasn't about horses. I heard Joe whinny, and I felt myself move. But common sense took over, and I came to a complete stop.

"Aah, I'd like to, but I have to, well…" I paused, looking toward the empty country road that lay ahead of me. "See, I'm taking this walk, and I really want to, hmm, finish it." I ended on a whispery note and hung my head, feeling like a fool. But I had no idea who he might be, and going on a ride with a stranger wasn't a good idea.

Gil pulled on his cowboy hat, giving it a slight tug. "Another time, Miss Dina. Just let me know should you change your mind."

"Thanks." I moved in the direction of the meadow that bordered the road, paused, and waved. "See you around." He waved back. *The end*, I thought. *Another missed opportunity*.

Yet that feeling of despair I'd grown to know so well had lifted, leaving me with a sensation that I was entering a private arrangement within myself. *I'll need time to think this one through*.

The dirt road was getting hot, and I could feel myself tiring, yet the day spoke to me of a journey that I must take. That was the reason for my walk, to try to make sense out of my new emotions. I guessed woefully that a horseback ride with a handsome cowboy wasn't included in those plans.

It was a warm day for fall, and I ran the back of my hand across my forehead. I was sweating from the exercise. *No, wait*, I thought, *that would be glowing*. Mom always said animals sweat and ladies glowed. The first time I'd heard her share that with me was one hot August day when my sisters and I were at the state fair. I'd made a reference to sweating like a little piggy; Rachel had giggled, but Jillian, being our older sister, had looked bored. The only common denominator we shared was the perspiration dripping from our faces onto the neckline of our matching white blouses. The temperature was in the 90's and our sun hats had plastered our hair against our scalps. I could see Rachel's curls had turned into moist ringlets while Jillian merely looked hot and annoyed. Sweat rolled down my back and just as I was about to elaborate on my piggy statement, Mom hushed me and ushered us into the shade of the Future Farmers of America tent, where she had shared that nugget of information and handed each of us a fresh tissue. Jillian had patted it delicately across her forehead and nodded at a boy from school, while I mopped under my arms making Rachel laugh and imitate my actions. Mom had sighed and handled us extra tissues while Jillian called us disgusting and looked frantically around to be sure none of her friends could see what we were doing. I smiled happily. This memory made me laugh. I would fold it up and pack it away.

My thanks for this idea went to the young woman who had headed the therapy group for cancer patients. We were all encouraged to participate at the meeting, and then we were divided into groups. After one session on "Preparing to Leave," I did just that. It seemed that we terminal patients had developed a strange humor and referred to the sessions as "Exit Strategy," much to the chagrin of friends and family. Still, I didn't fault the woman in charge. Even though her enthusiasm to help was eagerly embraced by most of the patients, I found her to be exhausting. Her one good idea was the memory suitcase, which I carried with me when I left her group. Though, on giving the concept additional thought, I decided that a duffle bag would be more my style.

Of course, I'd had to tell Rachel that I wasn't going to any more dying therapy classes, and she had soothed me by saying that something new was always being discovered and all I needed was a little more time. Worse was the call from Jillian that night as she went through the same scenario, but being a lawyer, she was more thorough, as well as more exasperating.

I plodded on, passing fences with chipped paint that held fields of dried grass. Several cows mooed at Susie, the herding dog, who took her responsibilities seriously by forcing the cows toward the barn. On several occasions Susie's former associates had herded all of us around the fields. I'd never known if that was just for sport or practice, but as I was little at the time and didn't like a dog nipping at my heels, I decided this was a memory I'd leave behind.

The sun still scorched the land even though summer was gone. A reoccurring vision of the shady kitchen at home kept finding its way into my mind, and I wanted a glass of ice chips. I comforted myself by thinking of chilly fall nights and rain that would come to cool the land.

A horn blasted its way into my thoughts, causing me to jump. Rachel, younger sister and self-appointed caregiver, pulled to the side and released her window. "Dina, you've gone too far from home." Her voice held an edge of concern. "And it's warm, too warm for you to be out."

"Hi! It's really good to see you, sis, especially your air-conditioned car." I smiled at her.

"Please get in and let me drive you home."

I stepped toward her window and felt the swooshing of cool air. "I like that. Feels good." Crossing in front of the car, I nodded and shouted, "You've got yourself a passenger." I opened the door and dropped into the seat. "Now this feels good."

"You look flushed." Rachel felt my head. "How do you feel?"

"You're fussing. Please stop." To take the sting out of my words, I tilted my head in her direction. "I'm fine, just warm and thirsty and looking forward to a nap." I smiled. "And ice chips."

Rachel nodded. "Gotcha covered." She swung the car back onto the dirt road. With the air blowing against my face, I began to feel better, and my thoughts returned to the cowboy. I wanted to go past the old gate again to find out if he was still there.

"Rachel, do you remember that old, wooden gate at the property line?"

"Nope." She closed her window and asked, "What gate are you talking about?"

"The one that's been there forever."

"You'd have to show me. I can't remember any gate."

"Around the next bend, look to your left." Hope inflamed me for a moment but quickly disappeared when the gate came into view. The horse was gone, the cat had disappeared, and there was no cowboy sitting on the fence. But still I noticed that the day had a sunny way of showing off the lopsided wood of the old railings.

"Oh, that old thing." Rachel was unimpressed as she spoke. "It's been there for years. I've never paid any attention to it."

"Do you remember the horses we used to feed at the old ranch?" I asked.

"Gosh, that was really way back. We were little kids. But no one's lived there for a long time."

"You sure?"

Rachel looked over her sunglasses at me. "Why?"

"Just wondering. I thought I saw some horses and, uh, people around there."

"Anything's possible, Dina. Land is rented out all the time."

I nodded my head and thought dryly that I may have just missed an opportunity to learn how to ride a horse, and time wasn't exactly on my side.

After a dinner of soup broth and soda crackers, I helped with the dishes. The food, little that it was, would help me keep the pills down and the pain farther away. Dying wasn't easy, and cancer was a mean disease. On the up side, I had a good doctor, and his medications worked well; but each day remained a challenge. Rachel worked so hard at keeping me fed and rested and cared for; I knew that she felt the struggle too.

Our old farmhouse was cooling off from the day's heat, but the warm air still hovered within the low ceiling spaces of the kitchen. I felt tired, but Rachel wasn't done with me yet.

"Will you try a little Jell-O?" She held out a pretty glass vase filled with red wobbly cubes. "I'll eat it too," she offered.

"Nope." I laughed. "Couldn't put either one of us through that." I tapped the spoon across the dish and added, "Only you could think of using one of Mom's cut crystal flower vases for a jiggling substance, pass it off as food, and make it look good." I felt happy. "But no, Rachel, I'm still going to pass."

A good-natured smile lit up her face. "Okay, what can I get you?"

"More ice chips would be nice. And Rachel, please don't put food coloring in them again. They were really gross."

"Sorry." Her voice took on an amused tone. "I just wanted to make them more, you know, appealing."

I joked back. "Oh, eye-catching they were, especially the green ones. They turned my teeth an odd color. Do you remember?" I made a silly face. "But appealing? No, green ice is definitely not appealing."

"Huh." Rachel pursed her lips before she spoke. "And imagine me thinking that those green ones would bring back happy childhood memories of your frog days." She looked pleased with herself and continued, "You always liked frogs."

"Yeah, when I was nine!" I made a gagging sound and fell into the chair.

Rachel flopped next to me and took my hand. "Is there anything you want to talk about?"

"Now that you mention it, yes. Boys."

"Boys?" My sister narrowed her eyes as she spoke. "What kind of boys?"

"Oh…" I sat back and gazed into space. "Good-looking cowboys."

"I like cowboys." Rachel nodded. "They have a way about them, sort of easygoing." Then she went into her alert mode. "I'm not talking about the ones who wear black hats because they're bad."

"What?" I sat up. "How'd you make that determination?"

"Past experience, and I'm not going to discuss it."

"Well, what if I told you I had met a handsome cowboy who wore aviator glasses and a tan cowboy hat?" I smiled.

"Oh, a tan cowboy hat, huh." She looked thoughtful before she replied, "A tan hat would be good."

"He even asked me to go horseback riding."

"You're on lots of meds, Dina. Dreams can seem very real." She gave me a curious look. "But if it sounds like fun, go for it."

"Oh, good answer!" I stood up. "And on that note, I'm off to bed. Where are my meds? I don't want to miss a thing." I kissed my sister and went to my room thinking what a waste I'd made of today. My happiness would come from my heart, not my mind overthinking a situation. The cowboy had offered friendship, and I had passed. I would walk toward the old gate tomorrow, and this time I'd have the courage to say yes to a new adventure.

The gray light of early morning was shattered when I woke to pain piercing my legs. My breath was lost in gasps as I tried to get out of bed. I fell and pulled myself up, forcing my legs to hold my body as I hobbled toward my bathroom and the bottle of pain medication. It took a half hour until I could dress and walk into the kitchen. I couldn't let Rachel know that I'd had another attack. She would never let me walk alone, and I wanted to get to the old gate again.

Luck wasn't on my side, and breakfast was a disaster. Nothing stayed down, and I was weak and irritated. Rachel irked me, and I hated myself. I had to lie down or pass out. The family room sofa was my choice, and once I was comfortable, Rachel left to go to the pharmacy.

After several minutes of lying down and watching the leaves drift away from their branches, I realized that the weakness was giving up its hold and my stomach felt more settled. I would try to take a walk.

As I headed down the dirt road, I felt the nearness of the gate, and I visualized it long before I rounded the bend. My feelings of anticipation crumbled as I stared at the decaying wooden structure. It stood all alone against a backdrop of abandoned pasture land and old trees. The gate was closed, just as when Rachel and I had passed it yesterday, and not a soul was in sight.

As I looked toward the sky of blue, I felt the sting of my tears. Pointing my feet straight ahead, I kept walking. Just what was wrong with me that I couldn't be more trusting, more adventuresome? Why had I said no when what I'd wanted to say was yes?

"Hey, that you, Dina?" A man's low-pitched voice, carrying a slight drawl, spoke from behind me.

I looked over my shoulder to see him moving toward me, leading his horse. It looked as if he'd come from the stand of trees. I noticed his long stride, slow and smooth, as he approached the gate.

He sure can appear from out of nowhere, I thought.

"Oh, um ..." *Easy now*, I told myself, *just act natural.* I waved. "Yes, it's me." I punished myself briefly for sounding dumb and wondered why I hadn't applied myself in social situations where talk flowed easily and people felt comfortable. I wanted to sound enthused, so I answered with a robust, "Hi, Gil!" *Maybe that was over the top.*

"Don't ya sound fine this morning?" His smile held the same charm as yesterday, but this morning the sun was behind his head, so he seemed surrounded by a golden glow. "Been thinkin' about takin' a little horseback ride?"

Pulling myself up to full height, I replied, "Actually, I have."

"Good to hear." Gil's voice was accented with warm tones as he pulled the gate toward him. Its worn-out creaking sound was music to my ears.

Slipping through the old gate, I felt less burdened. I paused to examine the change in my mood but let it go as a gentle feeling nudged me along the overgrown path. Gil walked by my side, making comments about the countryside, not talking too much, just a pleasant hum of words that felt good as they touched my ears. I glanced up and noticed his height, over six feet. He also had broad shoulders. I shook my head, wondering why I was doing this.

He whistled to his horse, which trotted along behind us. I smiled and looked up. "He's well behaved. You know, for a horse."

"Yes, ma'am." Gil grinned. "For a horse." The narrow path opened to the pasture, where the summer grass wore a mask of golden hues. Another whinny drew my attention. "That's Sweet Mary."

"She's saddled!" I exclaimed.

Gil nodded. "Seems to work best that way." He grinned. "Don't ya think?"

"But you didn't know that I would take a walk or say yes or ..." I frowned in puzzlement.

"Sweet Mary, meet Dina." The mare moved closer, curiosity clear in her brown eyes. Gil pushed his cowboy hat back. "She's saddled on account of my friend was called to another job and he rode this far before he caught the bus.

"Life moves in a funny way, Dina." His look was confident. "So if y'all want to ride Mary here, she's ready."

"Look, Gil, I should tell you up front I'm not exactly what you would call ..." I paused as Gil rested his hand lightly on my shoulder. I could smell something nice that seemed to float from his nearness. It wasn't cologne; it was more like the scent of fresh soap.

"Well ..." I hesitated as thoughts dashed around my head. "Truth is, I have ..." But the words didn't come out as I had planned. Instead I looked at him and saw that his face was washed with sunlight. It was a beautiful face of rugged lines and deep plains, and I felt my fears melt away.

The tone of his voice, low and sweet, brushed my emotions with unexpected excitement. "Do y'all want to ride?"

"I don't know how." I risked another look directly at him. "Like I said, horses are, well, they're big." Part of me wanted to say yes. After all, he was probably an expert, and this was the only opportunity I was going to get. That small voice in the back of my mind added that the man making the offer was very masculine and friendly and good-looking. I blinked at my thoughts.

He reached slowly for my fingers, holding them in his calloused hands. "Dina, if ya want to ride, you can do it. I'm here to help you."

"You are? I mean…" I felt flustered. "I mean that's good." I let out my breath, feeling a weak smile appear. "That's because I need help." I turned toward Sweet Mary. "I need help because I don't know how to ride a horse. But she does seem gentle and maybe friendly. I think." I raised my hand to touch her nose, and Mary lowered her head and gently pushed back. Her nose felt soft, almost like velvet, and I laughed. "This might just work."

Gil nodded. "Good to know." He bent down by Mary's side and cupped his hands together, indicating this was a service he was providing for my foot. I stared at the gesture. He nodded again, and gingerly I placed my left foot in the makeshift step.

With a smooth motion, Gil raised me up. I flung my leg over the saddle and was seated property. It felt right. I let the sensation pass through me and watched as Gil mounted Joe with a graceful swing. He looked at me over the top of his aviator sunglasses. I smiled as his sparkling blue eyes caught my stare, but I didn't turn away. "That was smooth. I mean the way you did that was smooth."

I felt foolish until he winked at me and added, "Years of experience, Miss Dina. Shall we?" Sweet Mary moved in step with Joe, and we rode toward the valley floor.

"Yep, there's lots to see. Lots to do." A playful note wrapped itself into his voice. "Tell me about you, Dina."

My buoyant feeling began to dissipate. I took another deep breath and let it out. My mind whirled with half-formed thoughts. *Should I tell him about my illness? Not now, not yet. Just let me have this day, cancer free.*

He sensed the change in my mood and spoke softly, "Life can be a tangle of emotions or sweet as honey, but usually, Miss Dina, it's everythin' in between."

"Yeah, that's the truth," I began with a sigh, whether expressing frustration or anger, I couldn't say. I was so ordinary that I had to smile. "Truth is that people just pass me by. Do you know what I mean?"

His head turned slightly so that the sunlight centered on the brim of his cowboy hat. "People passin' right by a pretty gal like you? I don't believe it."

"Well, it's the truth!" I laughed. "So here's how it goes. You see, my life has been pretty uneventful, but I've always had lots of happy memories. And without meaning to, I'd make people laugh."

The afternoon smelled like autumn, crisp and warm with the tang of ripe apples nearby. The light, musky aroma of pumpkins and squash mixed with the scent of rain in the air and the promise of frost to come. This was definitely my favorite season. I glanced at Gil, noticing the easy rhythm of his body as he moved with his horse.

"I like a good laugh, and I like a happy memory too. You gonna tell me more?"

"Sure. Let me collect my thoughts."

"Never rush a lady." His grin was spontaneous. "I'm willin' to wait it out."

"That's good," I joked back. The thought crossed my mind that I was flirting, but I pushed it aside with the theory that people who had terminal cancer did not flirt. I continued, "Well, there was this Easter morning when I was a little girl…" I thought back through the years. "I was the first one dressed for church, and my older sister was monopolizing the mirror, as usual." My tone changed. "My older sister, Jillian, always spent hours in front of the mirror."

Gil nodded. "Vain was she?"

"Oh no. Lovely, actually. It was always a rewarding experience for her to gaze into the mirror. But it was annoying for me, especially as her younger, unattractive sister. So I'd slipped outside to study my reflection in the windows. The next thing I remembered, I had fallen face-first in a mud puddle."

"How'd you do that?"

I shrugged. "Wasn't watching my feet."

"What happened next?"

"My cries brought my mother running to the door. My dad, I can still remember him pulling up his suspenders, was right behind my mom, who was holding Rachel; and Jillian, perfectly coiffed, wearing her new Easter bonnet, brought up the rear."

Gil's lips moved as if to smile, but instead his reply was neutral. "Must have been a sight."

"Oh, it was. The whole family stared as mud dripped off my pale yellow dress. Not knowing what to do with all the attention, I smiled awkwardly, and soon everyone was laughing."

He grinned and I smiled back. I explained how we'd been late for Easter service but my mother had shared the story of the mud puddle with everyone after church.

"I felt special all day, even after Jillian told me I was dumb." I made a face and continued, "She told me that a lot. But I never believed her. You see, Jillian was always so perfect, and I was, well, I was sort of sloppy … dirty face and sticky fingers kind of kid." I looked at Gil. "Anyhow, it really is a silly memory, but it always carries a smile from my heart to my face. And to this day, it makes Jillian shake her head in exasperation." I giggled playfully. "That alone is still worth a laugh."

A comfortable silence settled between us. Dry leaves crunched under the horses' feet. The perfume of autumn pleasantly infused the air. I turned my head toward Gil. "My Grandma Nana." I shook my head, giggling again. "Oh, I know that's a loopy name for a grandmother, but all my sisters called her 'Granny,' and I wanted to name her something that took longer to say." I grinned sheepishly. "That way, I figured she would pay more attention to me. I mean with my baby sister being so cute and my older sister being too beautiful … you get the picture?"

"Sure do." Gil looked toward the sky then back at me. "She was flattered that you took the time to give her such an endearing name."

"Really?"

"Yep. Really."

"How do you know that?" I asked.

With a shrug of his shoulders, he looked at me and replied, "I fancy myself to be a pretty good guesser. And Miss Dina, any granny would enjoy havin' an extra name bestowed on her." He turned Joe toward a path sheltered by trees and smiled at me. "With the understandin' of how important it was that the granddaughter who thought up the extra name just wanted a little more of her attention."

"Well then." That seemed to make sense to me. "I shall continue. My Grandma Nana once told me that what we reflect in words melts into harmony."

He nodded approval. "I gotta agree with that." The sunlight blinked like diamonds through the trees.

I moved comfortably in the saddle, wondering briefly why I'd never taken up riding. I'd always lived on a working farm with orchards and livestock and lots of chores. It was a good, healthy way to grow up. Family was important, and we had all pulled together. The orchards were my parents' pride, but even so, they were determined to send their daughters on to higher education. I wondered if they understood that keeping a small farm wasn't going to be a good investment in the years to come. Thinking back, I realized that most of the farm kids went on to college. There must have been something about the future that our parents just knew by instinct—keeping our farms would be a luxury, and other jobs would be necessary to earn a living.

I felt settled on Sweet Mary as she set a lazy pace. I thought back to the old ranch and wondered what had happened to the horses. I remembered walking down there with my sisters but not riding the horses. Seems it was in front of me all my life, but I'd never taken it up.

Well, it was one of the mysteries of my life. One of the "Why didn't I's?"

Gil asked what my plans had been after college. There was no remorse in my answer. "Oh, I had lots of ideas. Let's see, after college I was going to dance and travel. Meeting the man of my dreams and falling in love were high on my list."

"But that didn't happen?"

"Nope. When reality took over, I realized that I had to earn a living." I joked, "That was a shock."

"Was it now?"

"Yup. I was an adult and a job was a necessity. So I accepted a position as a teacher at a private school."

Gil nodded in understanding.

"So I'd come home for a summer break, and since I was unhappy with the teaching position, I agreed to live on the family farm for a year so Rachel could pursue her career in advertising."

I felt myself synchronize with the motion of the horse. I checked Gil's rhythm and nodded. "I feel good about this. This thing about riding a horse."

"Pleased to hear it."

I felt comfortable and smiled. "Well, where did I leave off?"

"You're living back on the farm."

"Yes, with Rachel. She's the creatively gifted one in the family. My baby sister is the idea person. She's also kind, stubborn, and loving. When I came back to tend the farm,"—I looked at Gil and continued—"I say that jokingly, as there isn't that much left to 'tend' except the orchards and the house itself. But I'd always liked the farm so spending a few years back here was fine with me. Plus, I could always sub at the local school. Anyhow, that allowed Rachel the extra time she needed to start a small company that dealt with advertising for local business, plus I could help her out. She was doing really good, even thinking of hiring another person, so I thought I should get a full-time position. I was considering a teaching post in a foreign country then ..." I paused. "Well, things didn't work out, so ..." I stopped again. "She had to take care of me for a while, but she'll be back at it soon enough. Her clients miss her, and she's really good at what she does.

"So you know about Rachel. Let me tell you about Jillian. She's beautiful, slender, and smart." I knew that I was talking too fast but couldn't stop. "She's an attorney, married to an architect, and raising her family back East. She is caring and bossy, in charge of her life and any other life that touches hers." I ran out of breath and had to pause.

My mind was buzzing with information, but I feared that if I let it slip that I had cancer, our relationship would come to an abrupt end. *Who wants a relationship with a dying woman?* It would be best if I stopped talking for a while. "Guess I had lots to say, huh?"

"And all of it interestin' information."

"Really? You thought my sisters were interesting?"

"Yes, ma'am, up to a point." Gil caught my attention. "However, I find you to be of greater interest."

"I see." My heart began to race. "That's a nice compliment."

Gil nodded. "Such was my intension." He looked directly at me. "Ever gallop?"

"Good Lord, no!"

"Wanna try?"

My eyes grew wide.

"Just move with Mary. She's goin' to do the work, and you're goin' to get the ride. Ready?"

I moistened my lips, considering the idea. Slowly I nodded yes, and Gil whistled at the horses. Their ears perked up, and I felt my heels urge sweet Mary forward.

The path opened swiftly to a meadow, and I felt myself gliding across the dried grass as if the horse had grown wings. The wind rushed past my face as sweet Mary picked up the exhilarated rhythm of the run. In my peripheral vision, fall's colors became shadowy waves of russet and gold, while ahead the sky offered a blue horizon without end.

I felt my fears dissipate into tiny pieces, like confetti tossed from the highest building. The ever-present sadness I carried with me was snatched away, discarded by the wind, as I flew across the open fields with Gil in the lead. Strength filled my body as I bent low over the horse, flowing with the gallop.

The idea of Jillian and her husband raising their sons, guiding them through life, flitted buoyantly through my mind's eye. My mom and dad filled another edge of my thoughts with happy memories. The image of Rachel in a white wedding gown softly touched my heart.

With blood pumping through my veins and the horse flying across the earth, I felt very much alive, as if I was free of daily pain and struggle.

As Gil slowed Joe, sweet Mary cut her pace. The horses began to snort as the sweat cooled against their bodies.

"What'd y'all think of that?" His voice was filled with energy. Strong color highlighted his cheekbones.

I offered a breathless answer. "Wouldn't have missed it for the world! I galloped. I really galloped!"

Gil's smile held enthusiastic approval. "Thought you might enjoy it."

"Thank you." I looked into his blue eyes. I felt my body race with the excitement of what I'd just done. "Thank you for making it happen."

He winked and pulled on the brim of his cowboy hat. "Pleasure was mine." He reached for his sunglasses. High-spirited energy from the ride spun around us.

"That's nice." I felt a generous smile spread across my face. "That thing you did with your hat. It was … nice."

Silence settled into the space between us as the horses walked off the heat of the run. I felt relaxed in the saddle. The sky remained filled with soft blue color. Gentle white clouds puffed at a leisurely pace overhead as a contented sigh slipped from my lips. I noticed that instead of feeling tired, I felt energized.

"Whatcha thinkin' over there?"

"How much I enjoy sunshine and a blue sky." I paused to look at the beauty around me. "I've always loved being in the middle of an afternoon."

Gil's smile was bright. "That so? How about night? Do y'all like evenings?"

"Sure. But as a very little girl, I worried about sundown."

"How so?"

"Oh, this is silly." I looked away.

"Hey, Dina." His voice flirted with me as he removed his aviator glasses. "I'm over here."

"I know."

"C'mon then. Tell me." He captured my eyes with a playful glance and held them. "Nothin' wrong with silly."

I shook my head. "Not unless you tell me a 'silly' too." Looking directly at him, I asked, "Promise?" And a second voice in me added, "That's a rule. Okay?"

He nodded seriously as he replied, "Cross my heart."

"Well, okay. A girl can't say no to that." I brushed my fingers hopelessly through my thinning hair. "Here goes. When I was very little, I thought that the sun, so full of pinks and purples at sunset, looked like it might bubble out around its corners." I risked a glance at him. "Told you it was silly."

"Sounds serious to me."

"Oh, and it was. I wouldn't feel that everything was all right until I'd see the wishing star high in the heavens." Smiling, I added, "Then I'd know that all was well."

Gil nodded. "Seems reasonable."

"I thought so too. There's more."

"That so?"

"Yes, indeed. I also knew that tomorrow would be on time, and it would bring a freshly born sun to light the new day."

"Mighty perceptive for a child."

"I was very bright for my years."

Gil looked sideways. "I'm sure you were."

"Yes. I always said in my next life I'd come back as a scholar and know positively everything. I still look for the wishing star. Did you know it's the brightest one in the sky?"

"Yes, ma'am."

I raised an eyebrow at his country expression. I had heard it used throughout most of my youth and always thought it to be gentlemanly, but people didn't say ma'am anymore. I was glad that Gil did. It felt friendly coming from him. "Well, once I know that star's in place, I'm at peace." An easy quiet shared the day. Minutes ticked by undisturbed by time. I smiled at him and cleared my throat. "Now it's your turn."

"So it is." Gil shifted in the saddle. "As a child, I wanted to lasso the stars and pull 'em down from the heavens. Keep 'em in a box under my bed so that I could look at 'em, maybe give one or two away to my best buddies."

I listened with interest as Gil talked. Having only sisters to play with, it never occurred to me that little boys enjoyed make-believe as much as girls.

"Told my brothers of my brilliant idea, and off we rode one night, ready to round up those stars. Our father was out on the path and asked us what we were doing out so late. I told him of my Olympian plan, and he listened real careful-like. Asked me if I was ready to take away such beauty and hold it only for my eyes."

Turning toward me, he grinned. "Sorta made me see the light in a simple sentence."

I smiled back. "Sounds like a wise man."

"Yes, indeed."

The horses stopped to graze. Looking at Gil, I asked, "Lasso stars?" I shook my head. "You must have had quite an imagination."

"Yep. From time to time, I would find myself smack in the center of some mischief. My father, now, he was a patient man. Took a lot of time with me." Gil made a clicking sound at the horses. "I was a lot of work."

"And it all paid off." That didn't sound right, so I continued, "I mean look at you now. Well…" I cleared my throat. "You seem fine."

"Thank you, ma'am." He put his sunglasses on and clicked at the horses again. They lifted their heads in acknowledgement.

Squinting at the sunshine, I joked, "I should have brought a sunbonnet."

"It's your lucky day." He pulled a squashed affair of beat-up straw out from his saddle bag. "One sun hat, comin' up."

He presented it with a flourish, and I accepted it with a grand gesture of thanks. I saw my reflection in his mirrored glasses and giggled.

The afternoon sun began its slide into the gentle hills as we rode back to the old gate. I knew the wishing star would be bright tonight.

Suddenly a brisk wind shook the trees, shedding the brilliance of their leaves in slow motion to fan out across the dark soil.

Without warning, my voice filled the space between us. "I miss that. The breeze lifting my hair." Embarrassed by the needy tone in my words, I knew that color would soon flood my cheeks. "Sorry. I didn't mean to sound like that." Quickly, I faced Gil. "I really had a lovely day. It was the gallop that made me think of how free I used to feel. The wind in my hair, that sort of thing." My voice trailed off.

His movement was without hurry as he turned in the saddle and looked over the top of his glasses. Sunshine filtered through the tangled branches of the bare trees, highlighting his eyes, turning them into sparkling sapphires. I wondered what kind of mischief he would have gotten into as a child.

He adjusted the brim of his hat. "The wind, huh?"

I nodded. "Yeah, the wind."

"Tell me, Dina. Tell me about the wind."

My eyes blinked rapidly. "Why?"

"I got me a couple of brothers who are into wind."

"Really?" My brows knit together. "What do they do?"

"Good stuff."

"Like what?"

"Let me think on it some." He shifted his weight in the saddle. "Mostly they like to cool off a hot day or carry rain across a parched field. That type of thing."

I laughed at his humor. "The basics, huh?"

"Yep. Basic stuff's important." He grinned and asked, "What about you?"

"I used to run. For exercise, you know?" I smiled, looking at Gil's lean body. "Well, maybe you wouldn't know. Are all your brothers as tall and lean as you?"

"Heck no. Got 'em in all sizes. Daniel now, he's the one who's into the wind; he's short and chubby."

"I can relate to the chubby part." I laughed. "I always had a small weight problem. Probably due to the fact that I used to enjoy food." I looked at Gil, noting the strong angle of his jaw.

"Nothing wrong with that." He had a droll look tucked in his smile. "Daniel eats up a storm."

I played along. "I suppose it takes a lot of energy to puff the rain across a dry field."

He nodded complaisantly and said, "That it does."

I felt my heart pick up a beat when his blue eyes engaged mine and he asked, "What's your wind story?"

"Mild, compared to yours."

"Miss Dina." His eyes danced with humor. "Ma'am. You have my undivided attention."

"Right." Grinning, I shook my head. "Well, my hair used to be long. When I ran, the wind would lift it off my face. I'd feel the cooling on my scalp, like the first snowflakes of winter melting on my skin." I realized I was staring at him. He didn't seem to mind. I spoke softly, "Winter is almost here."

Tranquil warmth settled around us as he met my eyes. His expression held understanding as silently he urged me to continue. My voice softened. "The idea of frosty days and icy winds helped me through some radiation that I had to have a while back. My skin would burn, and I knew there was more to come, so I would think of winter days and gray skies and pine trees heavy with snow. No colors, just cold shades of gray and white."

He didn't comment, and I was both grateful and relieved he hadn't asked any questions. I'd held so much inside that it felt good to speak frankly, at least about some of my treatments. The cooling of the day hastened my words. "That was my story. Now back to the wind...and your brother. What was his name again?"

"Daniel. The wind boy is Daniel."

I thought for a moment then asked, "Maybe he's a leg man too?"

"You don't say?" Gil's eyebrow rose in speculation. "Boy's always been a charmer, but a leg man, huh?" He seemed to consider this quite carefully. "Well now, that's somethin' he's been a-keepin' all to himself."

Shrugging my shoulders, I continued, "Well, I say leg man because when I was into running, the wind would gently blow across my legs, urging me to complete my goal. With each lunge of my leg and each pump of my arm, my hair would lift and fall against my cheeks with a teasing motion. When I slowed, my legs would feel wobbly with relief, and my arms would be heavy, but my hair would fall with the gentleness of feathers across my temples." I rotated my body and took a deep breath. Slowly I released it and looked at Gil. "It was sensual. Like a lover's hand lightly caressing my face."

"That so. Sensual, hmm?" Gil paused in thought. "Well, I gotta say, Daniel, now, he thinks of himself as havin' a good touch."

I noticed the lines at the corners of his eyes grow deeper as he carefully considered my words. "Mighty good touch, accordin' to him. Plus he's a real sweet talker to boot." Shaking his head, he continued, "Imagine that boy being a leg man and keepin' it all to himself! No wonder he waited so patiently in that long line."

Gil glanced at me with a raised eyebrow. "I'd say he got himself a real breezy job."

I giggled.

"No. I'm serious," he replied, holding in a smile. "The rest of us, why heck, we wanted glory jobs, but Daniel, now, he was farsighted. He saw the advantages of being able to puff through hair and drift across a lovely lady's face. Blow a bit on her legs." He tilted his head in thought.

"Mind you, all in the line of work. Why, as I think on it, that boy is right smart." He let his smile out.

I laughed out loud. "I love your sense of humor. It makes me feel so good."

He reached across his horse and gently touched my hand. "The journey is filled with joy, Dina."

A rush of wind crossed our path, and the horses lifted their heads. Sweet Mary snorted delicately. I felt the breeze brush against my warm cheeks. "Guess I have your brother to thank for that, huh?"

"Boy comes through at the darnedest times." Gil touched the brim of his hat, glancing toward the trees. "However, I am gonna have myself a talk with him about this leg man thing he's been doin'." He replaced his aviator glasses and spoke in an amused tone. "This was the first I'd heard about his job bonus. Imagine that." He turned to me. "And we talk often."

He appeared so serious, I had to laugh. Squinting my eyes against the rosy orange glow in the western sky, I realized all the radiance of autumn lay gathered in the path that led back to the old gate. I paused, holding the moment, feeling the wind.

Gil dismounted without hurry. "Tomorrow I'm gonna be riding down to the creek. If you like … that is, if you haven't any other plans, would ya like to join me?"

He helped me down, and I found comfort in his strength. His hands slipped from my waist as he set me on the ground.

Not knowing what else to do, I returned the old hat, immediately conscious of my scalp, still bald in places. My hands flew to my head as I said, "Oh! I must look awful. Next time I'll bring a scarf."

Gil gently pulled my hands away from my hair. He studied me intently for a long moment and said, "We see what we want to see, Dina." My lips pushed together as I looked away from him. Lightly he cupped my chin, lifting my face upward. "I don't see anything that would be unattractive."

His smile warmed me. I wanted to tell him to hold me tightly, but at that moment he took a step closer, and I felt a pleasant flow of happiness surround me, as if I'd been showered with an armful of flower petals. The good feeling was short-lived when that little voice inside of me asked, *How will you tell him you have terminal cancer, and what will he say then?*

I stepped back while pushing my fingers through my hair. "Well, that's really nice that you feel that way. Maybe I'm just too self-conscious, you know?" I clasped my hands in front of me and then let them fly out to my sides. "Thanks for understanding." I stopped moving and took a breath to gather my thoughts. "This isn't going well, and I really want it to. I had a great time today. Thanks for the good company. That's what I really want to say."

Gil leaned against the old gate. His words were slow in coming. "Now then, Miss Dina, might just be that you're afraid to shine."

I raised an eyebrow and replied, "And here I like to think of myself as a 'seize the moment' kind of gal." Pushing all thoughts of cancer from my mind, I said, "I would like to ride down to the creek tomorrow." With some humor returning to my frame of mind, I added, "I'm pretty sure that I can get you in my date book."

"That would be mighty nice." He stepped back and gave me a comical look. "Perhaps I'd best get me a date book too so that we can both keep track of these events."

I laughed. "Good idea."

The hinges made a grating sound as Gil pushed the gate open. I walked past him and realized that a fresh scent of meadows and trees surrounded him. It was nice. I turned to wave. "See you tomorrow."

Chapter 2

"Dina! You've been gone so long. I was really getting worried," Rachel fussed, looking close to tears. She put the watering can down and held the screen door open.

I could see water spilling from the saucers that sat on the floor of the front porch. Tiny beads of liquid had spread to the braided rug. I pointed. "You overwatered again." Shaking my head, I made the sound our mom used to make, "Tsk-tsk."

"Oh, Dina." Rachel glanced at the water and bent to wipe it up. "I worry so when you go off like that."

"Go off?" I smiled. "You make me sound mentally deficient."

"You know perfectly well what I'm talking about." Rachel stood up, and I could see she was serious. "Walking alone. I never know if you'll have a ... you know, a problem. What if you couldn't get home?" She took my arm. "This screened-in porch is not the warmest place for you to be." In an attempt to hurry me inside, she added, "Here now, let's get you a nice, hot bath."

"Nah, not yet." I felt good, better than I had in the past several weeks. But instinctively I knew that telling Rachel about my unexpected meeting with a man wearing a cowboy hat and riding a horse wouldn't be wise. Besides, Gil was going to be my secret. I disengaged my arm from Rachel's grasp and flopped down on the faded sofa, thinking about all the years we'd helped our parents prepare the porch for winter. It had been a family ritual, just like cutting back the roses and gathering the last of the squash.

Leaning back, I tipped my head toward Rachel. "Just about this time of year we'd help Daddy cover the screens with plastic to keep out the snow."

Rachel nodded. "He would patiently hold that heavy sheeting in place while we would tack it into the wooden windowsills with dozens of tacks that he would have to replace after we went to bed." We giggled together, and Rachel continued, "He never had a son to help with those chores, so he was stuck with us."

"And we were stuck with Jillian," I joked.

Rachel chuckled. "You're going to bring up the tarps, aren't you?"

I shook my head. "How could anyone other than Jillian supervise draping tarps over old furniture?"

Rachel began her Jillian imitation. "'You girls! Over here. You missed covering the arm. This is not a joke.'" Rachel pointed and wiggled her finger. "'The tarp is on the floor here.'" She emphasized each word. "'That's messy work.'" Then she rushed the words together just as Jillian had done so often, "'Oh, do pick it up. I mean it.'"

"You're good." I grinned. "And her most famous line: 'Okay, you two. Clown around and I'll call in proper help.'

Didn't you often wonder who she'd call?" I faced Rachel. "For a long time, I thought she had a special phone number in her diary titled 'Proper Help.' It used to scare me."

"Really?" Rachel thought for a moment. "Gosh, I was too little to think that far in advance. Just the idea of being replaced always shaped me up."

We laughed again, letting the day settle around us, and I realized how much fun I'd had with my sisters.

Rachel must have been thinking along the same lines as she smiled longingly. "Family stuff, huh?" Her voice softened. "I remember that throughout the winter months, the porch remained just cold enough to serve as a second refrigerator. We'd keep Granny's pies here."

I nodded. "And Mom's leftover turkey, the extra eggs, butter, milk…" I stopped to take a deep breath.

Rachel gestured toward the old card table by the side of the door. She cleared her throat. "Well, not that we use it that way anymore."

"No," I agreed with her. I thought back lovingly to the family dinners when the old farmhouse rang with the happy commotion of too many people in the kitchen. Each aunt and uncle, cousin and family member had a specialty dish, and they all appeared over the holidays. Mouthwatering aromas would fill the air. No wonder I was a chubby youth; everything was delicious.

The meal was always served at the large oak table in the dining room. When the table was separated in the middle, extensions were put in place, and pads were added to protect the wood. The tabletop stretched forever in the eyes of a child. Snowy white linen covered the surface, and Rachel said it looked like melted marshmallows. Chairs were brought from hidden corners and closets; even the old barn produced a few. But no matter how much planning went into it, there were never enough chairs for the main table, and somehow Rachel and I always ended up at the children's area while Jillian, without fail, made it to the adult table.

After the meal, the women would gather back in the kitchen for gossip and girl talk, and the men would smoke pipes and cigars, always outside. Mom had no tolerance for inside smoking.

Some relatives would spend the night, sleeping wherever they could find space. Blankets and quilts and pillows were brought out of storage weeks before the holidays so they could be aired and puffed. Everyone was comfortable.

A substantial breakfast was another advantage of big family get-togethers; buttermilk biscuits with gravy, egg casseroles, homemade cherry muffins, raisin cinnamon bread, jams, jellies, hickory-cured bacon and smoked ham—the selection was endless. Our life seemed centered around food and love and laughter. When everyone left the old house to return to their homes, suddenly the quiet was deafening.

It made me sad to think that the family dinners of our youth had disappeared over the years. I responded halfheartedly, "There isn't a need for so much food to be kept around." I gazed into space, and my voice took on a yearning note. "There's no reason to cook big dinners for the holidays."

Rachel nodded. "Who has the time to bake bread anymore? She paused in reflection. "Or plan reunions or celebrate birthdays and anniversaries around a dinner table."

"I know." A silence settled over us as we played within our personal thoughts. Finally I spoke. "Life is now fast and efficient."

Rachel agreed quickly. "We all have our favorite restaurants."

"Is that good?"

"I don't know." She wrinkled her brow. "Family get-togethers were nice. Lots of stories and jokes and warm fuzzy feelings. But things change." She sighed heavily. "And we have to change with them."

Just last week I'd overheard a phone call between Rachel and Dr. Bergman when she told him that she was going to hire someone to help her ready the farm for the season's change. I knew the heavy plastic that covered the screens and kept the snow off the porch was still waiting in the barn, along with the tarps to cover the furniture. After a lengthy pause in her end of the conversation, she'd added, "Oh, that's so nice of you to offer, but you really don't need to." There had been some more silence on her end, followed by, "Well, okay. If you're sure you have the time." My guess was the doc had volunteered a hand.

Thinking of the good doctor brought me back to the present, and I offered what I considered to be an innocent smile. "So what time does your date arrive?"

"Oh, Dina, he's not my date." Color flushed Rachel's cheeks. "He's your doctor." Her hands danced in front of us as she made signs for me to get up.

"Rarely does my doctor make a house call." I brushed at a speck of pretend lint. "No, Rachel, it is my opinion that Dr. Carl Bergman is most definitely your date." I was in no hurry to get up. "So what else is new?"

Eager to discuss anything other than her feelings for Carl, she replied enthusiastically, "Jillian called. I was just about to tell you. She wanted to talk to you."

"About what?" I patted the spot next to me, and Rachel sat down, causing us to fall into our familiar routine of plumping the back cushions and wiggling around a bit, each making an individual nest in the padding of the old seats. With that done, we turned our attention toward the damp spots on the old rug. I smiled. "Remember when Mom did the braiding for that? She let us help."

Rachel grinned. "I don't think we were a big help. Mostly we got in her way. Seems that Jillian was the helper." She made a goofy face. "After all, she was the oldest."

"Yes, but she didn't have an eye for color." I pointed toward the rug. "Look at that. It's orange and sort of yellow in that spot." I moved my finger in a line. "Here. Look, maybe red over there." I continued to traverse the braided rug, with my hand offering an airy wave. "Could be blue in that far corner. What do you think?"

"Purple, with orange, again." She cringed, indicating another area. "See. Over there."

"Hmm. You're right."

Rachel stared longer. "Or is that deep pink? I've never been sure."

Shaking my head, I looked at my sister as she squinted at the rug in the fading afternoon light. We had had this conversation many times. Jillian was smart, brilliant if you asked her, but both Rachel and I could have put more harmonious colors together for the braiding of the rug. "And you know what?" I continued. "Mom never complained. Not once. Never told Jillian that her ideas weren't the greatest in laying out the pattern."

I pushed myself farther into the cushion, feeling it embrace my back with familiar softness, and sighed. "Nice."

Rachel stretched too. "I'm glad we never replaced this sofa." She looked quite serious. "They don't make 'em like this anymore."

I agreed. "It's hard to get that musty old smell in something new."

"Do you really think it smells?"

"Not a bad smell." I smiled at my sister. "Sort of like an old sofa on a screened-in porch. One that's seen spring rain and wet autumns." Running my hand across the faded upholstery, I took a deep breath. "Some sun, some snow."

Rachel nodded. "It's a good sofa." Her brow creased for a moment. "I believe it was Jillian who said it smelled bad. We told her she was wrong."

Nodding, I agreed. "But she never did well with our constructive criticism."

Rachel snickered. "Didn't stop us. I always enjoyed pointing out the braided rug when we had company. You know, right after she would wow everyone with her latest achievement."

I wiggled my finger at her. "You were good. Always did it in a very innocent way."

"An advantage of being the youngest." Rachel looked guiltless. "I didn't know any better."

Looking at my baby sister, I said, "Me, now, I prefer the holidays. Right when she's telling everyone else what to do." I leaned closer. "Do you remember the Christmas she gave everyone a printout of their responsibilities?"

"You're right." Rachel slapped her forehead. "Christmas is the best time." She turned and gave me a high five. "There was the year she brought Tony home to meet the family. And she introduced him as Anthony, and he looked around like, 'Who's Anthony?'"

We both started to laugh. "Last time she did that," Rachel said, "it was also the year that she took over the kitchen and told all of us how to cook."

I nodded. "Which is not her field of expertise."

"Perhaps we were too sharp with her that year."

I shook my head. "No. That way Tony knew up front that she couldn't boil water. Or braid a rug."

"On the upside, she's good with lists." Rachel paused. "Mom understood that Jillian was doing her best with the rug. That's why she didn't say anything about the colors." Thinking about the winter evenings we sat at Mom's feet, asking her dozens of questions as she braided the rug, seemed to make Rachel sad. She looked up and spoke softly. "You know how Jillian and I worry." Her eyes clouded over as she tried gallantly not to cry. I felt my cheerful mood begin to disappear, but I wasn't ready to let go.

"Stop now." I brushed at the tears tumbling down my sister's cheeks. Her natural blonde hair curled around her oval face that was just slightly too long. But that had never bothered Rachel. It was the freckles on her nose that drove her crazy. Daddy used to say her nose had been kissed by the sun, but Rachel never saw the humor in his remark.

"You know we've talked about this a hundred times. Take a deep breath, okay?" Rachel tried, but her tears kept falling. "You'll look awful, and the good doctor will think you're overreacting again and want to send in a nurse who can cope with both of us."

I turned to the wicker table that was precariously balanced; a matchbox under one leg was keeping it even. Our eyes met, and we started to laugh. Rachel spoke first. "We've just got to get that fixed."

"So how long do you think we've said that?"

"Oh…" Rachel scratched her head, twisting a finger around a blonde curl. "Maybe twelve years, that I can recall."

I snickered and asked, "What do you think the chances are of getting it repaired?"

Tapping her lips with a finger, she offered a dramatic sigh. "Not so good, I fear."

I studied the table then looked at my sister. "Personally, I've always liked it like this."

"Me too." Rachel smiled. "It's always been my opinion that it has character you can't buy in a store."

Leaning over the arm of the sofa, I reached out to steady the wicker top. "Here." I handed her several Kleenex from the shabby-looking fabric box that had sat on the table for many years. "Remember this? It was an art project you did in, what was it? First grade?"

"Third grade, and you know it." She sniffed.

I touched the remains of red construction paper that had at one time formed a huge heart in the center of the box. Good things gather on an old porch. Pieces of white lace remained in a corner of the box. "Valentine's Day, yes?"

"Mother loved my Kleenex box." Rachel blew her nose. Makeup stained the tissue, causing me to grin.

"You'd better reapply that, or Dr. Bergman will know you have freckles." She raised her eyebrow, and I asked, "That's still our little secret, I assume?"

"You've never had to deal with spots on your nose." Rachel sniffed and fluttered her hand. "Oh, Dina, I'm sorry."

"If you keep this up, I'll have to call Jillian and tell her that you're in a funk and can't handle the situation here." I stretched my legs out and shook my head. "Heck, you know she'd be on the next plane, and we'd all be sorry." I turned Rachel toward me. "Listen up now. You know that she'd have us on a tight schedule, we'd be very well organized, and life, as we've come to enjoy it, would be condensed to notes and written instructions." I poked Rachel playfully and asked, "Do you want that to happen?"

Rachel dabbed at her eyes. "I'm getting better with notes. I've been posting them all over."

"I've noticed."

"Jillian means well. She truly does."

"Yes, just like you meant well when you gave mother that ugly Kleenex box."

"It wasn't ugly!"

"Was so."

Rachel looked at me and stopped sniffing. She narrowed her eyes. "Seems that I remember you gave Mom a box of candy—that you ate!"

"You make it sound like I ate every piece."

"You did."

"I never." Sitting back, I smiled. "I did leave one. A big one. And who ate that one, Rachel?"

"I was just a little girl, and you told me I could have it. I didn't know that Mother hadn't had any of the candy." An indignant note filled her voice. "You tricked me, and you know it."

"Do you know why?" I reached for her hand. "It was because I was jealous of the Kleenex box you made. Even then, you had a flair for art, and with that huge red heart sprinkled with glitter and the white lace, it was really a pretty box, and I wished I could have come up with something more original then a dumb old box of candy."

"Really?" Rachel squeezed my hand.

"Yes. Really."

"I spent a long time making that box."

"Oh, Rachel." I sighed. "Is this going to be a sad story?"

"No, I don't think so." She smoothed her skirt. "But you should know that the large glitter heart came off on the way home from school, and I had to glue it back on the fabric that covered the box. I used way too much glue, so it was really messy."

"My. That certainly was a pity," I commented dryly, knowing where this was going. "Made some extra work for you, did it?"

Smiling, she looked at me. "Do you remember what you did when I put the box on the table?"

"Oh, let's not bring that up again. So I sat on it. I apologized, and I pushed the box back into shape. As I recall, when Mom came home, we all had a good laugh about the candy and the box."

Rachel continued to grin. "Bradley came over to see you that afternoon. You do remember Bradley, your fifth-grade boyfriend?" She paused, looking into space. "Thinking back, I do believe you wanted to impress him."

"Sure I did. He came to the house to give me a valentine, and then we also had a good laugh about the Kleenex box."

"Not exactly." Rachel leaned closer. "He had a good laugh because the big red heart was sticking to your butt."

My mouth opened and closed. Rachel sat back and smiled. "Fair sense of humor for a little sister, huh?"

"You never told me!" I shook my head in disbelief. "I fessed up to eating all the candy. I took all the blame." I pointed at my chest. "I told the truth."

"So did I." Rachel smiled. "Just now." She pushed at her hair and pulled out a curl. After twisting it around her finger, she released it, letting it coil back. "So where were we about Jillian?"

I took a moment to center my thoughts. "I want you to think hard about her visiting. Let's start with diet. We'd only be able to eat healthy food." I could see I had her interest. "You don't like healthy food. Oh, and that wonderful dinner you're preparing for Dr. Bergman, forget it. Jillian would have lettuce with no dressing and skinless, boneless, brainless chicken breasts for the main course. Followed by an orange for dessert."

Rachel's dimples showed as she said, "No, not an orange. Something more exotic, like a star fruit. Never sell Jillian short."

"Okay. I'll give you that one, a star fruit." I let out a deep breath. "You know, I still can't believe you let me walk around with a huge heart stuck on my butt, knowing I had a boyfriend who was here. Right here, in this very house." I stood up and glared down at Rachel. "And allow me to point out that he was laughing at my butt. I always had a large bottom, and you knew how self-conscious I was. Shame on you, Rachel!"

A silence settled around us. Dust bunnies danced in the late afternoon light. Rachel stood up. She spoke softly, "I love you too."

We held each other and let time slip by. Past memories touched the present with a loving caress. We hugged again and felt our hearts beat in time with each other. I gently nudged her. "Now go powder your nose and fix that special dinner. I think I can still take a bath and set the table. Besides, I'm the one with the knowledge to do that special napkin fold that looks like a flower."

"Great! I love the way you do that. When are you going to teach me?"

"When the time is right." I grinned. "It's a secret that only Grandma Nana and I shared. Now about your nose..."

"I'm going." Rachel got up, collected her wadded-up Kleenex, and moved toward the door.

"Oh, being a little on the neat side, aren't we?" She waved away my comment, and I called after her, "Change blouses. Gray is not your color. Try that bright rose one with the scoop neck. You look hot in pink."

Rachel stopped and asked, "You don't think it's too splashy?"

"Sure it is." I smiled. "Wear it." I watched my sister go down the hall and called after her, "And don't cover it up with a bulky sweater either."

She muttered, "What are you, a fashion consultant?"

"I heard that," I shouted back. "Next time around I'm thinking of pursuing that line of expertise. Seems to me there's a calling for fashion consciousness…" I yelled louder, "…right here in this house."

I got out the linen napkins while thinking of my clever comeback. After congratulating myself on the fact that I still possessed a sense of humor, I let my thoughts return to the budding relationship between my doctor and my sister. It was my opinion that he was smitten by Rachel's loving ways. He'd obviously noticed that she'd been blessed with a natural sweetness and had observed firsthand her ability to offer support and encouragement. I laughed softly to myself. While we were growing up, people had joked that Rachel expressed the ideal traits for being a nurse, a mother, a teacher, or even a doctor's wife. They had no idea of my sister's strengths. Inside that blonde head was a wealth of ideas, the intelligence to separate the good from the bad, and the conviction to implement them.

My fingers made the multiple folds so that with a pull and a firm tuck the napkins became roses. I always thought that Grandma Nana was clever. I let my thoughts drift to Dr. Bergman. He was intelligent, good-looking, and quiet but didn't have a clue about his clothes. It was a good thing he wore white coats every day.

On the social side, he did have a sense of humor, enjoyed fine wine, and had traveled to interesting places, but he still appeared to be lonely. As I saw it, his only bad habits, other than his inability to dress himself, were nibbling the skin on his thumb and being a workaholic. I realized I was being picky, but I wanted the best for my sister. Carl needed to socialize more, a few friends, some help in the fashion department, and photographs on his desk other than of his dog (although I remembered that Rachel had commented favorably about the big, hairy pooch). I snickered as I finished making the folds in the last napkin.

Being late for dinner was out of the question tonight, so I hurried to my bedroom. Rachel had already turned on an electric heater in the old bathroom, and the little room was packed with cozy warmth. I filled the claw-foot tub with hot water and added some rose scent. Soaking was a pleasure to be fully enjoyed. As I felt myself completely relax, I let my mind wander back to my previous thoughts. If I were going to be totally truthful, in my mind, I had already matched Dr. Bergman with Rachel. After all, the pairing of two people to enhance each other was definitely a pleasant thought.

However, he was coming tonight to try, once again, to talk me into going back to chemotherapy. That was not going to happen.

At 6:00 p.m., Rachel opened the door, and I added punctuality to my growing list of attributes for Carl. He shifted his weight from one foot to the other and finally handed the flowers and candy to Rachel. *Way to go, Doc,* I thought. Then the thought flashed through my mind that perhaps he was nervous or maybe suffered from an overly timid social self. I'd read about that somewhere. If that was the case, Rachel would be able to draw him out.

I offered a beaming smile as I continued to observe them, wondering if my sister had noticed Carl's attempt to dress in a casual manner. I glanced in her direction to discover her face bubbling over with happiness. *Ain't love grand?* I mused.

Apparently, I was the only one who found his plaid slacks humorous. I thought of asking where he'd found them but realized it didn't matter. For me, it was the idea that he was actually wearing them, and Rachel either hadn't noticed or thought it was fine. It was going to be a long night with these two.

We moved toward the parlor. Not a good idea in my opinion, as the furniture took on a Victorian motif and wasn't comfortable.

Formal straight-backed chairs covered with burgundy velvet and little cushioning combined with prim loveseats in a meticulous flower print. It was my belief that they had less stuffing than the chairs, certainly not created for comfort like the furniture in our family room. It seemed that the living room had always been the dignified place for family announcements, such as Jillian being elected senior prom queen. Other decorous functions were made to appear more important as well, like my need to declare a new diet and six-year-old Rachel's presentation of her first watercolor, a blur of purple and blue.

In the parlor, even the doilies were officially placed on the chair arms. It was still a ritual that we wash, starch, and iron them frequently. *And who supervised that?* I asked myself. *Why, Jillian, of course.* She would call from her home thousands of miles away to ask us if we had done "doily duty," and Rachel and I would take care of it. Smiling to myself, I thought, *There must be something here that we want to hold on to. How many times have we talked of redoing this room but always let it slide?* And now, here we were marching like little tin soldiers into the stuffy parlor because it was correct. Besides the prudish furniture, it was necessary to navigate the spindly-legged tables just to get into the sitting area. Photos and bric-a-brac spilled over each tabletop, regardless of its size, and created a dusting nightmare, but I noticed that all the items were spotless and wondered when Rachel had time to accomplish that task.

We all took seats, and even though we had exchanged pleasantries at the front door, we did it again. With that out of the way a second time, polite conversation ensued, something I was never good with, but I attempted to look interested in what was being said.

With a glass of wine in his hand, the doctor seemed to relax a bit. He moved from the edge of the stiff loveseat toward the back and appeared to be more comfortable.

I let out a small sigh and nodded pleasantly at him. "That's better. Isn't it?"

Rachel gave me a warning look.

Carl crossed one plaid leg over the other and smiled back. "Actually, it is."

"Where'd ya get those pants?" It slipped out before I could stop it.

Rachel cleared her throat and stared intently in my direction. "May I see you in the kitchen?"

"Of course."

I passed Carl, and he replied, "Sears."

"Who would have thought? They're ...." I caught my sister's look of displeasure. "... really colorful. Our older sister, Jillian, is good with color. And I know that Rachel loves color. Right, Rachel?"

"Yes, I do." She blushed and hurried me toward the kitchen. "Dina! Be nice to him. Don't criticize his clothes!"

"Oh thank goodness. You noticed the slacks too." I made my hands flutter. "For just a moment there, I wondered about your fine sense of—"

"Just stop it! He's a doctor, not a fashion consultant. Please, please, be nice." Her voice had taken on a note of urgency. "Okay?"

"I couldn't help it. He's wearing plaid pants. Is he into golf?"

"Stop it!"

I shuffled my foot. "Golly. I am sorry."

"No you're not!" She was trying not to laugh, but her dimples were deepening into a smile. "Plaid pants are … well, they're …" Pausing for a moment, she shook her head. "He needs a little help, okay?"

"Yes." I placed my hands on her shoulders. "And the good thing is that you're going to take him on." I thought for a moment. "And hopefully take him shopping."

"I can handle it."

"Do the shopping thing soon."

"Just be nice to him. Don't embarrass him again."

"I don't think I did embarrass him."

"Dina! I'm warning you." Her voice was taking on a nervous edge.

"Okay. I'll behave. Besides, the flowers were nice." I kissed my sister and walked back to the parlor feeling glad that Rachel had talked me into the peacock blue scarf. I adjusted its folds around my head, thinking it did add a dash of fun to the evening.

Rachel brought out a tray of French and Italian cheeses surrounded with apple wedges, deep purple grapes and crackers. Carl poured more wine, and the conversation lumbered along. I wondered what Dr. Bergman's reaction would be if I told him about my riding a horse. For a moment, I wondered if the doctor owned any Levi's. Or a cowboy hat? Hopefully, it wouldn't be a black hat. Rachel seemed down on black cowboy hats.

I really liked the way Gil touched the brim of his hat and looked at me. I remembered how broad his shoulders were and how strong his chest looked. His body had angled down to a slim waist and probably a firm bottom, although I didn't know that for sure.

"So, Dina, what do you think of that idea?"

"What?" I felt jarred awake and all my pleasant thoughts disappeared.

They were both looking at me. "Dina, are you listening?"

"No." I closed my mouth then opened it. "Oh. I mean ..."

Rachel sighed. "Were you drifting off?"

"I believe I was," I replied seriously.

"Carl, she isn't always this way." Rachel narrowed her eyes as she turned to me. "Dina, Carl suggested that we all take a car trip one of these glorious afternoons and appreciate the fall colors."

"Well ..." I cleared my throat as if giving their idea serious contemplation. The thought of inviting Gil to join us surfaced and I replied, "Wouldn't that be fun?"

"Good." Rachel beamed. She looked at Carl. "We'll set it up. Make all the arrangements and have a splendid day."

She got up and moved toward the kitchen. "I believe it's time for supper."

Carl sprang to his feet saying how he wanted to help, and they disappeared into the kitchen. I looked after them, wondering how much help was really necessary to carry the food to the table, and decided that two people could handle the task.

Rachel and Carl enjoyed rare roast beef, potatoes mashed with butter and topped with fresh rosemary, vegetables with herbs, and the remainder of the wine. The doctor's praise for my sister's cooking was sincere. She encouraged him to eat more, and he did. They exchanged little gooey looks several times and thought they were being discreet. I, however, found the humor in it but kept from commenting. I was secretly relieved that he hadn't tucked his napkin into his shirt. Rachel might have thought that was nice too.

I realized they were in the early stages of a lifetime commitment, and even though it was a tender moment for them, I had to fight the urge not to giggle. My sister fussed over him, and he loved it. It was actually turning into a pleasant evening, all things considered. Thoughts about my afternoon adventure kept a bright smile on my face while I sat at the table and ate mashed potatoes, minus the frills, and drank ginger ale. These days, it was about all I could keep down.

I had insisted that Rachel bake an apple pie and serve it with French vanilla ice cream for dessert. It was my favorite, and I knew I could enjoy it vicariously if I tried. As I watched the pie being consumed, memories began to serenade the air around me like half-remembered music, daring me to begin a pilgrimage into my past.

I began to wander through the pathway of time, recalling family moments where the sounds of laughter and the smells from the kitchen blended softly together.

Deep inside my heart, I listened to the voices of my sisters as they shared a rainy Saturday morning, arguing over the card game that was being played on the kitchen table while they waited for warm cookies to emerge from the oven. I could taste the cold milk and the bittersweet chocolate pieces nestled within the cookies. I recalled the bright yellow of my mother's apron and Jillian's habit of drumming her fingers while waiting for Rachel to toss down a card. I thought of my cat, curled under the table, purring softly, waiting for his piece of cookie.

Thoughts of summer afternoons delighted my senses with memories of sunshine that glittered across the kitchen counters, while dirty little hands stuffed freshly picked wild-flowers into a mason jar. Mother always called my attempt at arranging flowers a bouquet of love. I glanced through the kitchen window that I had created in my mind and saw the path that led to the orchard where I and my sisters had picked the best apples for Mother's pies. Each detail offered its own joy. I felt content, a strong peace growing within me. Good memories were made in a kitchen.

The past and the present touched each other, and I returned.

The evening had developed a gentle Sunday pace, with Rachel and Carl wearing their best manners. Every so often, she would reach over and touch him to emphasize a point. I noticed how easily they shared a loveseat. He would nod and gently touch her back. I continued to enjoy the show.

The air had turned crisp, and Carl lit the fire. He did a great job, and I gave Rachel the thumbs-up sign.

She mouthed the words, "Stop it."

My lips worked out, "Do you want to be alone?"

She gave me an angry look, and I let it go.

I settled in to watch. Conversation ebbed and flowed until the dreaded subject came up. Carl talked about the new cancer center and how state of the art it was. Rachel asked a loaded question about new medications that gave patients back the strength the treatments took away.

Now it was my turn. I took a deep breath. "Okay, I'm going to say this one more time. And I really want you to listen good." Shifting to a more comfortable position, I began speaking slowly. "The chemo and radiation, along with the constant change of medications, made me very sick. You both know that."

Carl cleared his throat, but I raised my hand. "This is my speech. And that part of my statement only required a yes or no. Nothing more." I grinned, taking the edge off my rather sharp comment. "Sorry about that. I'm starting to sound like Jillian in court."

Rachel reached for Carl's hand and nodded slowly. He looked both sad and angry but agreed by saying, "Yes, Dina. We know how sick the treatments left you."

"And I was exhausted all the time. Don't forget that." I paused. "It's not a great way to live—unless there's hope."

Rachel tried to protest, but I shook my head. When I continued, my tone had developed a cutting edge. "Then the seizures started, stripping away what dignity I had left. At best, if I had continued treatments, I would have had a year. Isn't that right, Carl?"

"Dina, we can't say—"

"Yes, we can. An abhorrent year of misery and pain— each day growing weaker. Chemotherapy wasn't killing my cancer because it was spreading too fast. We all knew that."

I looked into my sister's eyes and saw that Rachel was close to tears. I knew I had to finish what I'd started. Even though I was growing tired, I took a breath and let my voice soften. "My days are numbered, and I accept that." Reaching out to Rachel, I whispered, "I wish you would do the same." Looking at Carl, I nodded. "You'll help her?"

"I'll be there for both of you."

"Good." *He's pulling it together,* I thought. Then I sat back. "So please, let's change the subject. I'm so tired of talking about me. Let's talk about you." I wanted to add "both of you" but thought I'd be pushing it.

Carl came to my rescue by offering to help wash the dinner dishes. We all rose together, almost bumping into one another. Rachel insisted she'd wash the dishes later, but Carl wouldn't hear of it. I thought of pointing out that we had a dishwasher and it too was from Sears, maybe even the same Sears location where Carl had purchased his colorful slacks, but I held back.

While we were all standing, I suggested that they enjoy a glass of port. It was the winning idea. We all sat down together and realized that someone had to get the port and glasses. I volunteered.

The living room of the old house was snugly tucked in firelight. I watched as moments of tenderness collected around my sister and Carl. He put his arm over the back of the Victorian loveseat, which I considered a feat unto itself considering the height and angle of the sofa's back. I was inordinately proud of this bold move and made a sign for Rachel to move closer. She ignored me. There was no hurry for them; they had a lifetime.

I turned toward the picture window, where wisps of clouds, filtered by an unseen moon, floated past. Far to the north lay the wishing star in a clear, dark section of sky. I smiled, wondering if Gil was looking at the sky tonight. It was a romantic evening, created for lovers. I excused myself; they protested, and I said that I welcomed the warmth of my bed. I let my comment hang in the air and wondered what ideas that might put in their heads. After all, I told myself, Rachel was my little sister, and I wanted to help. Glancing back, I noted that Rachel had moved into the arch of Carl's arm, and I realized she didn't need my help after all.

In the darkness of my room, I could feel the now-familiar pain as it grew slowly inside me, spreading from my lower back, pushing an ugly path down my legs, creating cramps and promising more misery to follow. Sweat beaded my body with fear as the cutting pain tore into muscles. I tried to be still, waiting for the painkillers to help me forget. Soon the usual ache in my arms softened, and I began to relax.

I thought of my ride on Sweet Mary, letting my mind lavish in the radiant autumn colors of a day spent with a cowboy named Gil, a stranger who had stirred up my forgotten emotions. I closed my eyes and could see his tanned, weathered face and deep blue eyes. The clean smell of his soap drifted around me, leaving me anxious for tomorrow's adventure. As I drifted to sleep, I realized I wasn't fighting this alone anymore.

Chapter 3

When I woke the next morning, my eyes opened to a bedroom drenched in fresh sunshine. Beams of light shimmered like liquid gold across the arched mirror above the old fireplace. I decided immediately that it was a grand morning to be alive. As I sat up, the flashing rays shifted in my line of vision, and the mirror softened the reflections of my room. I stretched happily. *Mornings should be filled with visual beauty,* I thought, *as well as a promise of magic to highlight the day.*

Lying back, I wiggled my shoulders into the feather mattress and realized how much I'd always loved the old featherbed, even now when society felt that a firm mattress was better for back support. I snorted to myself. Like I should be concerned with what was best for the long-term care of my back. It was the moment that I lived in, and as I'd learned to accept that simple fact, everything around me had become more precious.

I felt good today, always better when I didn't take the pills that suppressed the seizures. As long as the painkillers could keep my body numb, I'd get by. But how long could I go without the seizure medication? I didn't know. A week, maybe another day? To me, it wasn't important. What really mattered was that this morning I would take another walk down the country lane and meet Gil.

What a wondrous secret! I smiled to myself, thinking that the only other cloistered memory I had was the day when I'd bought my first bra. Otherwise, I'd shared everything with my mother or my sisters.

It seemed that my youth had been played out a hundred years ago, yet I still had a clear picture of myself peddling my bike into town and then courageously walking through the front door of Murphy's old department store. I smiled and tilted my head. I could still hear the creaking noise from the old, wooden floor as my feet carried me toward the sign that said, "Ladies Undergarments."

I remember making the decision to purchase a bra by myself based on Jillian making fun of me and my mother saying that I didn't need a brassiere yet. I had considered taking Rachel with me, on the back of my bike, but thought better of it. She was just a little girl and might have told someone by mistake. Besides, I knew instinctively that this was a very private matter.

Smiling, I snuggled deeper into the featherbed. There had sure been a lot of merchandise in that old store. In summer, the large display windows had been filled with stiff mannequins in starched wigs, each one attired in a colorful cotton dress. Boards had been painted a bright green to represent grass, and faded plastic flowers appeared to spring forth from the wood, like tiny miracles. I looked up at the ceiling with a half grin still on my face. Each season had a distinct display. When Mrs. Murphy changed the seasons, we all changed our clothes and attitudes to match the official calling. Her windows were our fashion guide.

I closed my eyes and recalled large hats with wide brims and colorful bows. Even then I knew that bright colors represented the newest merchandise, while faded colors were to be avoided. The hats sat on a rack in a back corner along with spider webs and a collection of dead bugs. Jillian, always being the most informed, had told us there was something to suit everyone's tastes at Murphy's, including small boys. It suddenly occurred to me what she had meant, and I wondered if her own sons had ever given her the gift of insects. I wondered if I should put it out as a suggestion to them. They were quick to catch on.

I toyed with the idea for a few minutes then returned to my prior thoughts. Even though Murphy's was my favorite store and Rachel's first introduction to advertising through window display, Jillian had preferred the mall that was being constructed ten miles down the highway.

I laughed, thinking again of how surprised I'd been at the variety of bras the old store had carried. Good heavens, there were numbers and letters and underwire and padding, and quite frankly, I hadn't been prepared to make such a complicated decision. Asking for help was out of the question, as my mind was firmly made up that I could do this alone. But not having anything to base my decision on, and liking bright colors, I'd quickly selected a red, cotton brassiere that was much too large. It had seemed fine when I looked at it, but my first clue that perhaps I'd made a mistake had been when Mrs. Murphy asked if the bra was for my mother or my grandma Nana. I had stood very still, realizing the bra was too large for me and maybe too colorful for either my mom or Nana. Thinking that Nana was more adventuresome, I had squeaked out her name. Then I'd paid for the brassiere, taken it home, and hidden it in my bottom drawer, where it remained for many years.

I snuggled deeper into the feather mattress, thinking that although my bra shopping experience hadn't yielded the results I'd anticipated, it still represented a part of growing up that was mine alone. To this day my adventure was still a delightful secret, if not a slightly embarrassing one, and I enjoyed having a secret.

Slowly I left the warmth of my bed and felt the morning stiffness as it settled into my legs. *Not today,* I told myself. *I will not be bedridden today.* Hobbling around the bedroom helped, and soon I felt a release of pain. It left me weak but motivated enough to take the muscle relaxer and several deep breaths. I was determined to think positive thoughts.

I dressed slowly in jeans and a red, plaid blouse and moved toward the kitchen. The thought of meeting Gil gave my spirits a boost of joy. We would ride again, this time down to the old creek, a place in the valley that I had always liked.

Sitting at the breakfast table, I thought of how handsome he was in aviator sunglasses and what a friendly smile he had. He had talked to me like he really knew me and wanted to be with me. A thought jumped out of my subconscious. It was unexpected but there right in front of me. Did he know me? It was as if he had been expecting me to stop at the old gate.

Rachel's voice brought me out of the daydream, but I made a mental note to give this new idea some additional thinking time. "Dina, please be nice to Mrs. Kopeck. I've asked her to stay until I get back." Rachel looked stressed this morning. "It will take almost the entire day to run the errands, and you know I don't want to leave you alone that long."

Her concern was sometimes stifling. I had to remind myself that she meant well.

"I promise to be nice to Mrs. Kopeck. Does that make you feel better?"

"Yes."

"How long did Carl stay?" I inquired pleasantly.

"He left shortly after you went to bed."

Rachel busied herself with my cereal. She was trying so hard to be nonchalant that I couldn't resist asking, "Is he a good kisser?"

"That subject is off limits, Dina."

"Oh!" I snickered. "Well, now, that must mean he is really a good kisser."

Color flooded her face, and my cereal spoon hit the floor.

"So, Rachel, you needn't tell me another thing. I've got the picture." I looked toward the floor. "Got a case of the dropsy's, huh? Shall I get that spoon?" I started to rise.

"Sit down!"

"Sure." I teased. "Just don't get snappy."

Rachel offered a long sigh, and I continued. "We were talking about Mrs. K. Tell me, do her chickens still lay blue eggs?"

Rachel placed a clean spoon in my cereal. "Of course." She carried the bowl to the table. "And she sells them at the specialty market, three eggs for two dollars."

I opened my eyes wide. "Wow. I remember when she used to bring Mom a basket full of blue eggs and Dad never wanted us to eat them. Something about their color put him off." I yawned, feeling less stress as the muscle relaxer began to work. "You do realize that Mrs. K. isn't a bundle of stimulating conversation, right?"

"I suggest you have a little social chitchat with her before you let her drink that special tea she packs." Rachel lowered her voice. "It has whiskey in it. You did know that, didn't you?"

"No!" I scoffed. "Are we the only two people in the entire community who have this knowledge?"

"Dina, being sarcastic doesn't become you."

"Oh, okay. Let me reflect on it some." I struck a thinking pose. "Oh, that's right. She's been sipping her special brew for twenty years now. I'm going out on a limb here, but I'll bet other people, besides us, know her secret. Well, in the interest of good decorum, I shall still remain shocked by your disclosure."

"Very funny, Dina."

"Why, that Mrs. Kopeck is just a tart!"

"Yeah right."

"However, I like her and her blue eggs. She's the first businesswoman I ever met. I have respect for that."

Rachel got a towel and wiped at the countertop. "Oh, Jillian called again early this morning." She carried her cup of coffee to the breakfast table. Its tantalizing aroma filled the air, causing me to inhale deeply. Rachel hesitated. "Does the smell bother you?"

"No, silly. I adore the smell of freshly roasted coffee. It's almost as good as drinking it. Did you know that I fell in love with the aroma first? And now that coffee and I don't agree, well, the aroma is still wonderful."

I smiled and asked, "So what did Jillian want that she called twice in twenty-four hours?"

"Two things." Rachel cleared her throat. "Number one, part A, is that she thinks the photo albums you're looking for are still in the garage. Number one, part B, is that she wants an apology for all the unkind remarks we made over the years while she took pictures and recorded our family history."

"Fat chance on the apology." I giggled. "Did she really do the 'number one, part A' thing over the phone?"

Rachel giggled too. "Yep. She sure did." Shaking her head, she took a deep breath. "Boy, was that annoying when we were kids." She elongated her neck and tilted her head like Jillian. "'Little girls, I want you to listen to me.'" Her voice took on a polished tone as she mimicked our older sister. "'Number one, part A, is that I want you both to clean up. Number one, part B, is that I want you to both disappear when my friends come over. Number one, part C, is don't make a lot of noise.'"

"Oh yeah." I nodded. "I remember how all of her instructions were dished out to us in grating detail. And it always worked 'cause we did whatever she asked."

Rachel scoffed. "Of course we did it. She was our big sister, and she knew everything."

I studied the bird outside the window as I thought about Jillian. "Don't you remember how totally invasive she was with her camera? Many's the time I could have smacked her silly, but looking at the old photos would be fun." I smiled wistfully. Feeling a tug at my heart, I knew how much I wanted to see the family pictures.

Rachel had a questioning look when she faced me. "Do you think we still have photos of that ugly pumpkin Jillian carved? What did she call it?"

"Oh, she had a name picked out, but when the pumpkin didn't win first place at the shopping center contest, she turned really grumpy, and Mom had to give her 'the talk' about good sportsmanship."

"Yeah, I was little, but I remember." Her forehead creased. "It was a hot day for fall, and you and I were stuck with loading that big pumpkin back in the trunk of the car. Then Dad took us out for root beer floats at A&W." The crease disappeared. "Gosh, were they good!"

"Yes, it was before the low-fat years took hold. Jillian still ate real ice cream then. Boy, that was a while back." We meditated on the lost years before I continued, "By the time we finally got home, the pumpkin had a total meltdown. What a mess. I can still smell it."

"We felt so bad that we made up a first-place ribbon." Rachel smirked. "And we stuffed that pumpkin in our coaster wagon and hauled it into her room so she could see her prize. Whew! Did it stink!"

"Oh, big mistake," I recalled. "We weren't allowed in her room, and neither was anything that smelled bad. Then when we heard her coming down the hall, we hid in her closet, another area where we weren't allowed."

"Yup, triple mistakes." Rachel nodded. "It wasn't one of our victorious moments."

"But, she did forgive us when she saw our sorry attempt at making the pumpkin a winner, and she told us we were the best little sisters ever."

Rachel smiled. "Yeah, that meant a lot. I still remember my pride peaking when I heard her say those words. You know that Jillian remembered the whole story?" Rachel leaned forward. "That's why she called. Jillian and Tony checked their personal schedules, and they each had some time, at the same time..."

I couldn't help it. I rolled my eyes.

"No. It's okay." Rachel waved her hand. "Let me finish. They took the boys to the pumpkin patch as a family adventure. They even had ice cream floats!"

My eyes opened wide.

"No, really, Dina. Our health-conscious Jillian let her sons eat real ice cream and drink soda in the middle of the day!"

I grinned. "Will miracles never cease?"

"Oh, it gets better! Really better. She actually told them the story of the pumpkin carving contest. The boys loved it! Tony had never heard it before, and he loved it too. She said the pumpkin patch was a wonderful family outing, and they were going to do it every year. And she wanted us to know we were still the best little sisters ever."

"Fantastic!" I reached for Rachel's hand. "That's what I want you to remember, the really good times, because there were so many of them." I squeezed her hand and smiled. "Promise me you'll think about all the fun. Do the secret cross-your-heart thing. Do it now!"

"Okay, okay." Rachel raised her finger. She made an X over her heart, kissed the tip of her nail, and blew the kiss into the air. She ruffled my thinning hair. "I wonder how many sisters have a secret oath."

I smiled back. "All of them."

Rachel kissed my cheek. "Your breakfast awaits."

"Get real. It's cream of rice, some breakfast!" I received a stern look as I shifted around in my chair. "You know, Rachel, today I feel as if I could eat bacon and eggs and cheese-fried potatoes."

"I know, baby. The thought of food is there, but you can't keep it down, and tossing your cookies…well, it makes you so weak." Her eyes began to fill, and she quickly turned around.

Even with the truth spoken aloud, I felt like eating real food. I continued to spoon the sloppy cereal around the bowl. It did remind me of glue, but I didn't want to hurt Rachel's feelings. I watched as she finished her coffee and began to search through her purse for the car keys.

A blue-haired lady rapped on the glass panes of the kitchen door. Mrs. Kopeck was armed with knitting, a book, her thermos, and a sweater, just in case the day turned cold.

I muttered, "She's equipped for anything. What did you do? Invite her for a week?"

"Stop it! She'll hear you." Rachel gave me a stern look. "Remember she was Mother's good friend, and she's here to help. I want you to behave. Promise me."

"Yeah. Okay. But Mom was never a drinker."

She whispered, "Mrs. K.'s tea taste has been embellished over the years. I'm sure of it."

I looked skeptical. "Are you leaving me with a person who may or may not have a problem?"

"Oh, Dina. Stop!" Rachel took a deep breath. "And remember, a little social conversation would be nice."

"Of course." I smiled pleasantly. "I am the picture of catchy chitchat."

Rachel looked at me with narrowed eyes then turned toward the door. "Good morning to you, Mrs. Kopeck!" she sang out cheerfully. "Please come in." My sister took a breath of the warm, sunshine-filled day and smiled broadly at our visitor. "Isn't it a lovely day? Dina is so happy to see you, and I'm so glad that you're here."

I muttered something about excessive enthusiasm, but Rachel ignored me as she took Mrs. Kopeck's sweater and laid it over a chair. She continued in her happy voice, "We both thank you for taking the time to visit."

I passed Rachel on my way to the teapot and whispered in her ear, "Overkill." I followed it up with, "Hello, Mrs. K." Rachel shot me a look. Feeling properly chastised, I freshened my tea and sat back down, resigning myself to contemplate my cereal as my sister helped Mrs. Kopeck settle in.

As usual, it took ten minutes to go over the list of my medications, which Mrs. K. already knew by heart but Rachel always covered as if it was the first time and everyone was enthused to learn of the many drugs that passed through my body. Finally, she handed over the sheet of paper with pertinent phone numbers printed in large block letters, just in case Mrs. K. forgot her glasses. Rachel asked her to read it back, always an embarrassing moment, and spent an extra minute on her personal cell phone number, another mortifying event she covered in detail. Then she handed one cell phone to me and put the other in her purse, a sign that the tedious instructions were finally coming to a close.

At last the cherished paper was securely taped to a kitchen cabinet, and with a to-do list in hand, Rachel blew me a kiss and added a promise that she would be home in time to watch our favorite TV shows together.

The door shut. There was a smooth silence, and I nodded to Mrs. K. "Bet you're glad that's over."

"Your sister is a lovely girl. Favors your Mother." She headed toward the windows in the small family room and lowered the shades. "Perhaps a bit more detailed than your Mom but has her coloring." Adjusting the hankie she kept tucked in her sleeve, she smiled. "Rachel's also very good with phone numbers."

"Indeed she is." Thinking of my promise for additional conversation, I forged ahead. "Usually someone who is inclined toward art can't make heads or tails out of math. It's a right brain, left brain sort of thing."

"Is that so?" Mrs. Kopeck looked surprised but not interested in acquiring new knowledge on the subject. She smiled in my direction and asked, "Do you need anything, dear?"

"Nope. I'm good."

"Well then." Mrs. Kopeck nodded and settled comfortably in front of the television. Using the remote, she quickly located her favorite game show. It created a soft buzzing of background noise as her fingers began to work the knitting needles. So instead of the affable communication Rachel had envisioned, we began our usual conversation. "How are you today, Dina?"

"Quite fine, Mrs. K. How are you?"

"Very well, thank you." Her blue hair was a beacon in the dimly lit room. I smiled, thinking it was rather pretty. Sort of the same shade as her gourmet eggs.

"How is your husband's health?" I inquired as I moved toward the rocking chair.

"Excellent." The needles made a clicking sound.

"And your children?"

"Just lovely, dear."

Faithful to my promise of practicing social manners, I indicated the colorful yarn with a sweep of my hand. "For your son?"

"Grandson." Adjusting the glasses on her nose, she looked at me. "Tommy."

"Yes, of course. Tommy," I replied lamely. "And that would be the son of . . . Walter Jr.?"

She grinned in understanding. "Sam and Kathy's youngest."

I sat forward in the chair, nodding my head in understanding. "Sure enough. Sam and Kathy. How are they doing?"

"Just fine." She pushed the hankie farther up her sleeve and reached for the knitting needles again. "How are your sister's boys?"

"Great! Growing, strong, really active in sports."

"And Jillian?"

I began to rock. "Why, perfect, as usual."

"Ahh, much like the child she was."

"Yes." I nodded. "Yes, indeed." I watched Mrs. K.'s fingers as they worked the yarn. "You remember my older sister well."

"Quite tall. Always in charge."

"That's right! You do remember Jillian."

Mrs. K. looked up and smiled. "She took good care of you girls. Loved you every day and made you mind your manners."

I took a deep breath. "That she did."

The needles made a metal tapping sound. Mrs. K. added, "She even made sure that Walter and Sam behaved too."

I nodded in complete understanding, rocking to and fro. In the shaded room, time slowed down, gathering around me like feathers. I could feel a nap coming on, but that wasn't going to happen today. I had important things to do. I stopped rocking and cleared my head by taking a deep breath.

I considered my promise to Rachel fulfilled; all social amenities had been covered, and I decided to move along. "Time for tea?"

"Lovely idea, dear."

"Allow me to get it." I stood and stretched. "And your book. Where did Rachel put it?"

"Kitchen counter." Mrs. K. correctly answered the quiz show question and turned back to me. "It's right under the note with that complicated cell phone number."

I grinned. "Please don't be hard on her." Using my best backstairs tone, I added, "She's practicing to be a mother." The needles stopped, and only the television played on. "So all those little details, like phone numbers, they're really important to her."

Mrs. K. turned around. "My goodness, is Rachel pregnant?"

I reached for the paperback. "Just in the thinking stage."

"Is that so?" Mrs. K. wrinkled her brow. "Didn't know she had a beau."

"That's because it's a clandestine affair." I carried the book to her chair. "Is the light close enough for you?"

"Oh, I don't need a light to knit by, dear. 'Clandestine,' you say. What does he do? Rachel's beau?"

"He's a professional." I put my hands up. "That's all I can say. Very hush-hush." I winked at her. "You know what I mean."

She nodded knowingly and put her needles aside. She stretched her arm toward the table lamp. "Yes, dear, it's within my reach, should I decide to read."

I handed her a mug. Filling it from the thermos, I inhaled deeply. "What a lovely, aromatic brew."

"Thank you, dear. Has a bit of lemon and mint in it."

"That it does. Where shall I put it?"

She reached for the mug. "How about a toast to your sister and…" Mrs. K. looked around the dim room as if someone might leap from the shadows. It occurred to me that she took clandestine seriously. Satisfied that we were alone, she continued in a quiet voice, "To your sister and her beau."

I felt good about that and reached for my own tea mug. We toasted to Rachel and her wedding, her future children and happiness for all. I liked Mrs. K. She was a fine lady. Her special brew was well scented and, I imagined, quite tasty. We had a toast to Walter Jr. and to Sam and Kathy and even little Tommy. In the spirit of the moment,

I proposed a toast to blue eggs, and that required a refill. Finally I held out her sweater. "This is for you. Just in case the temperature drops."

"So thoughtful, dear." She untangled the hankie and wiped at her nose. It disappeared back into her sleeve. The television sounds settled around the room, filling all the corners, allowing me to slip out of the kitchen.

Knowing Mrs. K. would soon be sleeping soundly, I went in search of my favorite sweatshirt. I even spent time applying lip gloss and studied my face in the bathroom mirror. I looked tired, and the skin was stretched too tight across my bones. Funny, I thought, that all my life I had wanted to emphasize my cheekbones, and now they were more prominent than I remembered. I could also see light blue veins through the skin around my temples. The eyes that stared back at me were weary, but when I looked deeper, they still held a sparkle. I whispered to my image, "Today I will feel good. I will be what I want to be. I will see what I want to see." The words seemed too ambiguous alone, so I decided to take something simple and verbalize on it. I looked back in the mirror. "Today I will see long, thick hair." Shaking my head, I realized I had overextended my positive thoughts. The reality of thin strands swayed across the bare areas of my head. I spent some more time trying on scarves, but they didn't feel right. I checked the clock and decided it was time to return to the kitchen.

My good humor was restored as I lifted the knitting from Mrs. Kopeck's lap and placed it on the table next to her empty mug. I felt a twinge of guilt but rationalized that I had only provided a mug and the occasional idea for a toast. I turned down the sound on the television and pulled the ottoman closer. I raised Mrs. K.'s legs so that they rested comfortably. She looked happy. I felt happy. Everything would be fine.

I walked back to the kitchen table and pocketed the cell phone and the pills that Rachel had left. The medication that prevented the seizures made me ill and sleepy, and I needed my strength to carry me to the old gate.

Chapter 4

I watched the sunshine rediscover the road through branches embellished with golden foliage. *Autumn, I thought, is particularly lustrous.* An invisible breeze brushed past my face on its way to the tops of the tallest trees, where leaves waited to embrace its movement. Some swayed in harmony; others shook free to waft toward the earth. I nodded to myself, smiling faintly at the performance of the season.

Gil waved when he saw me walking along the country lane. I looked up, still grinning. "So is that your brother directing the dance through the trees?"

"Hello to you too, Miss Dina." With a lighthearted gesture, he touched his hat in greeting, and I felt my heart flutter.

He looked up, squinting. "Yeah. That's Daniel. Leastwise, he's behavin' himself today."

"Well, that's good. Sounds like a younger brother to me."

He raised his eyebrows in surprise. "I never thought about that."

I teased, "He's obviously a talented choreographer. Look at the dance he's created." I pointed toward the country road where branches and leaves swayed in the wind. "He has those powerful trees at his command."

Gil rubbed his hand across his chin. "Thinking back, I do remember the boy seemed to enjoy dance and music. We all liked a good hymn."

"Oh yes," I agreed dryly. "A good hymn is a real sing-along extravaganza."

"Only the ones with an upbeat tempo."

"Did you add a few good hallelujahs along the way?"

He considered carefully before answering, "Sometimes."

I couldn't help myself from chuckling. "Does your whole family have a sense of humor?"

"Tends to make life a bit easier." He smiled warmly. "I believe your original question was about my brother's talent. And truth be told, Daniel always could cut himself a fine step."

"He liked to dance?"

"Yes, ma'am." Gil still looked puzzled. "But a choreographer ... Well now, I gotta tell ya, Miss Dina, that boy is full of surprises."

"Indeed he is." We stood together with only the old gate separating us as we watched the show. My voice was barely audible. "I miss dancing." I turned toward him. "Do you think there's dancing behind the pearly gates?"

"There are no gates."

He said it with such certainty I had to stop for a moment. What did he know that I wasn't getting? I smiled. "It was just a figure of speech." Gil looked perplexed as I went on. "My question was, do you think there's dancing in heaven?"

"Absolutely." He breathed in, and I felt myself drawn closer to him. He continued, "I think there's dancin' just about everywhere. It's an expression of joy, and folks like to feel good."

"Gotta agree with that." I raised my hands with the palms up and shrugged. "So ... am I early or late?"

"Neither." He pushed the gate open, offering me his hand. "As I see it, you're right on time."

"Well, I'm not told that often." Taking his hand, I walked through the gate. The weathered boards creaked on rusty hinges as they blew shut behind me.

I felt like I had entered our own private world. "Hi," I whispered. He smelled of soap and something else that was fragrant, like evergreens in the winter. My nose twitched, and I wondered if it was cologne and if he had worn it for me.

"Pine trees and yes." He spoke into my hair.

"What?" I looked surprised. "Did you read my mind?"

"I read your nose. It's cute when it wiggles like that."

"Ah. You're very observant."

"And I tend to listen well too. Daniel recommended the pines. He said ladies liked a fresh, outdoor scent."

I pulled away so I could look into his eyes. "And how did Daniel know that?"

"Experience, I reckon. What with the wind job and all, boy has learned a thing or two."

With a half-smile, I replied, "What's the name of the cologne Daniel recommends?"

Gil hesitated then shrugged. "Pine tree, I guess."

"Oh, Gil! You're such a straight man." I laughed. "By the way, tell your brother that it was good advice." I stood on my tiptoes, leaned forward, and inhaled. "Very nice. So who makes this scent?"

He swung an arm over my shoulder. "Daniel."

I giggled at his serious tone. "And just how does he do that?"

"Well…" He seemed hesitant to answer. "You sure you want to know this?"

I pushed just far enough away so I could look into his eyes. I lifted my eyebrow and replied, "Absolutely."

"Okay." He smiled down at me. "I met him early this morning so as I could have a talk with him about that caressing of ladies' faces. And about the possibility of him being a leg man." He held me at arm's length and looked over his aviator glasses, meeting my eyes. "Which is apparently all true."

"You seem surprised," I replied.

"Yes, ma'am. I was indeed surprised."

I giggled. "Do go on. Finish your story."

He cleared his throat and continued to look at me. "In the course of our conversation, he enlightened me as to the ladies likin' a fresh, outdoor smell." Giving a slight nod toward the pines that grew on the upper slopes of the ridge, he continued, "So he had me stand up there in the gatherin' of evergreen trees while he went around back and blew through 'em so that I'd have me up a pine scent."

I reached up and removed his sunglasses. I noticed that his eyes held an amused sparkle. "Gil, you wouldn't be telling me a tall tale now, would you?"

Bending closer, he spoke softly, "What's important is that you like it."

My laughter gathered deep in my throat. "That's a great story." I handed back his glasses, still snickering. "Really. I mean it, a great story." I thought to myself it was almost believable the way Gil had told it.

"Well, good then." He seemed relieved. "Glad to know that Daniel's advice was fine. Sometimes the boy has been known to play a trick or two."

"Is that so?" I replied dryly.

"Yes, ma'am. It is so. And now I'm thinkin' that with this here new talent of him directin' a dance, I'm gonna have to have myself another talk with him." His eyes twinkled as he leaned closer. "I dance a bit myself, you know."

"Well, no. I didn't know." I fluttered my eyes at him and realized how silly I must look, so I stopped. "But I will store that information."

Gil nodded. "You do that, Miss Dina. It might just come in handy." Just then the horses whinnied. He put his glasses in his shirt pocket and smiled at me. "The day waits. You ready to do some more ridin'?"

Leaving the dried meadows behind, we rode toward the canyon. I breathed deeply of the fresh air and felt a faint stirring of appetite, or at least I thought that's what it was. I told myself it must be about food because I was outdoors and doing something instead of being inside and bedridden. But then reality crashed through, and I thought of all the reasons I couldn't eat.

"There's a creek runs through the floor of the canyon. Best fishing hereabouts. Did you know that, Dina?" Gil squinted in the brilliant sunshine as he offered me the old straw hat again. "Do y'all like fresh fish cooked in an iron skillet? Say, over an open fire?"

I adjusted the brim and murmured my thanks as I peeked at Gil's profile. His dark hair curled around his ears, reminding me of someone else and at the same time bringing forth a sensual feeling that took me by surprise. I cleared my throat, giving myself time to focus on his question.

"Well, I used to like to eat. But ah, lately I, um, can't really eat much and keep it down." I risked a glance at him. "Do you know what I mean?"

He pulled his cowboy hat lower, offering a warm smile that softened the rugged lines of his profile. "Let me think on that some."

The sudden noise of water rushing over stones held sway over my ears and heart. "As a kid, I used to come here," I said. A grin tugged at the corners of my mouth. "But that was so long ago." I hesitated and gave a shrug. "Another lifetime."

"You come alone?" He put his sunglasses back on.

"Gosh, no. My sisters and I would pack up some sandwiches and put Kool-Aid in our dad's thermos. First we'd stop at the old ranch and ask permission to go on down to the creek. It's their property, you know?"

Gil nodded in understanding, so I continued. "The old man who lived there would ask us if we wanted to feed the horses, and his wife—he called her the 'missus'—would give us big bunches of carrots and we'd approach the corral." I looked at Gil. "I don't want to offend you or Sweet Mary or Joe, but honestly, horses are messy eaters."

"I'm wounded." He clutched at his heart. "And so are my friends."

"Well, I might as well tell you that after feeding carrots and sometimes apples to your friends, we'd have horse slobber all over our little girl hands."

He turned in the saddle to face me, a grin tugging on his face. "Any more insults you wish to hurl?"

"It's the truth." I smiled back. "So the missus would take us to the old pump where we could wash off. Gosh, that water was cold!" I snickered. "Jillian would inspect us to be sure we were really clean, and when she was satisfied, she'd nod at the missus, who would then offer us home-baked brownies and tell us to be careful and mind our big sister."

I glanced at Gil. "Nice people, the missus and her husband. I remember them as gentle and happy. But the horses were still big."

"That so?"

"Yup. Real big horses." I tried to show him by using my hands but realized I couldn't let go of the reins. He chuckled as if he had one up on me.

We continued to amble along, and my thoughts drifted back in time. I remembered the old ranch house being time washed in a soft gray paint. It was nestled among trees and flowers, and there was a swinging glider suspended from the deep overhang of the front porch.

Turning toward Gil, I commented, "I always felt welcome at the ranch. After the old couple moved away, I would go back just for the feeling of serenity that came from the land." I shifted my weight in the saddle. "I also liked the glider."

"Had a porch rocker, did it?"

"Sure did. A double-seater suspended with old chains that shed rust on whoever touched them. As a teen, I would swing my troubles away and dream about tomorrow." Smiling again, I added, "Until Jillian would be sent to fetch me home. Word was that the ranch was falling apart and not a safe place to be visiting." I stroked Sweet Mary's neck. "But I knew better. The ranch was a good place."

Gil nodded. "Smart and pretty too."

Just not honest, I thought, *and I've got to change that, but I'm not sure when.*

"Oh, you smooth talker!" I joked.

He cocked an eyebrow and replied, "Please do go on with your story."

I cleared my throat and continued, "So my sisters and I, armed with our warm brownies, would walk down here and spend most of the day." I pulled the straw hat lower. "We'd build little bridges with fallen tree branches. Once we even placed stepping stones across the creek."

"That so?"

"Truth be told, my older sister would give the directions while Rachel and I would do the hard stuff." I laughed. "It worked." I turned toward Gil and said, "But I don't remember the fishing. Maybe it was a boy thing."

The day was going so well that I didn't want to interrupt its flow, but I felt that I owed Gil the whole story. He needed to know the truth. I slowed my speech and continued softly, "I have wonderful sisters. They both care so much. Sometimes it's a little too much." I looked directly at him. "You can tell that I'm not very healthy."

Gil turned in the saddle. His eyes held mine. Tenderness swept across his face.

I took a deep breath and spoke simply, "It's cancer, and mine is terminal."

The day didn't change after my acknowledgment. The sky didn't turn black; no thunderclouds erupted. Autumn's radiance continued to surround me. I held up my hand for Gil to see that I didn't want him to comment yet. I wanted to continue talking.

"Jillian's a wonderful big sister. My cancer is very difficult for her to accept. She calls often and wants me to take treatments at an east coast clinic, but I declined after understanding the fatality of my disease."

Gil was a good listener, and I felt more words slip out. "The last two years I've fought the cancer with various mixtures of chemotherapy and radiation. And lots of drugs." Silhouetted against the lusty colors of fall, I realized I was hauntingly thin. "Boy, can those drugs make a body sick!" My skin's milky texture emphasized the sorrow in my blue eyes. I continued in an even voice, "Following the last set of chemo, I made up my mind—no more treatments."

Gil's brow knit with concern. His voice was a rough whisper. "I'm so sorry, Dina."

"Hey, the truth is that it's a relief to finally say it." Shifting my weight in the saddle, I focused on the sunlight as it collected in warm pools around the fallen leaves. *Well,* I thought, *if he wants to turn the horses around now, I understand.*

However, he remained silent, so I went on. "Besides, I have a great doctor. Did I mention that he's sweet on my sister Rachel?"

Gil's eyebrow rose. "That so?"

"Sure is. Oh, they don't think I know, but I do. Anyhow, where was I? Oh yes, the good doctor has powerful pain medication. As long as it works, I'll be fine." I rolled my shoulders. "Please understand that I'm not making fun of my disease. I'm coping the best way I can. Sometimes the burden gets so heavy that I go into my closet, shut the door, sit on the floor, and have a good cry. I feel so bad that Rachel is stuck with my care. It's so unfair to her. Her career was just getting underway when she had to put it on hold and play nurse maid to me." My throat felt tight. "I can't let her see me cry. It would hurt her too much."

Gil turned his head toward me and spoke with conviction, "She's stronger than you think."

"She is? How do you know that?"

"She's here for you, Dina. She's caring for you, and that makes her strong."

"Hmm. Never thought about it quite like that." I turned my thoughtful look toward Gil.

"Yep, it's the truth."

I grinned. "Well, that's good to know. One less thing to worry about on my end."

"Glad I could help." Gil grinned back.

I faced the trail, deep in thought again. "Now I can focus on my more immediate concern, Jillian, my sister who knows all. She's coming out in two weeks for a visit."

"Will it be nice to see her?"

"Not really. Oh damn! I didn't mean it like that. It's just that her plan is to relieve Rachel of her responsibility and personally nurse me back to a state where I want to continue this hopeless fight." My voice rose in frustration. "I'm sorry. I'm just so upset."

Gil gave me a minute. "Dina, people, like family, want to help so very much that sometimes they mess up. It's a fragile place to be."

"For them or for me?"

"For everyone."

"I'm trying to understand." I shook my head. "But my life is not exactly in a gentle pattern right now. The truth is that I dread Jillian's visit. I just wish that both my sisters would accede to the fact that the cancer is terminal. The best they can do is be there to help me when the time comes to leave." A wave of frustration passed through me. "I've tried hard to accept their cheerfulness and unending hope for a bright future. I really have. But in truth, it only serves to depress me."

I couldn't believe I'd told Gil, a stranger, this much about my private life. What had possessed me to babble on? Embarrassment flooded my face with color. I brushed at my cheeks.

His voice was understanding, soft and gentle. "How did you make the decision to stop the chemo?"

Well, I thought, *I've gone this far. I might as well finish it.* "About six months ago when I was in for a treatment, I saw a little blonde-haired girl who was there to begin her chemo. She was holding a beat-up teddy bear. Then, oh, I guess it was a couple of months later that I saw her again. She had lost weight and had an old look in her round eyes. She was clutching the bear this time." I shook my head and felt my voice quiver. "There is a huge difference between holding and clutching."

I ducked under a tree branch, noticing the air felt soft for a fall day. I cleared my throat. Actually, it felt good to finally tell someone the whole story.

"When I saw her the last time, we were both waiting in the reception area of the cancer treatment wing. She had a pink ski cap on her head, and around it her mother had tied a pretty satin bow. The little girl was very weak, and she was caressing this scruffy bear, holding it in her thin arms as if she were saying good-bye. Then she walked over to the children's toy chest and opened it. Inside there were lots of stuffed animals, and she tucked the bear on top, kissed its battered nose, and closed the lid."

I felt the horse move under me, and the day slid along. My emotions were raw, but Gil nodded at me to continue. I permitted my eyes to travel across the meadows, looking at life as it played out. After a few minutes had passed in silence, I took up my story.

"I asked her why she put the bear back in the toy chest, and she said that's where she'd found him. He was a helper bear, and now that she was going to play with the angels, Teddy would help other children. It was then that her Mom came and scooped her up. She waved good-bye and smiled at me, the sweetest smile I've ever seen. And in her eyes there was acceptance. Acceptance and..." I paused in thought. "...something like knowing a special secret and not being afraid anymore."

Light spilled across my face as we rode through a clearing. Dry leaves of flaming orange crumpled under the horses' feet. A quality of timelessness enveloped us.

"So I decided that if a little five-year-old girl could handle it, so could I. That's when I stopped chemo and decided to keep what dignity I had left. I was tired of throwing up and shaking, being dehydrated and having blackouts." I breathed in the air, letting it fill my body. "If there had been any hope, I would have never stopped…" I shook my head. "But there wasn't."

Gil cleared his throat. "What do you want to do, Dina?"

"Me? Heck, I want to live forever." My laughter, edged with razor sharpness, dissolved as tears swelled in my eyes. I sucked in a gulp of air and held it. I pressed my lips together as my chest began to shake with sobs.

Gil reached out to rein in my horse and offered me a handkerchief. "Let it go, Dina. You've kept too much in for too long."

I wiped at my angry tears, letting them flow. The release of emotions left me feeling lightheaded. I cleared my throat, stalling for time before I spoke. "Well, seeing that my first choice is not an option, I'll go with plan two."

"Which is?"

"Leave gracefully." I took another deep breath then pushed my insoles into the stirrups and extended my legs. "Sometimes I get cramps," I explained. "It's better now."

"Stretchin' always feels good." Turning his head, he smiled and continued, "Ya were about to tell me something else."

"Yeah." I settled back in the saddle. "So here's my take on it. Everyone is disappointed that they can't help. Each day there is more sadness and more anger and more dis-appointment. Then when it's finally over, everyone will breathe a sigh of relief and say, 'Oh, the poor dear. She was in such pain, you know. It's a blessing that she's gone.'

"And I agree with them!" I let out my pent-up emo-tions in a single huff and wiped at my eyes again. "I'm not hurt that they feel that way. I'm angry that I have to suffer so long, and that affects everyone around me.

"Gosh, I sound like I want to control the world, but I don't." I cleared my throat. My voice held conviction. "I just want some control over my life." I felt the steady rhythm of the horse. It offered me stability.

Gil tilted his hat against the sunshine, silently urging me to continue. "Truth is that I wish I could have left months ago when I knew it was fatal," I said. "It would have saved everyone, including me." I felt a flush of anger. "I don't think I'm being a selfish person when I say 'me.'" My hands made a helpless gesture, and I inhaled slowly. "It would have spared all of us stress, tears, agony … Each day I'm more tired. I fear the pain, and the cancer is winning. The only reason Rachel lets me walk alone is because the doctor told her to give me that time for as long as I have the strength to do it."

I squinted at the sunshine that filtered through the ancient oaks. Glancing at Gil, I smiled briefly and rolled my eyes. "Boy! Did I answer your question or what?"

He reached across to my reins until both horses stopped under the shade of an old elm. He removed his sunglasses and clipped them onto the collar of his worn denim shirt. He faced me and paused. His deep blue eyes held me gen-tly in their gaze. "Well, Dina, sometimes matters don't get resolved as we want 'em to. It's probably one of the harder lessons in life."

I took a deep breath and replied, "Well, thanks for your honesty." Facing Gil, I smiled. "If you would have said, 'Everything is going to be just fine,' I would have had to hurt you."

He released the reins, grinning at my humor. "That so?"

A lost emotion swept over me. I blinked, trying to recall the sensation. Was it a feeling of playfulness? "Yup." I smiled at Gil. "That's so."

My eyes took in the mellowness of the afternoon colors. "I'm not really a brave person. And I really don't want to talk about cancer anymore, especially when I'm outside enjoying the day and feeling pretty good."

We followed the trail that led toward a natural clearing where the creek pooled into a small lake. Autumn shades flowed throughout the trees in ripe colors. Gil tied his horse to a sturdy branch and reached up to help me dismount. Sweet Mary nuzzled my neck, asking for a carrot, which Gil produced from his saddle pack. His aviator glasses reflected a tranquil scene where shady impressions mingled with sun streaks to dapple the air. He was very close, and he seemed very tall. I could smell the fresh scent of his soap mixed with pine.

"I have something for y'all to see." Leading me beyond the trees, he pointed to a picnic basket where a red-checked cloth lay spread out, anchored in each corner by small rocks.

"What's this? How did…" I stopped, surprise spreading across my face.

"I left a bit early. Figured you'd enjoy a little picnic. So if you would open the basket and get us set up, I'll see if I can fish us up a main course." He gently touched my arm. "That seem all right to you?"

"Yeah." His closeness was intoxicating. I felt both warm and cold, depending on which part of my body was sending the temperature reading.

"Dina, did you know that fish is food for the soul?" He continued to stroke my arm. "I don't think y'all will have any problem with it."

"Oh." I took a deep breath. "Well, okay then."

He lifted a wrought-iron skillet from the basket and stood. His fishing pole was behind a tree.

I let out a sigh, followed by laughter. "Seems like you're prepared." I paused to inhale the fall air and grinned. "I like that in a man."

He touched the brim of his hat, offering a faint smile. "Do you now?"

"Yup." I smiled back. "I surely do. I also like fish dusted with flour, fried in butter."

"Me too. How about a squeeze of lemon and a few capers on top?"

"Now you're talking."

He grinned. "Have a look in the basket. Would ya?"

I moved toward the wicker basket and knelt on the checked cloth, where I began to look for plates and flatware. A fresh lemon, a small plate with flour, and a stick of butter lay on top. I shook my head in amazement. He had either read my mind, or we liked the same things. Which, to my way of thinking, could be good or bad now that I'd told him about the cancer. He seemed to understand, but that might just have been the shock, and then I had gone on and on about my feelings. I took a deep breath and thought, *why can't I just learn to be quiet about some things?*

A slight breeze lifted the brim of my hat, carrying it across the red cloth. I moved toward it, but after bouncing a few times, it blew toward the stream. Glancing up, I saw Gil move with a graceful measure, smooth and very much at ease, as he cast a line into the cool water.

"Hey, Dina, come on over here and see the fish jump."

I joined him, wishing I had more time.

"Yes, sir!" His spirited commitment to the task at hand was catching. "Look at that. Got us a good one!" Gil proudly displayed his first catch then motioned me closer. "Now then, Dina, how many can y'all eat?"

"Two."

He looked at me, grinning. "Hungry, huh?"

"You did say food for the soul, didn't you?"

"I surely did." He placed his aviator glasses back in his shirt pocket. "Come here. You ever get the hankering to try it?" He held out the pole.

As I stepped closer to him, his arms encircled me, his strength passing to my thin body. I felt him place the pole in my hands as I listened to his directions, hearing mostly the timber of his voice, feeling his chest and arm muscles work as he demonstrated how to cast a line. I stepped back to have a try and found myself pushed against his firm stomach. "Oh, sorry. Should I stand out more?"

"This is fine." His voice was husky. "Dina, I find this to be nice."

I took comfort in the warmth of his body until I felt the breeze on my scalp and realized what I must look like to him. I really wanted the hat back; however, it floated downstream with a life of its own. I tensed, but he continued to hold me close, slowly turning me until I faced him. "Dina, what do you see when you look in the mirror?"

"I don't like the mirror anymore." I turned away, looking downstream. "There goes the hat."

"Not to worry none." He draped his arm comfortably around my shoulder. "We'll get it later." We walked in silence toward the mouth of the brook, where it ran into the lake. The rushing water created light, musical sounds. I felt elated by his nearness but remained cautious.

"Now." He squeezed my shoulder. "Come on down here and take a look."

"No." Pulling back, I shook my head as I said, "It scares me to look." I turned to go when his lips moved close to my ear.

"You'll see what you want to see, Dina." His warm breath was gliding along my neck in a most pleasant fashion. "Have a look." The low pitch of his tone was touching me seductively. "I'm here with you. Ya have nothin' to fear."

So it was together that we knelt in the moist grass by the stream's edge, and I peered into the water. It slipped playfully over the stones as I saw a wobbly reflection of a girl with rich brown hair and a happy face looking back at me. Behind her was a ruggedly handsome man with a beautiful smile. Sunshine halos gleamed above his head. A nuance of memory floated just out of my reach. My breath caught in my throat. A clear lightness settled around me as my chaos dissolved, leaving me at peace.

Several minutes passed before I looked away. Gil gently pulled me toward him. "You see, it wasn't so bad." His eyes were deep blue, like the sapphires in Grandma Nana's wedding ring. I didn't move away, and his lips brushed my cheek with the gentleness of wings.

"Over everything, there is beauty that we remember. It's not necessary to understand; you only have to accept its pleasure."

My response was a murmur. "That's a very insightful suggestion. Spiritual, like it would come from an angel."

His fingertips combed sweetly through my hair, and the tender movement lifted the fragile strands, spinning them about and releasing them to cling lightly against my temples. I felt a single tear form. It was a tiny, wet bubble in the corner of my eye, and the breeze pushed at it until it toppled down my cheek.

My voice was scarcely audible. "It has a long journey from here to the sea." A calming iridescence gathered around me. "Some of us travel for a lengthy time." I looked into the blueness of his eyes. "For others, it's short."

He reached for my hand, holding it firmly. I felt his calloused fingers and thought of the kind way he had with the horses. The late morning hour was quiet. The presence of memories rested softly about me as the lone tear dropped into the stream. Gil gathered me close, and I sighed with a deep sense of loss. His voice hovered over me. "Dina, I'm here for you."

"Yes, I know." My body began to relax against his chest. Heat spread through me, giving an airy lightness to my body. The feeling remained as I thought back to the reflection that I'd seen at the water's edge. "I don't know how you did that," I said as I waved vaguely at the rushing stream, "but thanks. It's the way I think of myself, even now. When I know it's not so."

His voice, rough with wisdom, whispered in my ear, "It's the way you feel about yourself. Therefore, it's the way I see you." He held me at arm's length, "Angels know things." He winked.

"Yeah." I laughed nervously. "Well, I guess it's all the ripples and stones and water. You know?" I fidgeted, asking myself, *Is he serious? Does he think he is an angel? Do I think he's an angel?* I took a step back. "I mean, I see myself in many ways. I have lots of memories, and they all seem to have contributed to who I am today."

He spoke softly, putting me at ease. "Tell me about a memory."

Well, I thought, *if he is an angel, this might be okay, considering where I'm at in life.* Then I shook my head in an attempt to bring myself back to reality.

My voice was serene as I told Gil that I'd discovered ballroom dancing in college and it had become my passion. Phil and I were good at it, plus it was an incentive to keep my weight down. We'd enjoyed all music and had won several trophies.

Shaking my head, I recalled Phil's grace and leadership ability, his style and gentleness. He was definitely my first love of any significance, and he was gay. My disappointment had been bitter, and I'd felt cheated until understanding had softened my anger. Then Phil had become my best friend, and I'd missed him terribly when he and Randy moved to San Francisco.

I finished and looked at Gil. "That was the first story that popped into my mind."

"I believe you said that ya liked to dance."

"Yes, and I did lots of dancing, but there were other things that I never got around to doing because I always had tomorrow."

"Such as?"

"Well, I never made it off the bunny hill as a skier."

"Did you want to?"

"Sure. I wanted to swoosh down mountains and drink hot toddies in ski lodges and not be frightened of heights." I laughed. "But that didn't happen."

"How much did you want it?"

"Not enough to try harder. Thinking I had all the time in the world, I put it off until tomorrow. But now tomorrow is here, and I missed out." I looked away, lost in my own thoughts. "You know, it's funny how clear things become when they are no longer available."

He touched my face, bringing me back to the moment. Looking deeply into my eyes, he smiled faintly. "Careful what you wish for, pretty lady." I looked at him quizzically, and he winked. "Now how about we gather us some wood for a fire?"

Hand in hand, we moved toward the edge of the clearing, where kindling and dried logs were in abundance. Gil found stones and built a round burner, where he placed the wrought-iron skillet. I pushed the image that I had seen of myself in the stream out of my mind. It was just one of those odd occurrences and best left alone. I confined my curiosity to the inner packing of the picnic basket.

I pulled forth a plastic container and exclaimed, "Oh my God!"

Gil looked toward the sky, a note of surprise in his voice. "Huh?"

"Oh!" I exclaimed. "That must be an angel thing. The looking toward the heavens?" I joked.

"Ah." He seemed taken aback. "I never gave it that much thought, but as your askin', I guess it could be."

I held his eyes for a minute, trying to decide on something that didn't quite surface. I let it go when an herbal aroma teased my nostrils.

"It's potato salad! I love potato salad! Parsley. It has fresh parsley in it and...let me sniff again." I spoke confidently, "Yup, there's a hint of rosemary. And there's mustard. I love spicy mustard!"

"Whew! Glad the excitement is for the food." He glanced toward the sky and relaxed. "Do y'all like freshly ground pepper?"

"You bet!"

He reached over and rummaged in the basket, coming up with a pepper grinder. Then he dug deeper and produced a jar of capers. "What do you make of that, Miss Dina?"

"You're good. Real good!"

"Thank you kindly." He got up, moving toward the stream with his fishing pole. I stayed put, still enthralled with the items in the basket.

"Look! Hard-boiled eggs. Let's see...you mixed the yolk with onion and mayo? Is that garlic you added?"

Pulling his hat low, he cast his line into the stream. "Guilty as charged."

A tantalizing aroma drifted from the bottom of the basket. Wrapped in a cloth napkin, a loaf of freshly baked bread titillated my senses. I inhaled deeply, letting the yeasty smell of sourdough fill my being. I looked up and called to Gil. "Have a sniff of this bread." I held the loaf up. "When something smelled this good, my Grandma Nana used to say it was baked by angels." I stopped as soon as my words had spilled out. What was the matter with me?

He removed another fish from his line and tied it with the others, placing them back in the cool waters. Looking toward me, he replied, "Your Grandma Nana was a wise lady, said some nice things."

Grinning, I called back to him, "Yes, people say I'm a lot like her, so I'll say thank you from both of us."

"You're very welcome."

I returned to the basket, enthralled with its contents. "Oh, Gil! This is unbelievable. You brought everything." I continued my forage. "Hey, a pickle, a dill pickle!" I grabbed one, got up, and rushed toward the edge of the lake. My feet flew across the mossy grass as I carried myself into his arms. I landed with a thump against his chest. "Oops, sorry. Too much momentum. But look," I said triumphantly as I held the pickle toward his lips. "Try it. Tell me it's food for my soul. I really want to eat one."

The pickle crunched against his teeth, and he licked the juices from his lips. *There it goes again,* I thought as my heart flip-flopped and my senses heightened.

He grinned. "Messy but good. Yep, go ahead." Using the heel of his hand, he wiped his mouth. "Seems to me it would be all right for you to indulge."

Sharing the pickle, he touched my lips with his fingertips. I let my breath out carefully as I studied the angles of his jaw, permitting my eyes to roam across his features with unabashed curiosity. The tips of his fingers skipped across my cheek. I felt only the sensation as they moved up to my temples. Slowly, his lips met mine. I raised my hands to touch his face, feeling the rough surface of his cheeks. A tiny sound escaped from me as I pulled him closer. His kiss caressed my mouth, deliciously long, tasting sharp and tangy like the dill. His gentle response grew to a demand as his hands circled the small of my back, pulling me toward him. I could feel that this was our moment in time, a tiny space that we would forever own. I realized with a start that a sliver of my essence would remain here, and I felt a sweeping sense of fulfillment until Gil pulled away.

I felt embarrassed. Color flooded my cheeks as he moved farther from me. "What's wrong?" I asked.

His face reflected concern that I had not seen before. "I have feelings for you, Dina. Sorta sweet-like with a thumpin' in my chest." He held me at arm's length. "But I'm not sure how to deal with 'em." He turned and began to walk back to the picnic area.

My voice caught him up short. "Wait." I could still feel the warmth of his hand on my back. His kiss was still imprinted on my lips. "Is it because I have cancer?"

He turned sharply to face me. "No." His hands pushed against the back of his neck in an irritated gesture.

"Do you feel sorry for me?" My fear betrayed my sentiments and I felt a lump in my throat. "Is that why you kissed me?"

His voice registered outrage. "You know better than askin' such silly questions." He took my hand. "Come here." He guided me toward the checkered cloth. He took a deep breath and held the air in his lungs several seconds.

Shaking his head, he blew it out quickly and turned toward me. After a moment, his voice was under better control. "My, Miss Dina, you do have quite an effect on me."

Breathlessly, I nodded my head. "Good."

His eyebrows shot up. Surprise registered across his face, and he offered me a half-smile. "Yes, ma'am. I suppose that could be good."

We sat down, and I moved closer to him. My fingers began a gentle movement up and down his arm. His voice remained low as he pulled away from my touch. "I'm never going to catch us any more fish if you keep on interruptin' me."

I looked into the deep blue of his eyes. "Do you care?"

"About the fishin', no."

"How about my interrupting you?"

"Oh, I care." Lightly brushing the hair from my face, he leaned forward. "I truly care." He removed his hat and ran his fingers through his tangled curls. "And that might be my problem."

I lowered my back until it rested on the cloth. He towered over me, his powerful shoulders blocking the direct light, casting golden streaks behind him. "My sweet Dina, life is caught and held within the secret place of your heart. You must decide what goes there."

"There's a stillness at the core of my heart." My voice was soft but clear as I continued, "It represents the loneliness of terminal illness, and I don't want to be lonely."

"What do you want?"

"What do I want?" I murmured and closed my eyes, taking the moment to feel the powerfulness of his body.

Without understanding how it happened, I realized he had given me the gift of courage so that I could speak freely.

"That's what I want," I murmured. I opened my eyes, and positive energy flowed through me. Reaching up, I gently ran my fingertips through his tousled hair. "I want to spend more time with you. More time than I actually have, but I'll take what I can get."

A startled look spread across his face. "Is that so?" His eyes were bright with blue light that matched the sky, but his voice held a husky edge. "Is that what you truly want, Miss Dina?"

"Mm-hmm." My voice was softly quiet. "If it's all right with you?"

"Oh." His smile was provocative, and a moment passed between us. "I would have to think on that a bit." He lowered his head. "I think..." I could feel his warm breath on my cheek. "It could be mighty fine."

My ears echoed gently with his words. Was that a yes or no? His lips skipped across the sensitive skin of my neck, and I felt my body curve into him. "Cloud nine," I whispered.

"They're not assigned numbers." He continued to nibble his way toward my ear.

I turned my neck up, exposing more tender skin to his lips. "And why is that?" I replied softly.

His voice was a gentle caress. "Too many of 'em."

"Is that so?"

"Yes, ma'am." Gently he pushed himself back.

I felt a coldness seep into the warm day. Gil sat up, pulling me with him. Minutes ticked by, and no words flowed between us.

His hands moved almost without weight as tenderly he held my face. "We have this time, Dina. It's precious, and we must take great care of it."

Without warning, my stomach growled. I tensed and muttered, "That's not romantic."

He pulled away. "Dang, Dina! I let you go and get hungry. Here I'm suppose' to be lookin' out for ya."

I smiled at his distress.

"It would be my pleasure to invite you to a fresh fish dinner, served now." Leaning toward me, he kissed my forehead tenderly. "There is harmony in our souls, Dina. Yours and mine. But there are also things we need to discuss."

I opened my mouth, but he held up his hand. "And talk we will. Right after I feed you some lunch. That's a promise." He stood up and moved toward the water to retrieve the catch. I felt something had taken place between us that I was not aware of, and it bothered me. But Gil was good in offering a diversion.

No sooner had he started to cook the fish than my lost appetite resurfaced with a burst of energy I hadn't felt in many months. I was soon intoxicated by the aroma of freshly frying fish. I sniffed the air with eager anticipation, and my worries were pushed to the back of my mind. He turned toward me with a relieved smile, nodding with approval at the food I'd spread across the checked cloth. I'd sampled the potato salad, and it was sensational. We'd shared a full-flavored deviled egg that was perfect. I told him his picnic carried a delicious punch, and he was pleased. The scents of the mesquite fire combined with butter from the wrought-iron skillet and infused the air with ambrosial sensations.

Gil tended the fish like a mother hen watching her chicks while I continued the search for a spatula.

"While you're lookin', would y'all open up that bottle of white wine?"

This piqued my interest. "Where is there wine?" I begin an immediate search and located an insulated cooler sleeve with two crystal glasses behind the picnic basket. How had I missed it? The corkscrew was there too. "This is amazing." I looked at Gil. "You thought of everything." My voice held an incredulous note, and the word *angel* floated around the back of my mind.

His smile was slow in coming. "Now then, Miss Dina, you have given me a whole new type of inspiration for thinkin'." He glanced up with a sensual stare. "And I plan on doin' you proud."

"Well, all right." I smiled happily.

He winked and returned his attention to the pan. "How about givin' me that spatula and a glass of wine?"

The chardonnay was cold and carried an essence of pears and apricots. I handed both glass and spatula to Gil. He turned the fish, the hot butter sending up spatters and hisses in the pan. Mouth-watering taste buds came to life as the fish sautéed. He raised his glass in a toast. "To us, Miss Dina, and to this day."

I smiled peacefully and added, "To our moment in time." But my inner voice said not yet.

He extended his hand toward me, palm up. As my hand fit across his fingers, he tightened his hold, and his thumb softly stroked my skin. "To a sliver of essence."

Well, I thought, *we're thinking alike. Hadn't I recently had that same thought? So this can't be all bad. I'm just feeling insecure. After all, he didn't really say no.*

Our eyes met, and we clinked glasses then sipped the wine. It was crisp and fruity with soft apple flavors. I savored the taste. "This is so wonderful."

"I hope so." He grinned.

I nodded, thinking how sensual he was. "This is going to be so good!" Yet a part of me knew I was being overly optimistic. Everything necessary had been packed into the picnic basket, yet somehow I wasn't surprised. "The wine, it's lovely—complex, generous fruit, yet dry and supple. Those would be Jillian words." I shrugged.

Gil flipped the fish for a final time then swirled his wine. "Got a slight oak finish."

"American or French oak?" I joked.

He studied the glass, twirled the wine, and inhaled deeply. "American, I'd say. Got a good nose on it."

"Well, that's settled." I laughed. "You'd get on with Jillian."

"I get on far better with you." The fish was ready, and Gil motioned for my plate. Hunger consumed my thinking, and I ate with enthusiasm, savoring each taste as it came back to me.

"It's been a few months since I've eaten a complete meal." Much to my surprise, I felt fine and wondered how that could be. My stomach wasn't queasy, and that made no sense. Whatever was happening was good, and I decided not to interrupt the good feeling by questioning why. "This is really wonderful, but"—I indicated his plate—"I think you're going to beat me by one fish."

"Do y'all want it?"

"No." I laughed. "I'm teasing you."

"Thought so. Why, with the amount you ate, I don't know where y'all are goin' to put the chocolate cake."

"Cake?" Fresh excitement entered my voice. "Really? There's chocolate cake?"

"You bet." His face held a wry half-smile. "Baked it this mornin' with you in mind. Chocolate fudge with a cream cheese frostin'."

I felt giddy. "That's my favorite."

He opened a plastic cake plate and removed the lid. Creamy frosting was swept around the sides in thick swirls reaching up to consume the top. I stared, astonished at the height of the cake. He produced a knife and swiftly cut into the creation. Three layers of fudge cake with raspberry filling fell onto my plate.

"A touch of port with that?"

My voice went up a notch. "You have port?"

"Yes, ma'am. What's a picnic without chocolate and port to finish it off?"

"Good Lord, Gil. You must have had a wonderful mother who spent hours instructing you in food preparation."

"I was a challenge in the kitchen." He smiled dubiously. "But I did try hard."

I savored the cake, and I noticed he did too. Tiny sips of port accented the bittersweet chocolate. When it was gone, I leaned against Gil, smiling, and said, "I am complete. Does that make sense?"

"Sure does." He drew me toward him, wiping the last crumbs from his mouth. "Well now, Dina." He stretched and stood up. "How 'bout a short stroll followed by a long nap?"

"You got it. But you're going to have to pull me up. I'm so full, I can't move." I held up my hands, and he lifted me to a standing position. We made an attempt to enjoy the walk, but it was short-lived and accompanied by yawns and sighs.

Gil steered us back toward the blanket. "I'd say a nap is in order. But first off…" He nodded toward the tablecloth, where the cat was patiently waiting. "I'd say we need to feed Butch and send him on his way."

I bent down to stroke the cat's warm fur and was rewarded by a rumbling purr. "Friendly fellow, your Butch."

"Yup, that he is. Been around awhile." Gil offered him a plate of fish. "Best as I can recall, he never misses a meal."

We watched as Butch enthusiastically tackled the scraps. When the plate was spotless, he began a thorough cleaning of his face. Gil expelled a long breath. "Tidy fella, isn't he?"

"Very thorough." I giggled and stroked Butch, which he took as a good sign, curling up next to me.

Gil started to pick him up. "Off you go."

"No." I said. "Wait. Please let him stay. He's warm and sociable and nice." I gently scratched behind the cat's ear. "Besides, I like his purr."

"His purr, huh?" Gil held me gently, and we lay back.

"Butch has a musical purr. Listen carefully. It's almost like a hymn."

I paused, giving him time to add one of his more spiritual answers, but his response was normal.

"If you say so, Miss Dina. I'm not one to argue with a lady."

Gil tucked me into his arm, and the cat spooned against the back arch of my knees. I felt his body stretch out then relax, curling back against me. "Good kitty," I murmured.

"He cuttin' into my time?"

"Maybe."

Sleep came as the hazy sunlight silvered the canyon and the tastes of the day were stored in my memory.

Pleasant dreams filled the afternoon, so it was with a flash of remorse that I awoke. Reality quickly settled around me as I sensed the lateness of the hour. Pushing sleep from my eyes, I sat up. "Damn." I began to fumble with packing the picnic basket.

Gil rolled over smiling, playfully hushing my hurried frenzy. I fluttered my hands, explaining how long I'd been gone, the worry it would cause Mrs. Kopeck and Rachel. He nodded but didn't seem to be convinced of the impending disaster as I bumbled about in an attempt to pick up what was left of our picnic. The cell phone slipped out of my pocket and Gil handed it back to me. "Your phone?"

"No, Rachel's." I had to smile, "Well, maybe it is mine. We have two cell phones, actually. See how she prints in these big numbers?" I pointed at the back of the phone. "Rachel says that the large numbers are for Mrs. K. if she forgets her glasses, but it's really for my benefit. This is Rachel's number here and this is the number of this cell. She prints super large so if I'm having trouble with my vision, I will really see these numbers." I rolled my eyes and returned to pushing dishes back inside the wicker basket. "Anyhow, I thought I should carry the phone just in case there was a call I'd need to answer."

"I see." Gil grinned, "Then you'd best turn it on, don't cha think?"

"What?" I looked at the phone and pushed it toward Gil. "Doesn't matter. Look. No service here."

"Nice not to be interrupted."

"Yes, it was. But it's late and I really did give Mrs. K. too much tea. Actually, a large mug full of...let's just call it her 'special' brew."

"You did?" Gil opened his eyes wide. "Oh my."

I rushed on. "It's really hard to explain." I stopped, wondering what to say next, but Gil was looking at me quizzically. "Well, maybe it isn't that hard to explain." I leaned toward him. "You see, I wanted Mrs. K. to take a long nap so I could be with you. Her tea...it's sort of laced with whiskey."

"Not to worry." He smiled in understanding. "Nice lady, Mrs. K., but she tends to overdo a bit. That egg business can be demandin'. Probably needed a good rest."

"Oh." I looked puzzled as I said, "Well...okay. I don't feel quite so bad now. Gil..." I faced him and looked into his eyes. "Do you know Mrs. Kopeck?"

"Everyone in the valley knows Mrs. K."

"Yeah, I guess so." I blinked in thought and let it slide. "There's still Rachel. What do I tell her?"

"Why don't ya tell her the truth, Dina?"

I attempted to look stern. "Sure. Now here's what I could say. 'I encouraged Mrs. K. to drink so I could run off with a cowboy, whom I think is an angel.'" I looked at Gil, and he nodded with approval. I rolled my eyes. "Let's see." I paused in mock thought. "I could continue with, 'We had a wonderful picnic where I ate huge amounts of my favorite food. And oh, by the way, I didn't throw up. Now, Gil, does that sound like anything my sister is going to believe?" I shook my head. "No, it does not." I returned to packing the remains of our lunch and paused again. "That cake was unbelievable. A little slice of heaven on earth." I smiled at him, waiting for a response. His hand tightened on my arm. "I thank you kindly."

"That's it? No remark about heaven and earth?"

"Maybe later," he replied with a half-smile.

I could tell the air was growing thick with words yet to be spoken. I busied myself with putting dishes back into the large wicker basket, knowing that no matter how I fiddled with the packing, all these dishes didn't arrive in that basket—nor had the cake or the chilled wine. Even though I wasn't facing him, I became acutely aware of his presence. "Please help me clean up. I really have to get home."

"Let it be, Dina." He reached out and touched me in a quieting gesture. "I'll come back and take care of everything."

I stopped short, turned, and looked at him. "That sounds so final."

He continued to hold my hand. "There is a big difference between lovin' someone with your heart and fallin' in love with 'em."

I noticed deeper lines had formed at the edges of his eyes. He appeared weary, and I shook my head. "I don't get it."

"I haven't had that much experience with the fallin' in love part. That's a whole new set of responsibilities, and I gotta ask myself if that will interfere with what I'm doin'." He continued to press my fingertips.

My head was spinning. "What are you doing?"

"I'm here to take care of you, and now I need time to sort out my feelin's 'cause it's important that what is done next is what we will understand and face together."

"Are you . . ." Words escaped me. "Are you saying we're not going to see each other again?"

"Not for a while." He stroked my hand a final time and released it.

I felt as if the air had been ripped from my lungs. I stopped thinking while the autumn day tumbled around me in a mix of rejection and bedlam. I rose slowly, feeling as if I were in a trance. "I don't know what to say, what to do."

He stood up. A pained expression covered his face, and he reached for me. "I'm so sorry, Dina. I've done this all wrong."

"No." I backed away. "I don't understand what you've done or why, but I know that I don't want to be with you now. I want to go home."

Wind rustled through the thinning oaks as we mounted the horses and rode into the autumn afternoon.

Gil dismounted when we reached the gate. He assisted me down and held my stiff body against his. "Time, Dina. To sort and gather. Will you give it to me?"

I closed my eyes. "That's about the one thing I don't have much of."

He touched his hat brim. "What we make of the day is up to us." He mounted his horse slowly and looked back at me. He appeared tired, but I was too mad to be considerate of his feelings.

"Well, this wasn't your finest hour," I snapped. "And now my day is filled with confusion and doubt. You want time to think? Fine. Take all you need!" Tears stung my eyes, but I held them at bay.

Holding Mary's reins, he made a chucking sound, and the mare turned to follow Joey. I watched as he rode down the dirt lane, his back straight in the saddle, his body in rhythm with the sway of the horse. As he rounded the corner, he appeared to dissolve into the rosy gray horizon. I thought to myself, *Just like a cowboy.*

I knew the pain would come later because my spirit felt lost in an immense sadness. Had I really believed that Gil was an angel? One day he had appeared out of nowhere when I needed help, and he'd done some strange things. Did he believe he was angel? And what kind of an angel could he be if he broke my heart? I couldn't process this information. Angels didn't break hearts; they mended them.

As I started on my way home, I realized the dirt road was hot and dry from an afternoon of sunshine, but instead of feeling overheated, surprisingly I had enough energy to tackle the walk uphill. It was probably good that I'd had a big lunch. *Well,* I thought, *that's one of the strange events that happened when I was with Gil.* I was able to eat real food and not get sick. I knew this to be a non-happening in my life, yet it had happened. I looked around me and saw the loud vitality of fall in every tree, but nothing could change the hurt that lay deep within me.

Truth was that I had taken a chance with the cowboy and look where I was now...very much alone nursing a broken heart. I had known better then to fall in love with someone I had just met. Why had I been so silly to think that a relationship would work out? I wasn't going to be around long enough for anything to work out. So what was there about Gil that still made me want to be with him?

The truth, as I saw it, was that we had gotten along very well. It had felt right to me, and I thought he shared those feelings. Why, out of the blue, was it all wrong for him? Was it because I had told him about my cancer? I shook my head, trying to throw that idea away. My feet continued to move up the dirt road to our farmhouse

Of course, I realized that whatever time was left to me was limited and I wanted to make the most of every moment. Maybe the idea that Gil was an angel led me to actually think everything would be okay and, quite frankly, it should have been okay. I thought: *Angels make good things happen. It's part of their job.* Why did he hesitate? Why did he question himself when he knew my time was short and each moment counted? That wasn't good. It wasn't the way an angel worked.

Heartbreak came in all forms, and I'd had enough. I felt my anger rise to the surface. This was too unfair! I had some things I wanted to say to Gil, but I didn't even know how to reach him! Well, wasn't that just swell! I'd been played for a fool. I stopped, almost out of breath, and looked toward the deep blue sky. The sun glittered through the tallest trees, discovering new patterns within the rust and golden leaves. I thought , *Okay, and his brother blows the wind around! How stupid was I to buy into that?*

I could see my home as I rounded the bend. The farm sat on a rise of land as if it defied time and the economy. Nothing lasts forever, I realized sadly. At least my relationship with Gil had been over quickly while my feelings for the farm had been with me all my life. Unfortunately, both seemed doomed. I knew the farm would take the path of other farms if Jillian or Rachel couldn't afford its upkeep. Someone would offer my sisters enough money, the farm would come down, and a subdivision would go up. Such was the way of humanity. I was happy that I'd had my childhood memories in a more simple world, and I knew that Rachel and Jillian felt the same way. The only memory I wanted to forget was my meeting Gil.

Once again I thought of my responsibility to my sisters and myself. Helping them to understand that my death was near and helping them to accept it was my duty. I paused and realized there would be no more romances with cowboys and no more letdowns. I really didn't have the time for it. Plus, it was important to put on a good face at home, right up to the very end.

Chapter 5

Rachel's car was in the drive when I arrived home. *Oh, not good,* I thought. *This has been a disaster of a day.* I pushed my anger with Gil far away. The throbbing hurt would have to wait too. I would deal with those aches later. Right now I had Rachel to pacify.

Feeling the tension as I opened the kitchen door, I pasted a smile across my face in hopes of diffusing my sister's fears, but this didn't stop her rush toward me. Concern etched across her brow as she gathered me in her arms and held me tightly, releasing me only when she saw I was all right.

"You mustn't worry." I kissed her cheek. "See." I turned around for her full approval and extended my arms for another hug. "I'm fine."

"Don't try to con another hug from me. You know you're not supposed to go off anywhere without telling someone." She pushed her face closer to mine and spoke with authority, "That's a rule."

I nodded complaisantly, realizing she had to release her anxieties about my absence. I glanced around for a place to sit. Rachel was just beginning to shake her finger at me when Mrs. Kopeck opened the bathroom door.

"Pressure on the bladder is not good for a person my age. It's important to go whenever the urge strikes." Seeing me, she smiled happily. "There's our little patient."

With an overly bright smile, I greeted her. "Hey, Mrs. K. It's really nice to see you."

Mrs. Kopeck turned toward my sister. "I told you, Rachel, there was no need to worry. She just stepped outside for a breath of fresh air." Looking in my direction, she scolded lightly, "You should have told me, dear, that you were going to take one of your walks. Why, your sister came home and was all aflutter as to your whereabouts." She turned toward me and lowered her voice. "You know what I mean?" I nodded. Turning back toward Rachel, she inquired, "Have you seen my thermos?"

"Of course, Mrs. Kopeck." Rachel handed her the bottle. "It's very light."

"That's because it's empty, dear." She beamed at my sister. "So nice that you notice all the small things." Patting Rachel's arm, she continued, "Why, you'll make a wonderful mother." Mrs. K. gave me a wink. "Someday."

I couldn't help but take a peek at Rachel's reaction. Mrs. Kopeck caught my glance, so I felt obliged to add to the conversation. "Yes." I nodded my head. "Indeed she will."

I bobbed my head at my sister's confused look, adding optimistically, "A lovely mother."

When Mrs. K. went in search of her sweater, I whispered to Rachel, "Probably all that 'special' brew she drinks. I think you just have to go along with them when they get like that. The mind can wander, you know?" My helpful comment didn't reassure my sister. Her frown line was firmly in place.

With calm restored, Mrs. Kopeck gathered her knitting together. "Before I go, I want you to know that is a fine list." She pointed at the cabinet where Rachel had taped her list of instructions. "Your printing is big and bold and easy to read."

Rachel looked perplexed but smiled. "Thank you."

Mrs. Kopeck went on, "Shows a lot of patience, and that's necessary for raising children. Your mother would be very proud of you." She nodded at me and glowed at Rachel. "It's time I was on my way home." Pushing her arms into the sleeves of her cardigan, she nodded, saying, "Good that I had this. Weather's taken on a nip."

"It's seventy-five degrees out there," I muttered.

"Shh." Rachel gave me another cross look then turned to Mrs. Kopeck. "May I offer you a ride?"

"Nonsense. The walk will do me a world of good. Isn't that right, Dina?"

"Absolutely." I nodded. "And if you get a good clip on, you'll even warm up." I walked toward the screen door. "Physical exertion takes your mind off where you are and centers you where you want to be."

Pausing, Mrs. K. looked at me. "My, isn't that philosophical." She let the door shut with a bang. Turning back, she shouted, "Good-bye, girls."

Rachel bit her lip and watched. "Do you think she's all right? She seems…" She paused and looked at me. "Odd?" Following the departing figure with her eyes, she asked, "Does she look a bit wobbly to you?"

Leaning toward the window, I added a note of concern to my tone. "She sure does. Gosh, Rachel. Wow! Is she drunk or what?"

"Dina!"

"Oh, relax. Mrs. Kopeck looks just fine. You worry too much. Everything is fine." *No it's not*, I thought. *Gil is gone and my feelings are a tangled mess.*

Rachel continued to watch as Mrs. Kopeck wove slightly on her way down the drive and out of sight. She turned toward me with raised eyebrows. "Did you have a pleasant conversation with her before you let her drink?"

"I'm offended by that remark." But my try at indignation didn't faze my sister. She crossed her arms and waited.

"Yes, I believe we did," I replied meticulously. "We covered a lot of ground." I could see this wasn't enough to placate her, so I added, "You know, lots of chit-chatty things. Family? Walter Jr. You do remember him?" Receiving a passive look, I continued, "Sam and Kathy, their son, Tommy." Rachel raised an eyebrow, and I went on eagerly, "Got you there! You didn't know their son's name, did you?" My sister remained annoyed, so I jumped back in. "Also covered knitting, lighting, blue eggs, places, things…" I had no more to say, so I smiled, hoping it had been enough.

With a shake of her head, Rachel turned back to the bags of food that littered the counter. "Somehow I don't think I'm getting the whole truth." Her brow was still knit with questionable lines. "Am I, Dina?"

"Most of it." I knew how persistent she could be, so I shrugged. "Here." I laughed, feeling some of the tension leave my body. "Let me help with the bags."

Together we put the groceries into the pale yellow cupboards. *I will not think about Gil,* I told myself. Tracing the stencil of a faded rooster, I thought of our mom with love and remembered how she'd let her daughters apply the pictures of baskets and vegetables, fruit and barn animals to the doors of the cabinets. Even when Rachel and I had cleaned up the kitchen after our parents' death, we had decided to keep the worn stencils in place.

As the afternoon turned to evening, Rachel talked about the day and the traffic and her many errands, some of which she hadn't been able to accomplish. I had a glow to my pale skin and even managed to drink the adult formula, which kept her happy but was really unnecessary after the lunch I had eaten. I pushed that thought away. I knew I couldn't eat food like that.

I rested for a while, and when Rachel suggested that we watch our favorite TV programs, we settled together on the overstuffed sofa and the night offered a solace of love.

My fear, both from the pain and the tumors that had continued to grow in spite of the chemo, had kept me depressed, but tonight I felt different. The empty feeling that had haunted me for the past two years was banished to a remote part of my emotions. Even though I was weak, I felt better.

I teased my sister as I did when we were children. We laughed together as we played rock-paper-scissors and argued about which was stronger. Rachel finally shared her feelings about Dr. Bergman. I was pleased, knowing there would be someone for her to turn to when the time came. Carl was a good man; maybe he just needed to work on his social graces, or maybe he just needed to relax. Whatever, Rachel would figure it out and be able to help. Thinking back to the activities of the afternoon, I sighed bitterly over my loss of Gil. In a distant part of my mind, it registered that the news had come on and Rachel was staring at me.

"Well, are you going to tell me?"

Bringing myself back to the moment, I replied, "What do you mean, tell you?"

She nudged me. "You were gone a long time today. Wanna talk about it?"

I thought back to Gil's advice about telling the truth and was surprised that I had a thought about him that wasn't jumbled with resentment and anger. "You ready for this, Rachel?"

A compliant nod followed. "Is it going to be a good story?"

"Yes." I rested my chin in my hand as I thought about the afternoon's highs and lows. "Absolutely."

"Okay." Rachel pushed another pillow under her arm. "Let's hear it."

Shifting positions, I replied, "Well, the important thing to remember is that you're dragging this out of me."

She nodded. "Please start."

I tapped my hands on the table imitating a drum roll. "Here goes. I walked down the country lane, like I usually do, all the way to the old gate. There I met a handsome cowboy who had horses saddled for us, and we rode into the canyon." I paused for effect before going on. Her smile was still fixed in place, but her eyes had taken on a bewildered look.

"Well, he had a lovely picnic planned, but I was sad, and he confessed that he is an angel." Rachel gasped, only to be shushed by me. "You see, just by me telling you that part of the story, you know that I spent a most remarkable day."

With an effort, my sister closed her mouth, blinking her eyes several times. I rushed on. "So let me tell you about the picnic. We ate the most delicious pan-fried fish I've ever had. You know, over a mesquite fire with the butter sizzling in an iron skillet?" I looked at Rachel. Her head moved up and down in response to my vigorous nodding. "And the aroma, oh gosh, it was fantastic. Well, enough about food." I waved my hand in an airy manner. "Except I should comment on the cake. Yes, I really should." I offered a smile. "Three layers of bittersweet fudge with raspberry in between and port as a finish. He said something like, 'What's a picnic without chocolate and port?'"

I paused as the day came rushing back in full detail, and I felt forsaken. It was all so unfair! Catching sight of Rachel's frozen look of disbelief, I pasted a smile across my face and pushed my story home. "I've never met anyone like him. He even knew his wine. Did I mention wine? Well, maybe not. It was a bottle of chardonnay, pears and apricots up front, crisp, complex. Lovely bottle, actually." I felt myself talking too fast but wanted to finish what I had to say. "Of course, you know I've always preferred beer, but today, heck, it just called out for wine. He said it was aged in American oak. Imagine, he knew that by just sniffing it. So I told him he would like Jillian, but he said he liked me." Depression settled in deeper, but I kept my good face on and continued. "So wasn't that sweet? And, oh yes, we drank out of crystal glasses. Classy, huh?

"Then we took a walk, had a nap, and Butch curled up with me. Butch is his cat. Anyhow, we overslept." I felt my heart break all over again. "And then he broke up with me, and I've felt awful ever since. I walked home, mad enough to kick at stones; then I pouted, and that's why I was so late." Tears threatened, but I wouldn't give in, not tonight. Later I could lie in bed and let myself indulge in self-pity, but right now I had to be cheery. Nothing could destroy my evening with my sister.

"Uh-huh." Rachel blinked twice. "Does he know about the cancer?"

"Yup. Said it didn't matter, but I think it does." I stared straight ahead, feeling fresh ache rip through me.

The silence grew. She ran both hands through her blonde hair, speaking slowly, "You know my theory about drugs. Imagination can get out of hand. Hallucination can occur. You probably need to cut back a bit, and well, we'll see what happens."

"Other than the breaking up, it was a good day, and that's the way I'm looking at it." With great effort, I pushed my grief aside and focused on the evening that lay ahead.

Rachel nodded. "Sounds like an exceptional afternoon. That was ..." She paused. "... quite a story."

"As promised."

"I ... I ... didn't know ... what to expect." She tossed up her hands in an expressive gesture. "But it wasn't that, although the part about the cat was a nice touch."

My sister took another deep breath in an attempt to sort out her thoughts. "I only asked about your day because I have to leave you for a few hours tomorrow and Mrs. Kopeck can't stop by."

"Gosh, that is a pity. Oh, did I mention that my handsome ex-boyfriend knows Mrs. K.?"

"Dina!" Rachel's frown line sharpened. "I worry about you and this, uh, cowboy." Her voice took on a crisp note. "Mrs. Kopeck is dependable, and if there is no one here to look in on you, perhaps I shouldn't leave."

I began to think that some time alone might feel pretty good.

"Maybe I should reschedule?" Rachel's hand moved toward the calendar.

"Don't be silly," I replied. "I'll bet Mrs. K. has a big business deal going down regarding her blue eggs. Am I right?" I smiled as Rachel considered the thought. "But wait. I have a better idea than that." Leaning closer, I spoke softly, "Let's be honest. Having spent a portion of my day in conversation with Mrs. K., I do believe that I have insider information." My sister sighed. "I think I know where she's going to be tomorrow. It's her weekly trip to the hay and feed store for more of her 'special' tea bags. You do know that they sell hooch in the rear parking lot? Behind the old harvest equipment? It's to the left of—"

"I know where it is!"

"Good. For a moment, I thought you forgot about the time when Archie and you…" I sat back and threw up my hands. "Whatever. It doesn't matter because I'll bet that you have another plan all worked out for me." I patted her hand. "Now I say that because you're so good with details. It's the small things that you're tuned in to."

Rachel smiled, her dimples showing softly in the lamplight. "Are you going to tell me what you actually told her while I was gone?"

"You got me. I'm really into truth today." I shrugged again. "I said you were having a clandestine affair with a professional." The idea was so close to the truth it actually made me smile.

"Ahh." Rachel nodded. "A professional."

"Yes. I thought it was discreet yet smacked of reality."

She paused in thought then groaned. "Now be serious for a minute, will you?" She faced me, imploring me to listen. "I'll leave the second cell phone with you, and you can call me or call Carl's office. Anytime. I mean it." Her motherly nature was taking over. "And before I go, I'll look for the family photo albums so you'll have plenty of pictures to look at. It'll keep you busy." She forced a stern look and said, "And hopefully out of trouble." A smile played at the corner of her lips. "I don't want strange boyfriends in the house."

"Oh, he's not strange," I added grimly. "Well, maybe just a little. You know, with being an angel and all. But not to fret; he's an ex-boyfriend now."

"Dina!"

"What?"

"You know that I worry."

"Relax, Rachel. I'll be fine."

Pulling on a blonde curl, she focused her attention squarely on me. Tiny laugh lines created fine wrinkles at the corners of her eyes, and a smile highlighted her mouth. "Of course, if you're going to occupy tomorrow as you did today,"—she hesitated—"then I can only assume you'd rather be left alone."

I looked surprised. "That's very thoughtful of you, but ex-boyfriend means past tense. Gone, he's out of my life." Rachel was about to speak, but I jumped in. "No. I mean it. It's really considerate of you to trust leaving me alone. You know, sis, you've done a lot of thoughtful things for me. Like the time you told Justin Peterson that I was in love with his older brother, George. You do remember that? It was one of my most embarrassing moments."

"I thought I was being helpful." Rachel shrugged. "I was only twelve. Besides, you were," she added in final defense.

"No, I wasn't. You wanted Justin Peterson to take you to the seventh grade dance, and that was your way of getting his attention."

Rachel's tone was righteous. "That's not true."

"Is so."

Rachel folded her hands in her lap. "There may be a tiny bit of truth in what you say."

I leaned closer, smiling. "Who took you to the dance?"

"That's not the issue."

"Is so."

Rachel grinned. "I'm not saying anything else until I've talked with my legal counsel."

"I'm going to bed."

Rachel shouted after me, "Jillian will call you tomorrow."

Chapter 6

That night I closed my eyes, lulled to sleep by the rhythm of the rain as it softly patted the glass on my bedroom windows. My dreams were filled with white mountains and a night sky sprinkled with stars. I felt movement as my body glided over the snow with expert ease. My downhill ski cut firmly into the slope, my knees bent, and my body angled uphill as I went into the turn.

The freedom of skiing was a gift to my soul. Frosty air slid around me as my skis carried me into a bowl of snow. I felt myself fly up the curve, jump into the turn, and slide down with the grace of a ballerina. The moon winked in acknowledgment of my newly found skill.

Light flakes glazed my nose as the snow abandoned the dark sky to float softly to earth. I paused in the silence to study the shapes of the snowflakes and felt that I was surrounded by perfect patterns.

Pushing off with my poles, I rushed downhill, through the whiteness, and climbed another slope to soar across the mountain. The icy night rushed past my face, leaving my cheeks cold, my hair crusted with the fleshly fallen snow.

Another dip in the cavern of white carried me swiftly to the top of the crest, where the lodge came into view.

I went to the private place deep within my heart where stillness dwelled and let my ears pick out the sounds they wished to hear. The wind that whistled though the night was urging me home. I pointed my ski tips downhill, positioning my body into a racer's tuck, and quickly gathered speed. The night world flew by, with starlight twinkling in my vision until I careened into a sharp stop, my skis spraying a fountain of snow in front of me.

Instinct told me that Gil waited in the warmth of the lodge. I released my boots from the binding and stood my skis on end. My body quivered from the physical drain the mountain had extracted from me, but I looked once more at the white slopes that towered above me. I smiled as I moved toward the entrance of the lodge.

He stood next to the fire wearing a dark cowboy hat. I bent to loosen the snaps of my boots then walked toward him. He took my hand, and I looked into the deep blue of his eyes.

My face still burned from the cold of the slope. Water beaded in my hair as the snow melted in the warmth of the room. His touch was sensual as he offered me a hot drink. The rich aroma of brandy tickled my nose. I raised myself to reach his ear. "Only bad guys wear black hats," I murmured.

He removed his hat, placed it on the bar, and took me into his arms. "I'm not a bad guy, Miss Dina."

My dream floated into a silence that carried me back to my bed.

The storm had grown stronger, invading my room, leaving wet puddles on the old, wooden floor. The walls had swallowed up the dampness so that the air now tasted and smelled like the essence of autumn. Emotions swirled around me, evoking memories that I sorted through, enjoying and crying, loving, caring, and finally releasing them.

I woke later to a sky that was dark, polished with the night. One star glowed, sending a trail of light into my bedroom. The seductive silence soothed my senses, making my solitude absolute. Collecting my thoughts, I placed them close to my heart and drifted back to sleep, feeling as if an important task had been completed.

I opened my eyes to a morning that held a grape-blue mist and the waning memory of my dream. I knew that only Gil could have sent it to me, and I had to talk to him. But how? My body was exhausted, so walking back to the old gate wasn't possible.

The tumor in my lower back delivered a constant ache as I made my way to the breakfast table. Without the medications, I felt as if my head would explode and the cancer would consume me. My sight was affected today, only slightly, but it was enough for me to know that my days were short.

I shivered as I imagined what was taking place in my body. I couldn't have a seizure, not now, not when I had to find Gil. I wanted one more day. Letting my breath out slowly, I closed my eyes and began to search for his image.

As I sat down at the table, Rachel was talking about not finding the family albums in the garage but how she would look again when she got home. Her back was toward me as she poured coffee.

The cream of rice swam in front of my eyes. I shut out the nauseating sight, and slowly it wiped itself from my mind. That was so much better. I could breathe now. I inhaled slowly and felt a craving for real food. I willed my mind to focus only on that idea.

A tantalizing aroma of sizzling bacon teased my nose. I was afraid to open my eyes as the scent of eggs, cheese, and herbs filled the air. I peeked carefully through squinted vision. I blinked rapidly, and my mouth formed an "O" as I saw the breakfast plate in front of me. My only utensil was a spoon, but it worked just fine. The food was delicious, just as it had been yesterday. I didn't understand it, but I ate happily. Making small sounds of delight, I felt strength flow through my veins, giving my legs power and my arms momentum.

Rachel beamed with pleasure when she turned around. The cereal was gone, and I had a fresh glow.

After breakfast, Rachel settled me in the living room. Pillows surrounded me on the sofa, and Rachel continued to fuss with the afghan that covered my legs. "Are you sure you're warm enough? You're only wearing a cotton sweater and summer slacks. Maybe I should look for a sweat suit. They're so much heavier. And a winter blanket."

"Stop! Look at me. I'm in the sunshine, and I'm wearing a lovely shade of blue." I swept my hands down my body. "I really do feel pretty good about my day wear."

Rachel looked at me again to reassure herself. She finally nodded, and when I breathed out a sign of relief, she sounded matronly. "That wasn't necessary, Dina, but if you are comfortable, I'm good with it." She picked up the cell phone and held it toward me. "Let's talk about this for a minute." I moaned as she went on. "It's important that you keep in touch with me. Then neither of us will worry. Here." She pushed the phone into my hand.

I had to smile at her serious tone.

"So you understand, just push speed dial and you'll reach me. I'll carry the phone everywhere. And I'll only be gone for maybe three hours, that's the max."

"Okay, but let me check your instructions one more time for using that cell phone. Does it take photos? What is it that I push for speed dial?"

Rachel took the phone from my hand. "Here. Look, it says 'speed dial.'" She leaned back, and her eyes narrowed. "You're putting me on, right?"

I snickered. "I know how to use the phone." I shooed at my sister. "Just go, will you? You're slowing me down." I teased playfully, "Truth be told, little sister, you're interfering with my afternoon plans."

"Which are?"

"Haven't decided yet, but I'm mulling over my options. You see, I'm still mad at my ex-boyfriend, but I am considering giving him a second chance."

Pulling her sweater over her head, Rachel asked, "So about the same plans as yesterday?"

"You think it's going to be cold today, or are you trying to look like Mrs. K.?"

"There's nothing wrong with Mrs. Kopeck, other than her tea is a bit stout." Rachel stood straight, pushing her chest out. "I always had the smallest bust line in the family, but I think this sweater makes me look bigger."

"Yeah, that and your push-up bra."

"Very funny. Enough about me. Let's review your plans."

I smiled to myself. Truth was always best. Hadn't I been told that just the other day? "I'm thinking about meeting the cowboy again."

"Good for you." This time Rachel was prepared for my reply. "Then we're both going to have fun. I'm meeting a man too."

"You are?" I blinked. "Oh, I get it now. That's the reason for the push-up bra."

"That's not true!" Rachel replied passionately. She brushed at imaginary dust on the table as she softened her tone. "Carl is taking me out for a quick lunch."

I teased, "I'm relieved it's Carl. Thought for a minute you'd found a tennis pro or golf instructor."

"I'm going to ignore that last remark." Rachel pushed her hair behind her ears. "Carl has a break in seeing patients, and I'm meeting him at the sandwich shop by his office. Any comments?" She raised her index finger in warning. "Intelligent ones only."

"Put on lipstick and some of your new perfume. Readjust the left boob." I squinted as I looked up. "From this angle, it's a little lower than the right." I held out my arms to Rachel. "And let him see your freckles." I hugged her and said, "I'm so happy for you. The doc is a nice man."

Feeling Rachel's firm grasp, I smiled. "It's important for me to know that he'll be there for you. It will make my leaving easier."

Rachel trembled as she held me close. Tears filled her eyes and dropped softly onto the pillow. "I'll miss you, sis. When you talk of going, I can't bear the loss."

"Rachel, please look at me." I gently held her at arm's length. "I've been sick for far too long. You know that."

Rachel gulped air to fight her flow of tears. I reached for her hand and asked, "Do you remember how we used to watch the geese?"

A quiet yes slipped from her lips, and I whispered, "A flurry of emotions would tell them when to migrate. They would fly away because they were caught up in a flow of life." I squeezed Rachel's fingers. "Do you remember that?"

She nodded, and I let my breath out. "I feel the end of that flow. Just like the geese felt the need to migrate. It's the way of life, so you mustn't cry." I felt weakened as I wiped at my sister's tears. "The saddest part is leaving you and all the others I know and love, those who don't understand that where I'm going is beautiful." My voice grew in heated intensity. "I'm so close that I know this!"

Rachel stroked my forehead with cool fingertips. "Shh, Dina. Your skin is so hot. I'm going to fetch you a cold towel."

For half an hour, we sat in a tender silence. The cold packs felt good to me, helping to put out the fire in my body. My breathing evened out as I rested against the pillows. The lines of stress mellowed as I relaxed. Taking a deep breath, I attempted to wink playfully. "Go now, or you'll be late. I have lots to do myself." I began to wonder just how I would get in touch with Gil.

Rachel repaired her makeup, and I reminded her to add perfume before she left. She paused at the door. "Oh! I almost forgot. Jillian is going to phone. She wants to talk and tell you about some kind of new mud."

"Great." I shook my head. "I'm sure it will be informative. But it won't be the highlight of my day." I offered a faint smile. "Remember, sis, shoulders back, chest out." Nodding at Rachel's bust, I quipped, "Good adjustment on the left."

She rolled her eyes as she shut the front door.

I thought that something had looked different about her. Then I realized she hadn't covered her freckles with makeup. That made me feel good, and I smiled as I lay back on the pillows.

Chapter 7

While resting, I alternated my thoughts between what would I say to Gil if I found a way to get in touch with him and what I would say to Jillian when she called. I tried to remember if I'd seen Gil with a cell phone, but then what did it matter? I didn't even know his last name. I pushed the palms of my hands against my cheeks and released a sigh. *How silly I had been to fall head over heels in love with a stranger.*

The joy in being with him had been replaced with an empty void. I felt cheated and angry and nothing would fix that. But today I had to remember that my sisters were on the top on my list, and Jillian couldn't even suspect that I'd been hurt by a man.

I spent my time looking out the old picture window through the panes of wavy glass. I saw the yard blazing with russet and gold trees. They swayed as I moved my head from side to side. It had been a simple game I had played years ago with my sisters. We'd made up stories about what we'd seen in the distorted glass. For years, we had all talked about writing down our visions. It had never happened. I closed my eyes in thought. *Never put off to tomorrow what you can do today.* Leaves crunched across the patio. Grandma Nana had told us it was the footsteps of ancient Indians who had lived there long ago. I smiled, hoping that both Jillian and Rachel would share that thought with their children.

Opening my eyes, I remembered the day my father had laid the cement patio and how all the family had carved their initials in one corner. "For all the world to see." Those had been his words. After drawing an elaborate "J," Jillian had asked how many people from around the world would come to the farm to see their names. Dad had wiggled his shaggy eyebrows and said, "That remains to be seen." I'd always liked that answer and had used it often, especially when I was in doubt and didn't want to say, "I don't know."

The sound of Rachel's car vanished just as the phone rang.

Jillian was primed for the call. She spoke about her upcoming visit and asked how Rachel was coping with the cooking, cleaning, nursing, and shopping.

It was a loaded question, and I was ready with a fast answer. "Rachel's got it covered. Has notes posted all over the house. We're on a tight timeframe here. Hope you can keep up with us when you arrive."

"Very funny. Where is Rachel now?"

"Out."

"Left you alone?" Concern etched Jillian's voice.

"No, she took me with her. You're talking to a recorded message."

"I don't find that funny. I'm thousands of miles away, and I worry about both of you."

"No need to," I replied in a chipper voice. "I'm fine. Rachel had plans for the day, and so do I."

"And what might those plans be?"

I took a deep breath. "Oh. I hope to have a pressing engagement with a handsome stranger."

A lengthy pause followed, but I waited her out. Jillian's voice turned crisp as she said, "Okay, I'll bite. Who?"

"A cowboy."

"A cowboy!" Jillian's voice was indignant.

"Yes. A handsome cowboy. Yesterday we took the horses and rode into the canyon."

"No, you didn't."

I paused. "Why not?"

"Hey, got you on that one," Jillian continued in an authoritative manner. "Because you can't ride."

"Golly, in another life I must have been a cowgirl 'cause I did pretty good."

"Yeah, Dina," she grumbled. "Me too."

"Really? Do you think we were sisters then?"

"Oh, stop that!" Her annoyance was replaced with a note of curiosity. "Where did you meet him?"

I crossed my legs and replied, "Down by the gate that leads to the old ranch."

"Uh-uh, wrong answer." I knew in her tone that she felt smug as she continued. "Care to try again? I may not be living there, but I do remember the neighborhood history. Really, Dina, trying to bluff me?"

"Gosh, no. I guess I can only tell you the truth."

"That's better. Now I know for a fact that no one has lived at that ranch for years. The Jacob family kept horses there, and I would take you and Rachel down there to feed carrots to the horses. Then when the Jacobs moved, well, the ranch house was just left deserted."

"Not anymore. The corral has horses, and there are even ranch hands." I paused. "You know, people who work on a ranch?"

"I know what ranch hands are!"

"Good. I wasn't sure, with you living back east and all. But the ranch hands aren't on the ranch now because they're off on other jobs. That leaves Gil, who is taking care of the place for the owners."

"And who are the owners?"

"Don't know. Didn't ask."

Displeasure shot through the phone line. "Dina, you've always been fascinated by that old building. Every time you had a high school trauma …" I listened for her memorable, dramatic sigh. "… of which you had many." I giggled as she prodded on. "You'd walk down the road to that old ranch and sit on that rickety glider. This would, in turn, force me to go there." She paused, and I smiled again at the note of longsuffering that she could affect so well. "And I should mention that you usually picked a sweltering day."

I still found the humor every time I thought of Jillian's exasperation at walking down the hot dirt road to fetch me. "As I recall," I told her, "your first dilemma, before taking that walk, was finding the correct pair of shoes to wear."

"Hiking boots were necessary, of course. Correct socks and cool clothing. Sunscreen for my arms and legs, sun-block for my face."

Her outlandish preparations always made me snicker. "Then you'd have to cajole me into going back with you."

"Not an easy task." Jillian offered up another deep sigh. "On occasion, I'd even feel forced to sit with you."

"Do you remember the towel you'd carry with you to spread across the seat?"

"Of course I do." She snorted. "It was a filthy, old porch swing, and the wood gave off splinters." In a more contrite voice, she added, "I will say that it had a pleasant rocking motion."

"Yes, it did." I was glad that she remembered. "I appreciated the iced tea you also carried with you."

"Well, we had to quench our thirst," she replied righteously. "Dehydration can be a serious issue in hot weather. And perhaps even I solved a problem or two on that glider."

"I'll tell you true, Jillian, the old ranch was one of those places where understanding was jam-packed in the air. It would slip around me, and more often than not, I learned to accept what I couldn't change." There was a silence on her end, which I took advantage of. "So, big sister, there are valuable lessons here." I added arrogantly, "I may bill you for this advice."

"Right. Be that as it may, no one could possibly live at the ranch now. It's falling apart." Jillian's voice filled with a forced sigh as she went on. "Once again, tell me. Who is this cowboy?"

I replied righteously, "Well, as long as you're pushing, I might as well be really honest. You know I never could lie to you, Jillian."

"Don't try to snow me, kid sister. I'm on top of this one."

"Yes, of course you are. There's just no fooling you." I smirked. "What was the question again?"

"Really, Dina." Jillian scoffed. "I do this for a living. I'm going to win. Here's the question one more time: Who is the cowboy?"

"A very nice person." Heavy silence permeated the phone. "Hello? Is there someone there?"

"Of course I'm here," Jillian sputtered. Seconds passed for effect before she said, "All right, I'm ready to continue."

"Shoot, counselor."

"Why do you think he's such a nice person?"

"Because he can make me feel good."

"More specific, please."

"A specific, huh? Oh, I got one. He can bake a chocolate cake, and that always makes me feel good. Plus, just last night he sent me a truly wonderful ski dream, which I didn't especially deserve because we broke up yesterday and I was really unpleasant about it."

"Okay. Enough of this." Exasperation filled her voice. "We're going nowhere."

"Well, gosh, Jillian." I grinned to myself, keeping an innocent quality in my voice. "I'm just trying to keep you in the loop. I really don't know how to respond to the displeasure in your tone."

"Bull! We'll address the issue when I arrive. And I want to meet this cowboy friend of yours."

Well, I thought, *good luck in finding him.*

"For now," Jillian continued, "let's talk about something else. Something helpful. Something that I feel will be very good for you."

"You don't think the cowboy is good for me?"

"Enough!"

"Okay. Okay." My smile faded. "What do you think will be very good for me?"

Jillian rushed on as she answered, "I'm bringing special mud for you to soak your feet in. Don't laugh."

I looked toward my toes. "Do you still put pink polish on your toenails?"

"No, of course not. I'm a red person now. It's more mature. Let's get back to the mud and your feet."

"Why?"

"Because the feet absorb wonderful elements from the mud. Really! I'm going to mix it up for you, and I think it will help. Furthermore, if you believe it will help and Rachel thinks it will help, that will triple the positive energy in the mud."

"Really?"

"Yes, of course."

"Wow." No one ever said no to Jillian. Shaking my head, I smiled. "Do you remember how we made mud pies once upon a time? Mom got really mad, mostly at you because you were supposed to keep us out of trouble."

Jillian snorted. "It was okay until you and Rachel put the pies in Mom's clean oven."

"Had to bake them," I replied. Laughter followed. "And I also remember that time I wanted to go to the movies, but you wouldn't take me because you had plans with your friends and Mom wouldn't let me go alone. I was so mad at you that I went into the bathroom where you kept your lipstick and smeared it all over the mirror."

"You made a real mess."

I closed my eyes as I thought back to that day. "But even after I was sent to my room, I was still mad, mostly at me for doing something so dumb. But then you came to my room a few hours later and brought me that thing you baked."

"My first apple tart!" Jillian's voice bubbled. "I was so proud of it. How sweet that you remembered."

"You never were a cook, dear Jillian. But you had picked two apples, cut them up, put them between some dough, and spread butter and brown sugar all over them. You popped them in the oven and brought them to me warm with a scoop of ice cream that had melted all over the plate. You knew that apple pie was my favorite dessert."

Jillian's tone was gentle with memory. "You were so sad."

"But you made me happy. That was the best part. And you even forgave me right away. That homemade apple tart was the best dessert I've ever had." A question flitted through my thoughts. "Do you know how to bake now?"

"Heavens, no. God made bakeries for people like me. Without my constant support, they'd go under. But when I visit, I'll do another tart just for you." Jillian stumbled, followed by a moment of silence. "Dina, I'm sorry. I know you can't eat. I mean…"

"Hey, it's okay. I still remember the one tart you did, and that will hold me." I paused. "You've been a great big sister. The best. Did I ever tell you that?"

"Tell me in person. I'll be there in two weeks, and I'll take care of you and Rachel. I'll post correct notes where needed, reorganize the meals, and I'll find the photo albums that the two of you have misplaced." Jillian huffed like a wounded big sister. "All my hours of categorizing and documenting, and at last someone wants to see them. I'm so happy you finally appreciate my efforts."

I rolled my eyes and then spoke quickly, "Do you remember the images we used to see in the wavy glass?"

"You mean through the old picture window?"

"Yes. Why don't you document that? Call it, 'Fragments of a Simpler Life.' Rachel could do the art; you could handle the words." I paused. I could almost hear Jillian thinking. "You know it would be a lovely gift for your children and their children and so on."

"You might have something there. Not a bestseller, but a—"

"Family treasure?"

"Exactly! What a fantastic idea! I'm really surprised."

"Why?"

"Because usually the best ideas are mine."

I rolled my eyes again.

"I know you're doing that thing with your eyes! Right? Am I right?" Jillian sounded smug. "After all, you were my first client. I know you inside and out. Now tell me where Rachel is."

"She's running errands and having lunch with Carl."

"Carl? Who's Carl?"

"Dr. Carl Bergman."

"He's your doctor!"

"Well, I don't want to be greedy. Besides, as I've mentioned, I do have the cowboy, so I thought I'd share the doc with Rachel. Furthermore, they're in love."

"Why doesn't anyone keep me informed? And how do you know that?"

I settled myself against the pillows. "Because I can see it. He was here for dinner just the other night. The way they looked at each other...mushy eyes and all. Take it from me, it's a sure thing. So how's the family, big sister?"

"Great. The kids are busy. Tony is busy. And we're going to take that trip to Disneyland. Are you sure about Rachel and the doctor?"

"Mushy eyes never lie. You said that."

Jillian was lost in thought. "Yes, I believe I did."

"So listen, have a great trip to Disneyland, okay? Take the boys to Tom Sawyer's Island for me, if it's still there. It was always my favorite."

"That's because you were a tomboy."

I shrugged. "Doesn't make me a bad person." My voice softened. "Kiss Tony for me and tell him I miss his jokes. I love you, Jillian. I'm glad you'll be here for Rachel."

"I love you too, Dina. Just two weeks and I can put my arms around you and give you the biggest hug. I promise."

Tenderly, I whispered, "Good-bye, big sister."

Chapter 8

I lay still for a moment. The pain seared down my arms, and I gasped at its new swiftness. Feeling too weak to move, I feared the worst. My thoughts danced like stars, searching my memory for Gil's face. I focused on his image, hoping he really was an angel and that just by seeing him the agony would subside.

The phone rang, and I thought Jillian had one more set of instructions for me. I answered with a gruff, "Yes, what do you want now?"

"I'd like for you to meet me in the apple orchard, if ya got a mind for goin' there."

"What!"

"Dina, this is Gil, and I want you to meet me—"

"I heard you." My heart was suddenly thumping with anticipation. "How'd you get this number?"

"It was in large print on your cell phone. You showed it to me yesterday. Y'all do remember yesterday, don'cha?" There was a pause, and then he asked, "Well? Now that I've jogged your memory some, will ya meet me?"

Even though I wanted to see him, I was still upset with the things he had said, and I realized that a part of me was still sulking. "You don't have many phone skills," I snapped.

"And you, Miss Dina, answered the phone in a most unpleasant manner. I do believe the correct response is a simple 'hello.' Am I right? Should I start again?"

"No. That's not necessary." His reply had stung, even if it was true. But he wasn't going to come back into my life until I had an explanation and an apology. "I will meet you. I have several things I want to say to you, Mister, Mister...What is your last name?"

An awkward pause followed before Gil replied, "Can't say that I rightly have one."

"Well." His comeback required another deep intake of air. "Okay then." I didn't know what to make of his answer but was determined to have the final word. "I'll be out shortly."

I pushed the afghan from my lap and wondered how I was going to find the strength to walk outside. I forced myself into a sitting position, and as I stood, I felt better. When I moved toward the back door that led to the orchard, my spirits lifted. I knew I would make it.

Brilliant sunshine warmed the day, glinting off the fallen leaves that blew across my path. Someone was burning wood, and the pungent aroma mingled with the brisk smells of crisp air. I looked through the maze of apple trees. The harvest had taken place weeks before, and now their bare trunks marched, row after row, with half-empty branches stretching toward the sky. The summer's green leaves had turned to yellow and orange, and as the breeze nudged a path through the orchard, the leaves rolled with the currents of the wind.

As I walked it occurred to me we hadn't settled on a spot to meet. *Oh great,* I thought. *Just great. Where in the orchard am I supposed to find him?* I trudged along, selecting a wide lane between the old trees.

"Here, Dina." His voice filled the silence, and I looked up. "Blue is a pretty color on you."

I stood still. "It matches your eyes."

"Were ya thinkin' of my eyes when you got dressed?"

"I'm still mad at you." I moved toward him and put my hands on my hips. "I want you to know that guys have broken up with me before, but I've never been dumped by an angel." He stepped toward me, and I held up my hand. My voice held hurt and anger. "Let alone, my angel."

"It didn't happen that way."

We were nose to nose. "Yes, it did."

"No, it did not." Gil breathed in and out then continued talking. "I told you that I needed time to think. You know, Dina, it can be right difficult to think clearly about some things when I'm around you."

I listened to the sounds of the day as they cushioned my emotions. A horse whinnied in the pasture that bordered the orchard, and I knew Gil had ridden through the valley and not come up the drive to the farm.

He continued, "I needed time to myself so that I could observe people fallin' in love, to see how it happened, where they went with it, how it felt." His brows knit and he paused as he shook his head. "Dang, it can be a real unexpected feelin' and it can sweep you away in a moment's notice." He smiled faintly. "There was a lot to learn." He struggled with his composure, let out his breath, and said, "It's a good thing I have a bit of an edge of time so that I could properly review this phenomenal happenin'."

I took a baby step back. "What are you saying?" I was growing sensitive to the sounds of the day. Two horses moved to my left, and the wind carried the scraping sounds of their hooves across the autumn foliage.

"I'm sayin' that I had to study on it a bit."

I noticed that his cowboy hat was his normal tan one and felt an odd sense of relief. "And you did all that in less than a day?"

"Like I said, as an angel, I do have a unique approach to time, and I elected to use it, as this was an important decision for me to make." He looked me square in the eyes.

"You really hurt my feelings." I folded my arms across my chest and looked at my feet. I pushed my shoe through a gathering pile of crimson and golden leaves. "I'm still upset." The day grew quiet.

"Well now…" He cleared his throat. "That's what I figured, so I brought you a little present."

I glanced up to see him rotate his shoulders. He moved from foot to foot in an attempt to look comfortable. "I understand that when a fella upsets a gal, which I do bountifully apologize for…" He paused to look at me.

I made circles in the dirt with my other foot. "Go on."

"Yes, ma'am. I was sayin' that it's best to bring that gal a present, a meaningful present, so she knows that fella wants to make up—proper-like."

"Is that information you received from your 'wind' brother?"

"It is." He reached behind his back and brought out a shiny red apple. "But this here was all my idea." He held it for me to see. "Do ya like it?"

I looked from the apple to him and back to the apple. "Are you giving me an apple?" I asked in a disapproving tone. Is that your present?"

"It's a two-parter present."

"What's the second part?" I reached for the apple and realized that a dawning of crystal clear air now encircled us.

He voice was calm and steady. "It's a memory."

"Come again?" I felt bemused.

His glance carried me toward a tree farther out in the orchard. "Have a look."

"Where?" The day opened wide gates as I stared into the orchard.

"You're not trying, Dina." His eyes sparkled. "Y'all got to give it a shot if you want to get there." He nodded for me to precede him.

"In for a penny, in for a pound. Let's go." I moved forward but felt myself float slowly into the past. I continued walking along the rows of trees and followed the sunlight that flickered at my feet. I muttered, "Some present. I have to go to it."

His unruffled tone filled the air behind me. "Sometimes it just works best that way."

After a few steps I grew aware that we were not alone. Under a gnarled apple tree at the end of the orchard, two children sat, deep in conversation. Their voices touched the air with laughter, and I knew I was listening to an old dream. Nostalgia filled my heart, changing into a vibrant flow of recollection so powerful in its intensity that I wanted to stop the world from moving so I could be perfectly still. Perhaps that would allow me to understand what was happening to me.

The liveliness of the children continued with no regard to my presence. The little boy charged from under the tree, his curly hair bouncing across his forehead. The young girl ran after him. Giggles and shouts sounded from both children as they sped farther into the orchard.

A wash of memories enveloped me, years melted away, and I found myself back in the orchard, heartbroken at saying good-bye to my imaginary friend.

I looked for Gil and realized he was at my side. His hands reached for mine as he turned me toward me. My words formed slowly. "Is that me?" I pulled my hand from his and pointed toward the child. "Were you my friend?"

He nodded once and removed his hat. "Children need many things. You needed a friend."

"But my friend left me."

"Even then you knew it was right."

His words held the truth, and I felt his physical closeness grow stronger. I looked up at the man he had become and realized we were alone. "They're gone." I waved my hand toward the far reaches of the orchard. "The children are gone."

"But we're here." His words held simple wisdom.

I turned my head and looked thoughtfully at his face. Waves of sunshine caressed his hair, highlighting the dark curls, but no sunbeams danced over his head. "You no longer have the halo."

He looked calmly back at me through thick lashes. "Halos are for children. They're a starting place." He held my hand against his heart. "As you grow, the light comes inside, and you shine from within."

I felt the warmth of his chest through his denim shirt. I let his words settle. "Are you talking about people or angels?"

"Both."

Intense blue infused his eyes, and I felt calm in returning his gaze. There was a new level of understanding between us. I journeyed inside myself to find my shining light, but I wasn't aglow. "It's not there."

He released my hand and slid his fingertips across my cheek. "Let it be, Dina. Everything has a time."

"Did my friend need me?"

"Yes. You grew together yet apart. You had different paths."

"And now you've come back?"

"I never left you." His arms circled me, and I rested my head against his shoulder. He continued, "I entered this world with you, and I've watched you ever since."

"Okay." I sighed. "That's a lot to accept. I think I'd better sit down."

He guided me under a bare tree, and we sat on a carpet of leaves where the warm perfume of dark earth greeted us.

"Are you really my angel?"

"I am." He placed his hat next to us.

I sat for a minute letting that knowledge swirl around me while Gil waited patiently for me to say something. "What now?" I asked.

"I've been givin' that some thought, and here's what I've come up with. Lovin' is natural for me. We angels have that ability built in. It's what I've always felt for you.

Now then, near as I can figure, it takes centuries to under-stand this concept of fallin' in love,' which is where we're at, but we don't have the luxury of all that time. However, the fallin' in love part is a different concept from the lovin' part. Are you with me?"

"Uh, sorta."

I liked watching his lips move, and when he saw my interest, he offered an inviting smile. "So here's what I've been thinkin'. I'm willin' to learn as I go, if y'all are willing to accept that."

I was growing aware of his pine scent again, and my heart did a flip. "You sure get to the point."

"When presented with a situation, I find it best to deal straight on. Would ya agree with that?"

"Yes, I would." We sat facing each other much the same way as when we were children. I set the apple close to his cowboy hat and shyly reached for his hand. "It's been a long trip, coming to the end for me, and I have much to do." Leaning against him, I wished for more time. "Will you help me?"

He pulled me toward him, wrapping his arms around me. "I can give you time to sort out your thoughts."

I snuggled closer. "And the courage to do that?"

Stroking my hair, he replied, "You already have the courage. Y'all need to find your peace."

The wind blew across my cotton slacks, patting the fabric against my legs. I smiled up at Gil. "Is that Daniel again?"

"I felt the wind blow across your legs too, you know." He turned his head toward the pines on the upper ridge. "Bit frisky on his part, I thought." Looking back at me, he continued, "I plan on havin' myself a long chat with the boy. High time he up and found himself his own girl."

I laughed at his serious tone, feeling relief from the stress of the day. I wondered if he actually had parents and which parent gave him his sense of humor.

"Yes. Both." He looked apologetic. "Sorry, sometimes I do that. I wasn't found under a rock, ya know. I'm an angel, not an apparition."

"It's a lot to accept." I found myself staring at him. Without his hat, I noticed his dark hair was longer and windblown. "I guess angels don't ever turn gray, huh?"

"I do believe, Miss Dina, you could change that."

"I don't know whether to be insulted or flattered by that remark."

An easy smile crossed his face as he tipped his head to one side. "That's your choice."

"If you think you're going to be a show-off with smart quips like that, this may not work out."

"No, ma'am." He looked confused.

"And I don't expect you to act dumb either."

"Yes, ma'am, I will not."

"Good. Then I think we can say, overall, I've been an easy job for you."

"No, ma'am. That we cannot say. Frequently you paid no never mind to my tugs on your conscious or my taps on your shoulders."

"I'm human."

"Delightfully so." He lifted my fingers to his lips.

I was flattered but had more to say. "And you're, well, with your family and all, you're..." I paused to take a different approach. "You understand having a brother who is the wind is unusual."

He held back his smile. "I appreciate Daniel's helpful nature, but it's not necessary."

"No," I replied. "It certainly isn't."

His head bent down, and the air moved between us like silk as his lips touched mine. My eyes closed, and I felt his kiss caress then tease my mouth. I began to float, feeling complete, as if someone had woven a magic spell that made me well and whole again. I saw a small light, deep within me, begin to shine. The words "This is my time" slipped from my lips.

He nodded in understanding and sat up. "That it is. And as this is your day, it's high time we got on with it."

"Are you asking me out?" I quipped.

"Miss Dina, will you consider this our first official date?"

"The other times didn't count?"

"Everything counts. Time is a gift. But now, today, this moment, I'm makin' it our first date. And, as a first date is an important event, I want y'all to know that I plan to special it up some." He reached for his cowboy hat and settled it on his head. "Y'all notice, it's not black. Right?"

I smiled and nodded.

"Got yourself an eye for color, you have." He touched the brim and winked at me. "So now, where do you want to spend the afternoon?"

We peeked up at the sky from between the branches of the old apple tree. Dark clouds began to roll across the ridge. Gil commented, "Looks like rain." He stared at the rumbling sky. "I like rain. Got a personal involvement in it. How about you, Dina? Y'all like a good lightning and thunderstorm?"

"I enjoy a rainy afternoon." We both stood up. Shaking off the leaves, we moved from the shelter of the tree. I continued, "Thunder, lightning—it brings out the best in a person. Besides, now that you're all grown up, I'd like to know about what you learned when we were apart. You know, like the subjects you studied."

A note of amusement entered his voice. "I see."

"Well, I assume you went to some kind of school. Right? So you can tell me about it."

Moving closer, he spoke softly, "How about I show you?" His smile was seductive. He made a clicking sound. Sweet Mary appeared from the end of the orchard, and Joe followed her. "Say we take us a ride over to the old ranch?"

"I haven't seen it in years. Are the new owners taking good care of it?"

"You tell me."

"That would be great, but..." The sun that had been tangled behind a dark cloud broke loose. I took it as a good omen and replied, "Yes! Let's go." My voice became hesitant. "Maybe I shouldn't be so quick with that yes answer. Rachel will be home soon."

"No need to worry so." He tucked my hand back into his. "It will all work out."

Laughter bubbled up as I shook my head. "Yeah. Right."

"Butch will be there." He squeezed my hand. "He'll purr."

"Well, how can a girl say no to that? I'll run inside and get a sweater and as we girls say, 'freshen up.' Give me about ten minutes."

I felt joy spilling over as I dashed through the Victorian parlor, headed to my bedroom. This was going to be a fantastic first date. I grabbed my toothpaste and looked for the brush at the same time. I was as giddy as a teenager. I took a few minutes to preen and came to the same conclusion that I reached every time I tried to smarten my look; there wasn't much I could do. So be that as it may, I grabbed a tan jacket, flung it over my shoulders, and headed toward the kitchen door. I felt another presence in the hall and instinctively stopped.

"Dina, where are you going?" Rachel was out of breath when she reached me. "I called you on the cell, and there was no answer. I came right home. Where were you?"

"Oh, hi. I was in the orchard."

"Why? You were supposed to stay put inside."

My thoughts rushed around my head in spinning circles. *Did she see Gil?* I walked toward the parlor window and peered outside. "I, uh, felt like getting some air. So I took a stroll." The orchard was empty; neither man nor horse was in sight. I felt both relief and alarm as I sat on the old loveseat. "Am I in trouble?" I joked.

"You're never in trouble, Dina." Rachel sat down next to me. "But you expect too much of yourself."

I folded my hands in front of me in an attempt to look chastised. Rachel held out a new bottle of pills. "During lunch I told Carl of your hallucinations and that, coupled with your walking alone, and all your prescription medications, well..." She looked worried. "We need to make some changes."

"Like?" I eyed the bottle of pills.

Her voice held a crisp edge. "I know how you value your independence, but for your safety you cannot keep walking alone."

My breath caught somewhere in my chest, and I knew this wasn't going well. My mind ran with options, but no coherent thought pattern surfaced.

Rachel went on, "As long as you'll cooperate with me and I can watch over you, you'll never need twenty-four hour care." She shushed me by lifting her hand. "But if you insist on wandering that old dirt road alone, I will continue to fear for your safety. It's my responsibility to know where you are and what you're doing." Her voice took on a pleading note. "Let me do that for you."

I could see frown lines etch across her forehead and knew there would be no arguing with her. My date with Gil was fading away, and with it all hope.

"You look so tired, Dina." She reached out to touch me. "Your face is white. You need to rest."

"Please, Rachel, let me go!"

"No. I can't do that. Besides, you might as well know that Jillian called me after she talked with you. She said that part of your conversation made sense; the rest of it..." Her voice trailed off. She held my hand. "She's very concerned."

I pulled away. "So you and Jillian decided what's best for me?"

"No…maybe. Dina, some days you take your meds; some days you don't. You're all over the board with them. I know that some pills you spit out, and you double up on others. Your medication has been carefully measured out for your body, and when you abuse them, well, this is what happens."

"Uh-huh. So you've had a consultation with my doctor?" I tried to act outraged. "And I wasn't even there?"

Rachel moved toward the kitchen. A wash of sorrow swept over me. I looked toward the empty fall afternoon and realized that I was very much alone.

She returned with a glass of water. "This pill is new. It's meant to help you relax. You don't need food with it, and it won't make you sick. If you take it as directed, it's not habit-forming."

My temper was flaring. "Oh! Well, Rachel, habit-forming isn't one of my immediate concerns."

"It will offer you twelve hours of relaxation. Carl said you might feel sleepy to start with, but when you wake up after a snooze, you won't feel all of your anxieties."

I knew I had to accept the pill or Rachel would be forced to take other actions. Months ago we'd discussed hiring a private nurse but had decided against it. I had agreed to do what the doctor advised and Rachel had agreed to assume responsibility for my personal care. If I put up a fight about this new medication, she'd never let me out of her sight until other arrangements could be made.

I accepted the water and pill, placing it under my tongue. Making an ugly face, I swallowed and glared at her. "Should I lay down now?"

She seemed tired, and her eyes held mine for a long second. "It also dissolves quickly under your tongue."

There was a bitter taste in my mouth as the pill disintegrated along with my final hope of meeting Gil. I felt betrayed.

"You want to be outside; I can fix that." She sounded relieved. "Come with me."

I followed her to the grassy area outside the family room. The old hammock was tied securely between two old trees. I stared at it while Rachel brought out a pillow and light blanket. "You'll be outside, you can rest in the hammock, and I'll know where you are." She spread the blanket over me and kissed my cheek lightly. "After you wake up, I'll walk with you. It won't be so bad." She joked, "I'm good company."

Layers of frustration built one on top of another, weighing me down, but the little pill was doing a good job. I felt tired and told myself that I would shut my eyes for only a few minutes.

Time passed slowly in a dark sleep. All my troubles were gone, but so was the sense of myself. It wasn't uncomfortable being there, but it didn't feel right either.

My eyelids were too heavy to open, but from a distant part of me, I was conscious of a presence. I sensed a movement and forced my lids to rise so I could look through narrow slits where a cowboy hat faded in and out of my vision. A corner of my being whispered, *That's a good thing*, but my body wanted to fall back into the dreamless sleep where I was alone with no cares or worries and no one could tell me what to do.

A low voice with musical overtones kept invading that space by calling my name. The drugged part of me wanted to ignore the sounds from outside so I could drift away again, but a tiny light at the end of a long hall kept blinking at me in a most irritating manner, forcing me to be more observant.

From a great distance, I felt cool fingers trace the lines of my face. I heard my name called again, but the dark space that was filled with sleep wouldn't let go. Neither would the low voice. They fought each other until a kiss, feathery light, brushed my lips. I wanted to respond, but nothing seemed to work.

"What's it goin' take to wake ya up, sleepin' beauty?"

My nose picked up a scent of fresh soap and pine for a quiet moment before the drug resurfaced to claim me again. I felt air being forced into my lungs, and when I exhaled, more air came surging in. A mouth covered mine, filling my chest with another breath of air, again and again. I picked up the pleasant rhythm of breathing and felt I was rising to the surface. This time my eyes opened wider.

"Breathe deeply, Dina."

The low voice was commanding, and I sucked at the crisp air until I felt an awareness enter my body.

"Take the air all the way into your stomach. That's my gal. Now release it. Good work, Dina. Do it again."

The fog that filled me began to thin, and I was breathing without the commands. I grew aware of the trees overhead and the slight sway of the hammock.

"Well now, good afternoon to you, Miss Dina. Seems that you were takin' yourself a long time to freshen up some so I thought I should come callin', and what do I find but you takin' yourself a snooze in this here hammock." Gil's sunglasses were hooked at a corner of his shirt, and they flipped forward as he leaned over me. "Welcome back from your little nap."

Tilting my head, I stared into the mirrored frame. My voice was weak. "I look awful."

Gil pushed his hat back from his head and studied me straight on. "Oh now, I wouldn't say that. A bit worn out maybe, but it'll pass soon enough."

I looked up. Gil's eyes were seductive under half-closed lids. "A couple of clear breaths and you'll see the light."

I felt tired, and talking was a chore. "It's not shining. It's just blinking, and it's only a dot that's far away."

"Gotta start somewhere." He spoke with knowledge. "Deep breaths now, Dina. That's right, keep 'em slow and easy."

With more oxygen in my body, I felt awake, if not fully alert.

"A big gulp of sunshine will truly improve your condition." He grinned at me.

I looked dubious. "Is that angel talk?"

"Yes, ma'am, it is. If y'all knock back some of that crisp fall air and have yourself a guzzle of sunbeams, why, you'll be wantin' to sit up and take notice in no time."

I tried to rise up, but the hammock swayed dangerously until Gil caught it. "Easy there."

"Where's Rachel?" I mumbled, holding my head.

"Busy."

"Can she see you?"

"She's not lookin'."

"That's good." I swayed a bit. "Oh boy." Gil helped me to stand, but the world was still spinning. "She had a new medication for me. I think I'm really relaxed."

"Deep breaths, Dina. In and out. Breathe."

I filled my lungs with fresh air. "She won't let me go. I'm a prisoner here."

Gil helped me take some steps. "Not being an ornery kind of fella, I still have to say this." He looked me over with care. "I'm a mite tired that so many people insist on interferin' with our date. I have planned a lovely afternoon, and I do want us to enjoy it."

I took another deep breath and asked, "Does Rachel have an angel?"

"Sure does."

A pleading sound entered my voice. "Maybe you could have a word?"

"Already did." He spoke with authority. "That's why she's not lookin'." He helped me to maintain my balance. "Here, lean on me and we'll breathe together."

The dizzy feeling was subsiding, but weakness replaced it. "I'd better have another swallow of that sunshine."

"Good idea. Tends to speed up a recovery." His arm continued to support me. "Now then, it's a good thing I have that edge on time so we can work on this new little hitch with your breathin'."

"Gotcha." I filled my lungs with the autumn air. "My sisters think you're a hallucination." I looked at Gil carefully and saw his familiar face. His eyes held a tenderness that made my heart weep. "Touch me so I know you're real."

"As I live and breathe, Miss Dina, I'm real to you, and that's what's important. Do y'all agree with that?" He kissed my nose, letting his fingertips softly trail down my cheek.

"Okay, I felt that." A pleasant shiver tickled my back. "I think my feet are going to move." I scrutinized Gil's face. "You sure about your edge on time?"

"Sure as I'm standin' here." He grinned. "We got us all the time we need to celebrate our first proper-like rendezvous."

My senses began to tingle, and I found that my eyes could stay open without as much effort. "Don't take this the wrong way, but have you ever had a first date before?"

He laughed. "Why now, I do believe that y'all consider me to be backward on my social skills."

"I meant because you're an angel," I protested.

"Angels do socialize. We are not misfits, and we have manners." He kept his arm around me. "Keep breathing that air in. Inhale through your mouth." He filled his chest with air and let it out. I did the same. "There you go. Feelin' better?"

"Yeah, I am." I felt better, almost cheerful. "Maybe one more sunbeam and I'll be good to go."

"That's was I was waitin' to hear!" He squeezed my shoulder. "I want you to be tip-top so ya can enjoy the preparations I've made for us."

"You didn't decorate with crepe paper, did you? I used to have a maypole on my birthday decorated with crepe paper streamers."

"No, ma'am." He winked at me. "I thought I'd take us dancin', not maypole twirlin'."

"Oh, that's right." I winked back. "You know all about my little girl birthday parties. You must know everything about me."

"Not everythin'." Gil leaned close to my ear. "But I am fixin' to make some improvements in that area as the day goes by."

"Oh, I like the sound of that." My heart began to race.

"Well, Miss Dina, we are goin' to have us one fine afternoon. God willin' and the creek don't run dry."

I looked deeply into his eyes. "Since you're the angel, the first part is up to you. As to the creek, we've had a rainy summer, so I'd say it's flowing just fine."

"Then that's a cut of good news!" His jubilant mood lifted my spirits, and he spoke cheerfully, "Let's get into our day."

"What do you have planned?"

He raised an eyebrow. "Didn't y'all tell me that you liked surprises?"

"I did."

"Well then, I'll untie Sweet Mary and Joe. Got 'em over by the far side." He leaned toward me playfully. "Didn't think I should upset Rachel none. She feel the same way as you about horses bein' big?"

I smirked. "Yeah, pretty much."

Feeling fresher with each intake of air, I directed my feet to move toward Sweet Mary. She snorted her pleasure at seeing me. I rubbed her velvety nose and quietly spoke of sweet nothings, ending with a promise of fresh carrots to come.

Gil laughed. "She's playin' ya some, 'cause she's already had herself a couple apples."

"And Joe?"

"Yup. Him too. He's not slow in the treat department. Had himself one or two while waitin' on ya."

I glanced toward the house and didn't see Rachel. If Gil was right about time, we had this afternoon to share. He unhooked the aviator glasses from his shirt then dug in his saddlebag and handed me a hat. "What we make of a day is up to us." His smile was catching, and I grinned back.

"It sure is."

We rode away from the farm, leaving the hammock behind to sway in the breeze. The old fence came into view, and Gil rode ahead to unlatch the gate. His tall frame was outlined against the sky, and from my vantage point on Sweet Mary, it appeared that he was supporting the clouds on his broad shoulders. I paused to enjoy the view, smiling to myself.

He looked over his aviator sunglasses at me. "Whatcha thinkin', Dina?"

I dismounted like a pro, and his arms slipped around my waist. I looped my hands behind his neck as if I'd known him forever. The essence of evergreen lingered in the air. I took a long breath, letting it travel through my body. The effects from the pill were nearly gone. Gil's lips touched mine in a gentle kiss, causing my heart to miss a beat.

"I like the way you do that."

"Do you now?"

"Yup. It's very thorough. Plus, I think you're really enjoying it too."

He laughed. "You got me nailed there." He pushed his glasses back on his nose. He released me and took my hand. "If you're feelin' good enough, I thought we'd walk to the ranch." A tilt of his head indicated the road beyond the gate.

"I'm doing fine. Lots of fresh oxygen helps get rid of the bad stuff."

"That it does." He looked questionably at me as if expecting more.

I grinned. "And the sunbeams. They were a really big help."

Gil nodded and whistled for the horses. They followed behind us. I felt the calloused skin of his palm as his hand held mine with a comfortable firmness.

"Oh." I paused. "Thank you for letting me swoop down mountains last night. It was like flying through snowy air." I squeezed his hand. "I loved the feeling. That dream meant a lot to me." My eyes glanced upwards. "I am sorry about the black hat comment."

"Apology accepted. Us angels, why we tend to be toward the good side of things." He grinned down at me, "That's why we wear tan hats." He joked, "So y'all can tell us apart."

"I think I understand now."

"Glad we got it straightened out," he teased.

"Me too because after the incredible sensation of night skiing I know for sure that I'm coming back as an athlete; probably a skier. Definite Olympic material."

Gil nodded thoughtfully. "Guess we should put that scholar idea of yours on the back burner for now, huh? Give ya a little time to sort out your options."

"It's like you said." I grinned. "There's lots to see. Lots to do."

A slow smile curved across his lips. "I'm never sure when I talk if people hear me or not." I watched his face with pleasure as he leaned closer and whispered, "But I'm right pleased to know that you've been listenin' up a storm lately." I felt his breath on my ear. "'Cause you are right on the mark, Miss Dina. Lots of new ideas to explore."

"Is that so?" I reached up a finger and tugged gently on his sunglasses.

His eyes, the color of sapphires, sparkled back at me. "Yes, ma'am." His voice took on a husky note. "Right on the mark." He lowered his face until his lips brushed mine. "Shall we walk?"

The lane was awash with a carpet of leaves that crackled underfoot. I replied pleasantly to the rustling sounds, "Indian steps."

Gil nodded. "Wherever man has lived, his essence lingers." He glanced up smiling. "Sorta looks like rain, Dina. We'd best hurry a bit."

"Rain! No way. It's bright and sunny and..." I looked toward the west, where steel gray clouds silently approached. "When did that happen?"

He turned me toward him and raised my chin. "I thought a rainy afternoon was your favorite," he teased as his eyes flirted with me.

My heart began to beat rapidly. "It is." I took a calming breath and replied, "But I don't get it. I mean ..." I looked at him questionably. "It was sunny."

He folded his arms around me and whispered in my ear, "Who can explain the weather?" He rubbed his shoulders as the dark clouds smothered the sunshine. "So did y'all talk to Jillian this morning?" He reached for my hand again, and we continued to walk.

"I said good-bye to her. It had to be done because I'm not going to be here when she visits. But Rachel will need her. I'm glad they have each other."

Dappled light splashed across Gil's face. He nodded in understanding. "That was a big step." He stopped. "Did she know you were sayin' good-bye?"

I looked into his eyes. They reflected a shade of blue that reminded me of the lobelia flowers I had planted every summer with my sisters when we were children. "She's really pretty smart."

He pulled his cowboy hat lower and nodded. We walked in silence, being swept along by the golden lure of the day.

I smiled sadly. "They were the best sisters. Sometimes ornery, sometimes fussy, but we could always count on one another when it really mattered. We argued, competed, shared, and loved ..." I bit my lower lip to keep from crying. Taking a breath, I shook my head. "...often at the same time." There was a catch in my voice. "Guess that's part of being a family." I wiped at my eyes. "Sometimes this is really hard ..."

He offered me a freshly pressed handkerchief, the kind my Grandma Nana used to give me whenever I had a good cry. After wiping at my tears, I moved wordlessly into his arms. His voice was soft when he spoke. "We travel forward, Dina, but it only takes a blink to be in the past. Listenin' to good memories is a fine part of life."

I was drawn to the comfort his words offered. He reached out and held my tears in his fingertips. It was a tender gesture, and I rested my cheek against his chest, feeling soothed. I knew that today belonged to us.

The air was rapidly turning cooler, and the smell of rain was close. The old ranch house was as I remembered it, a simple structure of logs and stone tucked into a clearing. Several horses stood in the corral, lifting their heads at the sounds of approaching people. Gil opened the gate, and Joe and Sweet Mary joined the other horses.

The sheltered porch still embraced the house while the old glider, moving to the call of the wind, beckoned us to enter. Hand in hand, we scrambled up the stairs.

"Careful," I warned Gil. "The third step has been weak for years."

"Gotcha." Nodding, he reached for my elbow.

"No," I teased, pulling away. "I didn't mean you had to help me. I was giving you a heads-up so you didn't fall."

"Well now, why don't I be a gentleman and offer you my assistance anyhow?" He extended his arm, and I laughed.

"Okay. That way we can help each other climb the stairs."

"Exactly." He paused in thought, looking deeply into my eyes. "That's a mighty good plan."

We passed under the weathered trellis. Strips of gray paint peeled back from the wooden slabs that held the remains of late summer roses. I stopped, touching the petals that were as brittle as potpourri. As the wind picked up, the withered blossoms fell from my fingers, filling the air with a shower of faded white. I suddenly felt tired and very sad.

"Don't look so gloomy, Miss Dina." Gil turned me toward him.

Over his shoulder, the sky filled with fast clouds of gray mist. I focused my attention on the sculpted lines of his face. In the dreary light of the approaching storm, I studied the chiseled angle of his jaw and noted the creases by his eyes were not as deep as earlier in the day.

His fingers slid under my chin as he spoke. "The roses bloomed profusely all summer long, real bright and sassy-like." His face warmed with a friendly smile, and I saw again the boyish charm that I had noticed the first time we met. "They're taking a much needed rest." I felt myself respond to his words as he bent his head down and kissed my cheek. "They'll be back." He reached for my hand, hurrying me across the porch.

At our heels, the rain came swirling, soft as down. When we reached the kitchen door, we rested in each other's arms. I tilted my head back, and he cupped my face in his palms. "I have some work to do here. Y'all want to take a seat for a minute?"

My nose twitched at the bold, smoky aroma that stirred the kitchen air. The scent of freshly ground beans left me giddy with pleasure. Gil had begun looking through the small freezer compartment above the old refrigerator while I continued to inhale the robust scent of espresso.

A mouthwatering pie, with warm fruit dribbling out of its golden crust, was sitting on a glass plate. Delicate whiffs of cinnamon and nutmeg scented the air. Instinctively, I moved toward the wooden sideboard, aware that my feet made a soft padding sound on the flooring. I glanced down at the old linoleum. It had yellowed with age and showed several cracks. Speaking over my shoulder, I said, "Looks like you'll be replacing this floor pretty soon."

Gil looked down. "Here I thought your attention was on my pie."

"Maybe." I shrugged playfully.

"Tell ya what. Why don't I let you deal with that old floor? Seems that fashions and decoratin', that kind of stuff needs an expert." He winked and turned back to the refrigerator. My mind jumped around a bit at the familiarity of his words. I had to remind myself that he was my angel and he did know certain things about me. I smiled and faced the pie. "Did you bake it?"

"Sure enough. I have several areas of expertise."

I laughed. "Oh, I know that now."

Grinning, he faced me. "I was lookin' for vanilla ice cream. Would that be okay?"

"Pie and ice cream go together." Turning around, I noticed that the windowsill behind him needed paint, but the curtain was freshly laundered and pressed.

He followed my line of vision. "One of my half-finished chores. Look over here." He indicated the next window. "This one is complete." Fresh, white paint outlined the rainy day. "You know, sometimes everything just doesn't get done."

"Oh?" He looked at me as I cocked my eyebrow and spoke quietly, "I know that."

Reaching out, I touched the cotton fabric of the curtain. It was stiff with age and faded by the sun in its sheared folds. "I'm just surprised that you could wash it and press it without having it fall into pieces."

"Well now, Miss Dina." His deep blue eyes were sparkling with mischief. "Today I'm just full of surprises."

I pulled myself back to the moment. "Rachel bakes a fabulous apple pie. My doctor really enjoyed it." I smiled at the memory. "Jillian does sort of an apple tart. Hey, almost forgot to mention that my big sister told me this old ranch was deserted."

"That so?" He shut the door of the freezer compartment. "I think of it more as an old softness. Sorta the work of quiet years spent with the land." He glanced at the curtains. "Maybe a touch faded, but we're here. Does it look deserted to you?"

"Not after that explanation." I let my eyes take in the diffused light of the rain-lit room. A mason jar filled with wildflowers sat in the center of a scratched Formica table. I spent my time enjoying the sight, recalling the perfume of past flowers. Four chairs with faded vinyl seats were pushed against the table. Brown stuffing was poking through the cracked vinyl in the chair closest to me. I turned to Gil. "I'm going to guess they were yellow."

"Bright yellow." He seemed pleased that I'd noticed and gave me a wink. "Just like sunshine."

"Uh-huh. And where did you find wildflowers this time of year?"

"Faith, Dina. Y'all gotta have faith." Moving past me, he replied over his shoulder, "I'm tellin' ya, it'll move mountains."

"And grow spring flowers in the fall?"

He shrugged and smiled. "So far I'm guessing that ya like my surprises."

"Okay." I laughed. Using my finger, I pushed the stuffing back into the chair and sat down. "Heck, I feel honored to be here."

"Me too." His voice rang with a teasing note as he asked, "So, Dina, y'all like apple pie and ice cream, huh?"

I bounced up and stepped toward the wooden sideboard. "Sure do."

Moving closer, he let his eyes drift slowly down my body then gradually back up. Pressing his face into the curve of my neck, he spoke softly, "The only pie I know how to bake is apple." His voice turned gravelly. "I was hopin' you'd like it."

I stepped back suddenly. "I'm sorry." Moving away, I felt embarrassed. "Yesterday was, well, it was like a miracle. Eating, being active, riding horses..." Emptiness filled my tone. "Truth is, I can't keep food down. Even if it's my favorite."

"Now then, Dina," Gil chided me as he stepped closer. He delicately stroked my face. "I gotta tell ya, folks have said some strange stuff about my pie, but no one has ever told me they were going to throw up from it." He stopped my protest with a light kiss, letting his lips dance slowly to my temples. "No need to concern yourself with a bad thought. My apple pie is straight from heaven." Gently, he tilted my head upward. "So's my coffee. I want you to know that."

I listened attentively to the raindrops splash against the windows, and soon a tranquil clarity slipped around me, making me aware only of his nearness. I realized that our bodies were already fitting together. The afternoon had turned cool, with enough wind and rain to create a snug retreat within the old ranch, a private space where I could live for the day.

His name slipped past my lips. My hands reached out to touch his chest. "I can feel the beating of your heart. It's strong."

His mouth found mine, slowly settling into a deep kiss that made my senses whirl. "Do you like that?" I whispered.

"Well now, Miss Dina, the first time we thought about this, you took me by surprise."

"Did I?"

"Yes, ma'am." He gathered me closer, and I felt the heat of his body. The excited flutter turned to a hammering in my chest as he drew my mouth toward his. The intensity of his kiss left me breathless.

Breaking away, he led me to a small bedroom, where faded paper covered the walls. A large, pine bed claimed my attention. It dipped in the middle under its own weight of softness. Two ornate posts rose from the headboard, disappearing into the pale grayness of the room. The taste of rain was in the air, cool and welcome. Creamy lace curtains fluttered in the breeze from the half-open window.

He led me to the bed, wrapping me in a patchwork quilt before standing up and walking toward the fireplace. He sparked a match to the papers stuck under the pyramid of logs. Firelight blazed, highlighting the deep tones of a ruddy brown armoire and showing me that the faded wallpaper had once been blue.

Nestling into the eiderdown of the bed, I watched Gil remove his shirt and hook it over the armoire door. The simple movement held my attention as the fire clutched at the dried wood, sending a hail of orange flames up the flue. He faced me, and my eyes followed the line of his broad shoulders as they angled down to a flat stomach.

The belt slipped from his Levi's. His smile was provocative. He looked at me with a firmness of purpose. I wished again for more time but understood that my destiny was in place.

The down bed curved in with his weight as he sat down. He turned toward me, and his thumb circled the hollow in my cheek for just a moment; then he pushed the quilts away from me. The coolness of the room felt good against my heated skin. His hand slipped to the buttons of my blouse. I tipped my head upward to study his face. The deep blue of his eyes stirred my senses, leaving me breathless as I moved my hand toward his hair. I reached out, burying my fingers in his rich, dark curls, pulling his head toward me. His kisses covered my face as he gently pushed me back into the softness of the bed.

Very slowly he began to undress me, unconcerned where my clothes fell. Moving to the foot of the bed, he slid my jeans away.

He bent over my feet as his thumbs pushed gently into my soles, creating wavy circles of pressure that left me breathless. The heels of his hands kneaded against my arches; his fingers found joints to massage as his warm breath brushed across each toe. I gasped as pleasant vibrations raced through my body.

Sliding upward, his fingertips massaged my calf muscles. Suddenly his tongue was brushing a path along my leg, seeking the soft spot on the inside of my knees. I cried out with a new sensation.

I felt him tense slightly and then relax. He let his fingertips create tiny circles on my inner thigh.

His attention moved toward my abdomen, his mouth tracing a line across my skin.

His body moved seductively next to mine, causing me to quiver with anticipation. He turned me on my side as he pressed the center of my back closer to him.

His kisses moved down my neck with a new intensity.

I felt his face, rough with the beginning of an afternoon beard, as he brushed his mouth across my tender skin. Inflamed with heightened desire, I moved seductively under his touch.

The darkened afternoon mellowed the room, softening all the corners. Slowly, he let himself return to my lips. He drew my lower body toward his in a tight embrace.

I opened my lips for his kiss and pushed myself against him, feeling the roaring beat of his heart. Pleasure filled me, building to a crescendo as heat surged through me, taking me to new heights. We remained there as our bodies soared and dipped with the flow of life.

When I drifted back to earth, I realized that Gil was holding me tightly while our breathing slowed and our bodies cooled. Time slipped by peacefully. I felt his breath on my neck and smiled. He rolled over and stretched. Totally relaxed, I pushed up on one elbow. Feeling impish and seductive, I looked into his eyes. "I'm wanton."

His eyebrows elevated. "Is that how I made you feel?"

"Would you like that?"

His face reflected both thought and puzzlement.

"You mustn't look so serious. I was joking." I smiled blissfully, lightly touching his lips. "You make me forget," I said as I leaned closer, resting against his shoulder, "so that my life rolls away to a better time, when I felt the joys of living."

"You're loved, Dina."

"By you?"

"Yes."

I raised my head so that I could look into his eyes. "Are you *in love* with me? Or is it the angel version?"

"I've been thinkin' on that, Dina. I do believe it's a bit of both." His fingers stroked my face tenderly. "I gotta say that even though bein' *in love* with you is new, it's powerful, yet it's tender. At times, it right takes my breath away and leaves me a tad giddy." His eyes held mine. "I wouldn't change a thing about such a blessed feelin'." I felt the depth of his emotion fill my body all the way to my toes.

"Well then." I stretched, turning toward the window, watching the gentle patter of raindrops. "What shall we do with a wet afternoon?"

He sat up, slowly pulling me with him. "Let's stroll with it."

"What?" My curiosity was aroused. "You mean like walk in the rain?"

"Told ya I had a nice afternoon planned for us. Y'all asked to see one of my classroom skills." He grinned playfully. "Bet I can find us some yellow slickers." He pushed off the bed and looked back over his shoulder. "Besides, I want to show off one of my talents."

I boldly let my eyes sweep across his lean body and answered back, "You already have."

"Thank you kindly." With a self-conscious laugh, he met my stare.

"Gil, are you embarrassed by my ..." I paused, searching for a word, and settled on, "Forthrightness?"

Rubbing his hand through his dark curls, he grinned. "Yes, ma'am. But don't you give it no mind, 'cause I'm workin' on learnin' how to deal with it." He winked. "Life's full of new lessons." He turned to me with a wry half-smile. "And I think I'm catchin' on right quick."

"Oh yeah." I stretched luxuriously. "Right quick."

He looked down at me with narrowed eyes. "Now if you keep on a'doin' that, Miss Dina, we're goin' have ourselves another set-to, here and now."

I pulled the quilt higher. "Not until we have that stroll."

Chapter 9

Dressed in our clothes and protected with rain slickers, we ventured outside. The rain caressed our awareness of each other. The sky was a symphony of pewter and dove gray. Winds chased the clouds across the heavens. Gil glanced up and smiled patiently while I joked, "Is that Daniel again?"

"Boy's a real show-off, isn't he?"

Thunder shook the earth, and I covered my ears. "Another brother?" I shouted.

"Matthew's specialty," he called back. The noise subsided, and he squeezed my hand. "I'm not as loud."

I laughed, letting his humor wash over me. Freshness swept the land as the storm brooded overhead, sending a swift wind to bend the tall grass.

Gil sighed. "I do enjoy an autumn rain. Gets things right, has a soothing way of cleansing the land, prepares us for winter's rest. And I have to confess that I feel mighty good just now. Bein' in love and all fills a fella up with a monumental sense of passion and strength. Makes him feel right proud." He smiled mischievously. "Do y'all like lightnin'?"

I pushed the hood of the yellow slicker back so I could see him better. The scent of pine lingered around him, but now it was mixed with the earthy smell of fresh rain. Damp curls clung to his forehead. Reaching up, I pushed them away from his face. He took my hand, stroking the back of it as he kissed my fingertips, letting his eyes direct my look to the east. I sensed a powerful intensity surface from Gil's body.

Sudden white streaks cut into the sky, splitting the gray with flashing light. "Ain't that somethin'?" His voice was etched with pride as he looked toward the heavens. "Never ceases to amaze me." The wild sky settled back into its blue-gray shades.

"As a family, you work well together." I smiled. "What a display. Did you study that when we were apart? Is it basic angel training?"

"Basic, no." He rolled his words. "It's more like a specialty course."

"Well, you were busy." I spoke in an amazed voice. "I guess the poetry of a storm lies in the heart."

"That so?" He stopped walking and turned me toward him. "Can't say I ever heard it described that way before."

"So I've given you a first to think about?"

"Yep. That you have." Nodding in thought, he replied, "In more ways than one."

"Well, I'm glad. And the lightning was beautiful." Gazing into the depths of his eyes, I whispered, "Truly beautiful."

"Thank you." Gil scuffed his feet on the wet earth. "It's one of my better talents, and I don't use it often enough."

I lifted myself up and brushed my lips across his. "Thanks for letting me in on your secret. You have learned wonderful skills."

He gathered me in his arms, and we enjoyed the heat that radiated from our bodies. Kissing the top of my head, he replied, "The pleasure was mine."

Wind beaded the raindrops that fell on our yellow slickers as we walked hand in hand. Soaked and happy, we splashed across the porch. He tossed the rain gear onto the kitchen chairs and returned with thick towels, handing one to me.

"Hey, they're warm!" My surprise was natural. "I don't see a dryer. How did you..."

"They feel best that way. Don'cha think?" His smile was kind. "Dina, comfort is a dimension of awareness." Turning me toward him, he kissed my forehead. "I'm here to cover both areas."

"That's good by me."

"Dry off or shower?"

"I don't want to wash the rain away. I feel too alive, too fresh, too new." I spun in a small circle and stopped, facing the kitchen table. I noticed that some of the more delicate flowers had shed a few petals. I looked at Gil and said, "Know what? Now I really want apple pie and ice cream." The nutty aroma from the coffee pot drifted past my nose, causing me to breathe deeply. I smiled. "And coffee. I want a cup of real coffee."

"You got it. It'll take the chill off." He gestured vaguely overhead as he said, "Dishes are in the upper cupboard. I'll cut the pie and spoon out the ice cream." He looked over his shoulder. "I found it earlier but was distracted." Our eyes met, sharing a lively exchange. "Do y'all like French vanilla?"

"Yup. I do." I turned toward the cupboards. Through the glass inserts I could see dull shelf paper that had once been an array of fruit patterns. *Typical of an era,* I thought pleasantly. When I opened the door, a faint whiff of forgotten spices, cocoa, and sweet molasses greeted me, and I realized with a pleasant sensation that this must have been the spice cabinet when the missus lived at the ranch. Maybe her brownies had originated from this space.

My search for dishes rendered clean but chipped mugs and plates. I admired the spotless glass inserts in the cupboard door and assumed this was one of the projects Gil had recently completed.

I watched as he found forks in one drawer and white linen napkins in another. He appeared to know his way around a kitchen. I considered that a desirable trait, wondering if he had baked his chocolate picnic cake right here.

As he spooned generous scoops of ice cream over slices of pie, I filled our mugs with the rich, dark coffee. Gil found an old Coca-Cola tray, and we loaded our food onto it. Commenting favorably on our hefty portions, we moved toward the main living quarters of the ranch.

A fire was waiting to be lit in the oversized hearth. Heavy pine furniture gathered around the room in comfortable silence. Gil placed the tray on a polished table then spread a rosy colored quilt over the cracked leather sofa, adding a cheerful burst of color to the rainy day. He tucked the blanket into the deep cushions, commenting, "A few splits around the edges but still mighty soft from oil rubs."

"I know. My dad had a leather chair that he frequently rubbed down."

Gil nodded, indicating I should sit first. I tucked my feet under me, sinking deeply into the sofa cushion. "So nice." I sighed. "Got one at home like this. It's in the family room." I smiled. "Parlors can be formal, you know? Still carry some good memories though. A lot of warm memories in a family room. Now the kitchen, that's where the fuzzy memories are. And the front porch, oh, don't get me started!" I indicated the pine sofa with a broad swoop of my hand. "This is a gold mine, you know?"

"It is?" He seemed astonished by my remark.

"Yes. It has that worn chic look that city folks go for."

He looked at me quizzically. "They do?"

"Yup. Overstuffed cushions, dark green leather." I grinned. "Hand-carved pine furniture."

He moved toward the hearth. "Well, if that's the case, just wait till I show you how pretty firelight is on mahogany stain. Why, we'll have them city folk beatin' a path to our door."

"Nah. Don't think so," I said. "This is our little secret."

He returned to the sofa and slipped his arm around me, pulling me toward him. He whispered into my hair, "Right glad you feel that way."

I tipped my head back. "You do plan a lovely day. I'm sorry there was a delay."

"Not to worry none. We're here now."

We listened to the sounds of the afternoon with our hearts as the rain swept over the ranch, isolating us from the world. I spoke gently, "This is a good place to be."

The pie disappeared from our plates, and Gil refilled them. Melted ice cream pooled in the bottom of the dishes, and I called for Butch, who lingered in the hallway. "Gotta share the goodness. Happiness spreads more happiness."

The cat sauntered over to the plate as if he was doing us a favor, drawing a smile from me and a shake of Gil's head. "Dang cat. Thinks he owns the place."

Butch cleaned the dishes and jumped up on the sofa, settling himself in my lap. I stroked his ears, and my reward was a loud purr. I looked at Gil. "My mom said that thing about sharing goodness."

Gil leaned back, clearly content, and patted his flat stomach. "A lot of wise ladies in your life." He rose gracefully, heading in the direction of the kitchen. "More coffee?"

"Half a cup would be great." I looked out the window where curtains had been pushed open to let in the rain-sodden day. I was glad of the fire and the warm cat on my lap.

I liked the sentiment of the old room. Pine end tables flanked the sofa, each holding a faded doily. Stained glass lamps were perched in the centers of the starched lace. A pull cord caught my attention, and I gave it a tug. A small glow burst forth, revealing a cascade of lively radiance from the multicolored panes.

Gil returned with an old enamel pot, carefully holding a red dishtowel around the handle. "Might hot," he said as he filled our cups, adding cream to both. When he sat down, the sofa welcomed him with a dip as he pulled the second cord, and we were rewarded with another illumination of light. "Electricity was added to most of the rooms years ago."

"The lamps are pretty—art deco?" I asked.

Gil shrugged. "Could be. Lots of people passed through here. They all left a little somethin'."

I thought about his answer as I lifted the coffee and sipped. "That's very true," I replied.

Comfortably, we settled into our day, and I asked, "Tell me about you, Gil. You mentioned more brothers. Do you have a large family?"

"Very large. Christmas is our favorite time."

He drew me toward him and settled me securely in the embrace of his arm. "As often as possible, my brothers and I join our Father in Rome to celebrate the holidays."

"Tell me about what you do."

"Well, one year I wanted to see the Sistine Chapel, the ceiling in particular. Bein' as I was sort of an independent kid, I went off on my own to do just that. Standin' there lookin' up, well, I got to tell ya that I was amazed," he said as he grinned self-consciously. "But I was not tendin' to where my feet were goin'. Then I heard this voice shoutin' at me, 'Basta! Basta!' I was shocked. How someone could be usin' profanity in such a holy place."

Grinning, he shook his head as he recalled his youthful adventure. "I wasn't to be distracted by such talk. No sir, not me. I kept right on lookin' up, admirin' such marvelous work. Never did see the box in front of me and bam! I fell hard, hittin' the floor and sprawlin' out like I had four feet and six legs. It was a sight to behold!

"When I collected myself sufficiently to get up, I saw one of my older brothers laughin' like a fool. In between him gettin' his breath and a'gigglin', he told me that someone shoutin', 'Basta! Basta!' at me required my immediate attention. Asked me if I'd been studyin' my foreign language and told me that in Italian 'basta' meant stop."

Gil laughed. "Instead of bein' shocked by what I thought I'd heard, I should have been listenin' to what was said and, of course, watchin' where I was puttin' my big feet."

He folded both arms around me. "Do y'all like Christmas?"

Giggling, I placed my ear against his chest and listened to the steady rhythm of his heart. "Yes. We always told family stories. You know the kind? They make you embarrassed, but every year they come out to be told again and again until you finally see the humor in them. Must be some kind of lesson there. Like how to laugh at yourself."

"Suppose you tell me one." He got up to shift the logs, and fresh warmth filled the room. The new glow softened the aging furniture. Sitting down, he gathered me back into his arms. "I do enjoy a good story."

"Promise you won't laugh at me."

His lips brushed my cheek. "I make no promise that I can't keep."

"I like an honest man." I rested my head against his shoulder. "Okay, here goes. This is a story about Christmas break. It was back when Jillian was about to graduate from college, and I was in my first year at the same school.

"Rachel had her driver's license and had talked Mom and Dad into letting her take the car by herself and drive to the city to meet our plane. Jillian had been a sorority girl"—I rolled my eyes—"and was very good at it, I might add. So now that she was about to enter law school, it was her fondest wish that I take over as sorority queen of our family. She'd been grooming me and introducing me to all the right girls for most of the year. Up to that point, I'd made a decent impression. After all, I was under Jillian's tutorship, and she would let me do no wrong.

"Several of her sorority sisters had flown in with us and were about to catch other planes to head to their home-towns for the holiday. Well, on the flight in, the older girls had been drinking champagne, and they'd given some to me. Basically I was a beer and chips kind of gal so to actually drink the bubbly, I felt very mature and quite worldly.

"I really needed to go to the bathroom while I was still on the plane, but as things happen, it was occupied; and when that person left, someone else went in. Then the plane started its descent, and I had to wait. By the time we landed and taxied, I really had to go. So as soon as I got off, I found the bathroom in the airport, and even though the sign said, 'Under New Construction,' at that point, I didn't care.

"Rachel was there to meet us, beaming with pride at her newfound independence behind the wheel of the family car, but I sort of flew past her, so she followed me into the john. Jillian and her sorority sisters were chatting about something ever so cosmopolitan and never noticed my urgency.

"While I was sitting on the toilet, it flushed without warning, and I felt a little stuck to the seat. That's when I realized the toilet seat itself was flush to the rim of the toilet. The airport was installing the automatic flush in all the bathrooms, but it wasn't quite right on the toilet I occupied because it kept flushing and before I realized it, my butt was really stuck to the seat."

I heard him swallow something that sounded like a laugh and pulled away from his shoulder. Teasingly I scolded him, "You're not laughing at me, are you?"

The corners of his mouth twitched as he replied, "Not out loud."

"Good enough for me. I'll continue." Snuggling back into his chest, I smiled to myself. "Well, the suction created by the constant flushing held me captive."

Gil made a sound through his nose. "S'cuse me." His hand covered his mouth. "I was just clearin' my throat."

"That's all?"

A small silence prevailed as I watched him. I raised my eyebrow and asked, "Shall I continue?" Butch chose that moment to begin another rumbling purr as he stretched out across my lap. I rubbed under his chin as he looked at me with loving eyes. "At least someone here is being respectful of my feelings."

"Yes, ma'am. Both Butch and I wait with bated breath to hear how this all ends." He offered up a smile. "No pun intended."

I sat up, wondering why I was having such fun telling this story. "Naturally, I was mortified by what was happening to me, plus I couldn't reach the door lock because of, well, you know…" I pointed toward my derriere. "The suction was…"

"Oh! I got the picture." Another twitch started at the corners of his mouth, causing me to look at him closely. He took a deep breath. "Do go on."

"By this time, my bottom was slowly being sucked into the toilet bowl, so I called out to Rachel for help. She ran out of the bathroom and over to where Jillian was standing, where she announced in front of all the sorority girls that I was being pulled into the toilet bowl because my butt was stuck to the seat. Poor Jillian. Her mouth hung open in midsentence. Her year of preparing me for a more sophisticated lifestyle evaporated in a puff of smoke.

"Rachel began swinging her hands in an effort to get someone to do something. Then all of the girls moved at once toward the john, where they were greeted with the sounds of a toilet flushing and me moaning.

"The sorority sisters, being quick to assess the situation, realized that someone had to crawl under the door to save me, and they pulled paper towels from the container to pave the path for Jillian, who scrambled under the door, took stock of the circumstances, and stuck her hand under my leg, which broke the suction. I got up, glad to be alive.

"Jillian asked quite calmly if I was all right and if I had any money. I told her that my butt was sore and asked how she could think of money at a time like this. She just held out her hand until I reached in my purse and found a couple dollars.

"When she opened the door, her sorority sisters were gaping at us. Then they started asking questions all at once, until Jillian, using a very authoritative gesture, raised her hand for silence. She announced that she had a retainer from her first client and that we planned to sue the airport for their lack of toilet maintenance, leading to abusive, physical damage and mental duress."

"You serious?" Rich tones of laugher bubbled up, and Gil added hastily, "Butch and me, now, we aren't laughin' at you." He looked around for support and finding none, shrugged his shoulders and said, "Well, shoot. We're laughin' with you, Dina."

"Sure you are." I smiled, remembering the many times the airport episode had been told. "Every year that story came up at Christmas. Daddy used to say my bottom was a part of the holiday celebration, just like the wreath on the front door."

Gil's laughter erupted again, and this time I joined him. All the noise caused Butch to jump down. "See what we've done? We've upset his afternoon nap," I joked.

"Right sorry on that, Butch. I'll make it up to you."

With a twitch of his tail, Butch dismissed both of us, disappearing into grayness.

Gil's brow suddenly knit in a line of concentration as he asked, "Wonder where I was when you were gettin' your bottom attached to a toilet seat."

"Where *you* were?"

"Yep. I should have been there takin' care of y'all."

"In a woman's bathroom?"

"Granted, bein' a guy, I wasn't welcome everywhere with you. But being your angel, I did have a responsibility."

"So you weren't perfect?"

"I did try, but as I mentioned earlier, you were not the easiest person to guide."

"Oh, Gil!" I brushed my lips over his cheek.

He drew me into his arms. "Truth be told, your bottom looks fine now. So no serious damage was done."

I felt the moment fill with seriousness and asked, "Have you really always watched over me? I ask because it's a difficult concept to get around."

Gil blinked. "God knows I have applied myself to the task at hand."

My quick response was, "What's my favorite dance?"

"Waltz."

"Yes! I've never told anyone that. Ever!"

Gil stood to help me off the sofa. Moving toward the staircase, he let his arm drape casually across my shoulder. "The dining room is over here, and if we move the table off to a corner, there'll be plenty of floor space. See this?" He pointed toward an old gramophone and a stack of records. "I think I can find us a waltz." He rummaged through the dust-covered albums and looked over his shoulder. "I'm proud to say I've been around long enough to know how to waltz."

I looked deeply into his eyes that twinkled with mischief.

He returned my stare. "I can also boogie."

"Get out!"

"You wound me." His hand covered his heart. A humorous note slipped into his voice as he asked, "Is that the way y'all talk to the man of your dreams? Your special angel? Who has promised y'all a lovely day, filled with surprises?"

I stood with my hands braced against my hips and shot back an answer. "It is if he's putting me on."

"Well now," he said as he let the twang slip into his words, "Ah am offended that you find me anything less than honest." A seductive smile lit up his face. "Y'all wanna move on over here, ma'am." Reaching for my hand, he nodded at the table. "Come on. Help me move this, and we'll see who can cut a good step."

I cocked two fingers at him. "You're on, cowboy."

The rain had returned to a fine mist, and dampness seeped through the wooden walls of the old ranch. Gray fog hugged the dining room, protecting it with diffused light.

Gill dragged a chair to the center of the room. He climbed on top of it and grinned down at me as he positioned himself under the ceiling light. "Bet y'all have never seen one of these. The old lights cast a pretty glow that I think you'll like." Smiling, he produced matches from his jeans pocket.

Touching the wicks with the glowing match, he quickly lit the candles in the overhead fixture. "Sorta old-fashioned-like, hangin' a wagon wheel from the ceiling to make a chandelier.

"Do you remember Mr. Jacob?"

I thought for a moment. "An old man. That's about it. I was just a little girl when I fed the horses."

Gil grinned. "Well, he was quite the romantic. Him and the missus never had this ceiling fitted for electricity."

I smiled up at him. "Feels like a good place."

"Yep," he said as he stepped off the chair. "Lotta love in these rooms."

The glow from the candles cushioned the edges of time and dimmed the wood, tossing benevolent shadows across the old pine floor. "You want to do some swing, working up to a boogie, and going into a waltz for the grand finale?"

"That's quite a program. I pick the first song."

"Do it." He nodded toward the dust-covered albums.

I found an old Elvis Presley album. "This is great." I blew at the dirty cover. "I've always liked his music. It's one of those unexplained things." Facing Gil, I said, "I heard him sing when I was just a little girl. My mom and dad had his records. Even back then, his voice always moved me. Why, he could make me laugh." I paused, letting my thoughts collect. "And he could make me cry."

As I gazed into the blurry room, my tone grew gentle. "Then when I was older, he even made me want to fall in love." I looked at the album cover of a young man who had affected the world with his talent. Slowly I handed it to Gil.

"Good choice." He smiled approvingly as he removed the record from its album sleeve. "A man of faith. A life of temptations. Some of us do better than others, but it all gets sorted out in the end." In a graceful movement, his thumb traced a line across my lips. "He sings with another choir now. Has a beautiful voice." His head tipped toward the gramophone. "Do you want to crank it, or should I?"

"There's really no electricity in this room?" My eyes scanned the walls for an electric socket.

"No, ma'am. You won't find any electricity in here." Leaning closer, he whispered in my ear, "Boss says Mr. Jacob was right. Electricity interferes with the mood, and I gotta tell ya, I share that opinion."

Smiling happily, I nodded. "Well then, crank away."

Gil put the needle on the record. Clean, crisp music filled the room. Drums and guitars offered a rock 'n' roll introduction to the rich, sensual voice of the youthful Elvis.

"Hey, that's really good sound." I swayed with the beat. "I thought it would be scratchy."

"Faith, Dina, you gotta have faith."

My hips and shoulders moved in unison. "Makes me want to dance."

He turned and said, "Happy to oblige."

He took my hand, and we tested each other on a few dance steps. Gil was a natural leader. His hand rested firmly in the small of my back, guiding me into dance moves. I could follow with little instruction as I turned under his arm and flew back into his arms, never missing a beat. He rolled me out and caught me on his other side. Our feet moved in unison as the rhythm filled my body. Our arms crossed over our shoulders, behind our necks, and we slid out of position, holding each other's fingers as we did a circle movement. He spun me into a double turn and pulled me back against his chest. He led me through the more difficult steps that I knew by heart. I felt as if I could dance all night until the needle scratched the end of the record, leaving me slightly breathless.

"That was incredible!" I hugged Gil with joy then pulled back. "You're a dancer!" He looked at his feet, and I hurried on. "No, I mean it. You're really a great dancer! You know all the moves." I blushed. "What I meant was ..."

He reached for me. "You done yourself proud on that one."

"Thanks. Flattery works for me." I stepped back and swiveled my way into a circle. "I love dancing! Where'd you learn?"

"Seems after my little experience at the Sistine Chapel, my Father thought I should learn something to help my feet so they weren't fallin' over each other. He suggested dancin', and I took a fancy to it."

The room felt warmer as Gil selected the next record. "You up to a tango?"

"Why not?"

Gil straightened his back, lowered his chin, and looked down and over his shoulder at me. He beckoned me with his eyes. Tossing my shoulders back, I approached him in a haughty manner. He took me in the tango position, holding me formally for a long moment to establish the intimacy of the dance before he began the sideways steps. We became aware of the sexuality in the music as our bodies lunged together in the disciplined moves.

Outside the sky remained leaden and dull, covering the reality of day. Inside the house, golden light shined from the windows.

Laughing, trying to catch my breath, I turned back to the old gramophone. "Whoa." I wiped moisture from my temples. "I haven't had a healthy sweat in, well, I don't know how long." I frowned. "Oh my, that didn't sound right."

"It sounded okay to me."

"Actually, women glow."

"Is that right? Gil mopped his forehead. "How about a beer?"

"I'd love one. You have any? I mean, I didn't see any in the fridge."

"Didn't need any with our pie. Tell ya what, you pick the next song, and I'll find us a couple of cold ones." He headed toward the kitchen.

I watched his long legs stride comfortably across the timeworn floor. His jeans fit him well, and I realized that I had been right about his fine-looking frame. I felt a flush of red on my cheeks and shook my head. He was back within minutes and handed me an icy beer. "Just so you know, I'm a man of my word. I made up with Butch for both of us."

"You did?" I accepted the beer.

"Ya. Gave him two kitchen treats. Told him one was from you, the other from me."

"And he understood that?"

"Sure did." Gil raised the can of beer to his lips, took a drink, and continued, "I told him the biggest treat was from you."

I smiled, very pleased. "You did?"

"Ya. He was on your lap when our ruckus behavior disturbed him."

I nodded and held the beer to my lips. "That's true." Looking at Gil, I replied, "That was nice."

He pulled two dining chairs over to the table that had been pushed against the wall. "Butch is a good fella."

With country western music humming in the background, we sipped cold beer and talked about line dancing. Gil demonstrated some boot-slapping steps, and I showed him a spin and fast stop. He hooked his fingers into his jeans as we made up our own moves, finally swinging into a two-step as I twirled under his arm.

We dropped back into the chairs, reaching for our drinks. Around us the room remained bedded in a dreamy light. Gil sang the lyrics to a country song about trains, whiskey, and old dogs while I listened, entertained by his choice of words.

"I enjoy country western. It always tells a story, plus it's got a beat. You can't ask for more than that." I watched as Gil took a swallow of beer. "You have a wonderful voice. Please do one more."

"I'd been hopin' that you'd ask. This is one I think you'll like." In a voice patched with rugged edges, he sang "Love Me Tender."

The words floated like gossamer bubbles into the air, imparting a sense of fulfillment to my heart. He leaned closer, his lips lightly brushing mine. His thumb wiped away my tear.

"It's one of sheer joy."

"Yes," he said as he held my eyes with his. "I know."

"Thank you. That was beautiful." I cleared my throat and began to get up. "Time to crank up our entertainment center. I forget it isn't surround sound."

He grinned back at me. "Isn't it?"

"Well," I said as I thought about it, "the music does come from all corners of the room." I sat back down and looked at him. "Did you ever sing professionally? I know,"—I held up my hand—"dumb question. But you have a great voice. So I asked."

The jewels of candlelight fell across his dark hair and softened the rugged lines of his profile. "Miss Dina, only singing I've done was in church."

I narrowed my eyes and leaned across the table to face him. "Same choir as Elvis?"

"It's a big choir." He hooked his boots through the chair legs and watched me. "Been around for a long time. Changes voices now and again."

"That's my answer?" I leaned closer. "'Cause I expected more detail from my angel."

"Did ya now?" His mouth wrinkled into a grin.

I smiled back. "It must have been a loss for them when you left."

"It was early trainin'. I moved on to other things." He winked. "More important, I'd like to think." He wiped his lips with the back of his hand. I kissed him, tasting the malt of beer from his mouth, and breathed deeply. Memories of sunshine and apple blossoms filled me. My chair bumped the old phonograph where the needle rested on the next record. It began to play, and the sweet notes of a waltz whispered in the air.

Slowly, as if entering the canvas of a beloved painting, I felt myself rise. Gil took me in his arms, and the dance began as we moved across the floor, locked in the voyage of life. Music drifted like falling petals around my head as his arms carried me into the sky, where stars blazed and breezes cooled my heat. In waltzing swirls, I felt the moments of past and future splash in drops around my being. Wrapped in love, my body dipped and swayed at Gil's direction as we waltzed in a golden room, sharing unspoken wisdom.

As the tired notes played out in softness, our feet floated across the pine floor, and Gil led me back to the overstuffed sofa in the main room of the old ranch. We lay in each other's arms, quietly watching as the logs burned in a fire show, with all the colors that went into the making of the day.

We made love sweetly, touching and exploring with a gentleness that left me weak with desire. He traced the lines of my face and spoke words of love against my cheek. We fit together perfectly in the cushions of the leather sofa.

I clung to him afterward, watching as the sky lifted its heavy gray covering, yielding to a grape-blue mist. A path was cleared for the late afternoon sun, and the purple colors gave way to shades of rose that began to light the sky. I knew I had more to do, and reluctantly I released Gil.

Chapter 10

The waltz played again in my mind, quietly touching my heart, and I knew that the time I had left was drawing to a close. My fingers traced a line down Gil's back. I liked the feel of his skin; his muscles rippled under my touch, and he drew me closer. I thought: *Life is so precious.*

As I surfaced to a more conscious state, I stretched until all of my muscles relaxed. I sighed as I said, "It's the quiet times like this when single memories come to mind."

He raised himself on one elbow, and I noticed a few dark curls had tumbled across his forehead. I rolled toward him, he put his arm around me, and I wedged myself against his side. "Do you know what I mean?"

"Tell me, Dina." He tucked my head under his chin. "Tell me about what's important to you."

"Oh, I guess it's the small things that you forget in the rush of a lifetime." I looked at the creamy doily on the table and thought of the doilies in the parlor and the many times our mom had cared for them. Now it was our job, and beneath all our complaining, a feeling of family kinship still lingered.

I smiled, bringing myself back to the present. "I like wildflowers. I like the way they spill out of the mason jar in the kitchen." Closing my eyes, I smiled. "Like a pretty spring meadow early in the morning, still fresh with dew. Each petal on every flower is an exquisite creation." I sat up, leaving the warmth of his body for just a minute. "Nature is a wonder. A symphony of miracles."

My smile faded slowly. "But we often miss the single flower because we focus on the whole meadow. And then we see several meadows, and they melt together, and we begin to take all that beauty for granted." My voice was barely audible. "It's such a loss."

I turned back to look at Gil. "Something wonderful happens to us, and we skip over it. Events merge together because we're so busy keeping pace with living."

Gil sat up, and I placed my head gently on his chest, feeling it rise and fall with each strong breath. I remarked quietly, "When you have time to appreciate the small things is when you're dying. That's when you become keenly aware of the world around you because you know it's all going away." I pulled back and looked into his gentle blue eyes. "There's a message in what I just said." I paused in thought. "There is also an injustice."

Gil's face was bathed in the buttery glow of the late afternoon. His lips brushed my forehead, and I became aware of the fresh pine fragrance that floated pleasantly around him. His voice was soft as cotton as he asked, "What do you propose to do, Dina?"

"Not let it happen again." I shifted into a position where I could wrap my arms around my knees. "Pack a memory suitcase. You know, an enthusiastic woman suggested that back in cancer therapy. I called it the "Exit Strategy" but dropped the idea of a suitcase because a duffle bag was better suited for me. However, the idea is the same. I can take it with me. Study it like a student who's trying to learn a new subject." I asked curiously, "Can that be done?"

"The idea is sound." He smiled and shook his head. "But the term 'Exit Strategy' ... now that is harsh."

"You think?"

"Yes, ma'am. Quite harsh."

I felt myself smiling and gave my shoulders a shrug.

His hand reached out to brush the hair off my face. "I'm here when you need me. The time that's left is yours to use as you see fit." He leaned closer. "You have the courage."

"Good."

I stared at the glowing embers in the fireplace for a long moment. Raising my eyes toward the windows, I noticed that weak sunlight filtered through the lace curtains. I asked, "Do you believe we get messages from our loved ones who have died?"

Gil reached for my hands and pushed them firmly against my chest. "It's what you believe here. It's what your heart tells you."

"You asked what was important to me." I took a deep breath and relaxed into him. "From the time I could remember, I always had a big, white cat as my constant companion. Truth is that we had a lot of barn cats, but this one was different. He was my friend, the one I took all my troubles to." I snickered quietly. "Plus he got along with all the other cats and kept order among them. Even then Jillian appreciated that and often pointed it out to us by commenting on how organized the barn was."

I released my tight hold on this thought so I could slip back in time. My voice softened. "He walked me to the bus on my first day of school and met me afterward. He continued to do so until I was fifteen. The kids would tease me, saying he was really a dog disguised as a cat because only dogs walked their kids to the bus." I smiled. "Vinnie, his name was Vinnie. And he never cared if I ate an extra candy bar or had a bad grade on a math test."

Gil stroked my arm, giving me a moment to collect my thoughts. I continued, "He had a way of solving my childhood dilemmas as well as sharing in my joys by looking at me with his big green eyes while I poured out my woes or told him a new joke. Then he'd rub against my leg and purr, and sure enough, everything would be okay in my world." I stared into space, remembering. "On rainy days in the spring and snow-filled days in the winter, I'd go out to the barn, and he'd curl up on my lap, always willing to listen and give me a portion of his time. I couldn't imagine life without him."

After clearing my throat, I continued, "But one day I came home and instead of Vinnie, my mother met me. She told me that Vinnie had fallen from the hay loft and was hurt. I rushed to the barn, and he was lying on his side. Grandma Nana had examined him and said she couldn't find any broken bones and we should let him rest. He purred when he saw me, and I checked on him until I had to go to bed. By morning he was up and making his rounds like usual.

"As the weeks wore on, we all noticed that he began to bump into things. His walk was hesitant, and he seemed confused. When I looked into his beautiful, green eyes, I could see something was very wrong. It was then we realized that he was slowly going blind."

I paused to take a deep breath. Sometimes it hurt just to remember, but I went on, "I spent hours with him, teaching him to come to the sound of my voice. I would even tap the ground so he could get his direction. If I wasn't around, the other barn cats would walk next to him, guiding him. It worked really well. Even though he sort of leaned sideways, he didn't let it slow him down.

"A few weeks passed, and I began to notice that he was getting thin. He didn't have his usual big appetite, so I started feeding him by hand. I had to really encourage him to eat. Soon after that he lost interest in keeping his white fur gleaming, so I would brush him and rub a warm washcloth across his coat to help him groom."

I stopped, feeling the rush of tears just under the surface of my words. Gil held me closer. I took several deep breaths and went on. "I was fifteen, and Vinnie was sixteen. The realization slowly dawned on me that he had been hurt when he'd fallen from the hay loft. It had probably caused his blindness and maybe even internal injuries. He was hurting, and he was shutting down. It was more than I could bear."

I put my hands over my lips and held them there for a moment. Taking another deep breath, I waited and then exhaled slowly. Still my voice trembled. "Vinnie knew that I still needed him, and he was trying so hard to stay that it broke my heart. I knew what had to be done. I gathered all my strength and went out to tell him that it was okay for him to leave."

I shut my eyes and could recall the dim light in the barn. When I inhaled, the smells of hay and dust filled my memory, and my grief came back in a rush of emotions. "He was in a corner, lying on the fresh pile of straw that I'd given him. Tiger, another barn cat, was sleeping next to him, keeping him warm. When they saw me, Tiger rubbed against Vinnie and left. I paused to watch as another cat approached and rubbed noses with Vinnie."

I let it play through my mind. "I continued to watch from the door as the other barn cats did the same. It was all very dignified."

I grew silent, remembering the anguish that had ripped through me that day. Gil turned me toward him, looking deeply into my eyes; he spoke no words but gave the slightest nod of his head.

I continued quietly, "I waited until they had all said their good-byes to Vinnie before I called to him. He tilted his head toward the sound of my voice. I tapped the barn floor like I always did so he could get his direction. He got up slowly and came toward me. I took him in my arms, and once again, for the last time, his white fur caught my tears. I carried him back to his corner of the barn and placed him gently on the straw. I told him how much I loved him and how brave he was to have stayed so long for me. My heart was breaking into little pieces, and I thought I might even be sick.

"Then Vinnie looked up at me and begin to purr—a soft, slow purr. He kept looking at me with his wise eyes that were no longer green but now bore the dark circles of his blindness. He was telling me that his time had come. I promised to be brave." My voice cracked, and I felt Gil's hand tighten on mine. I sniffed and swallowed hard. "He put his head back on the straw."

Tears begin to drip down my cheeks. I wiped at my face and took a deep breath. "Guess you know that I was inconsolable, huh?"

Gil's thumb stroked the tears from my face. "Go on, Dina." His voice held compassion. "There's more to tell."

"Yes, there is." I straightened my back. "The next day, the whole family had a funeral for Vinnie, and we buried him by Mom's rose garden. Grandma Nana took a cutting from a white rosebush and told me to plant it by Vinnie's resting place; maybe it would grow. But it turned from green to brown. A cutting is a fragile thing, much like life itself." I smiled dryly at Gil as his fingertips touched my drying tears. "Well, I missed Vinnie terribly, even though everyone tried to compensate for my loss. Mother met me at the school bus stop, which was really silly 'cause it dropped me off on the road in front of our house and, after all, I was fifteen.

"Rachel, who was only thirteen, tried to make me laugh at her dumb stories. Jillian even invited me to visit her at college. I learned that just because my heart was broken, life didn't stop.

"Before winter came, I placed stones around Vinnie's grave so I could find it when we had snow. Fortunately, we had a mild winter followed by a wet spring. One day, Grandma Nana asked me if I had been to visit Vinnie's grave. She told me there was something I should see. Even though it was raining, I went outside to look, and there was a tiny, green sprout poking up from the dirt."

I looked at Gil, my voice still filled with the wonder of the moment. "Somehow a single root, not even the thickness of a piece of thread, had survived and sent up life. I watched all summer as it grew stronger and put out a few delicate leaves. One day early in the fall, just about the time Vinnie had died, a small white rose appeared." I whispered, "Vinnie's rose."

Gil's breath tickled my forehead. I tilted my head up to look at him. "I believe it was his way of letting me know he was there if I needed him. Each year that rosebush dies back, and each spring it grows again. The best blooms are always in the fall." My mind drifted back in time. "Beautiful, white roses from Vinnie. I always thought I'd make my wedding bouquet from them."

Gil gently tucked the blanket around both of us. I felt its warmth against my bare skin. His voice was softly rough. "I was hoping you'd tell me about Vinnie."

I nodded quietly as a newborn strength filled me. I sighed with deep satisfaction and said, "You knew, didn't you?"

His breath tickled my ear. "It took courage and faith to let him go."

"Yes, it did." I sighed.

"And Dina…" He paused. "It took a lot of love."

I wanted to put my arms around him and press my head against his chest, but I knew I had more to tell him. He was looking at me as if he were waiting for me to finish.

"Gil," I began and then stopped, not knowing how to go on. Giving myself a moment, I studied the crosspieces that supported the ceiling beams. I could sense his smile as he said, "It's easier, Miss Dina, if you just say it."

"Well, okay." I continued to avoid looking at him and let the words slip from my lips. "I also believed in the concept of reincarnation before I knew there was a word for it."

Gil held my shoulders, turning me toward him. "All concepts start with a seed of thought."

"I couldn't have been more than five or six years old when I got this seed, and it certainly didn't come from my parents." I laughed nervously. "They were churchgoing people, and reincarnation was not a thought they entertained." I grinned sheepishly. "Probably the most radical thought they had was to stay up late and listen to Elvis sing love songs after we girls were in bed."

"I told you that he's a good guy." Gil pulled me back on the sofa. He lay on his side next to me, and once again, we were surrounded by the old leather cushions that felt soft as a cloud. Gil continued, "I don't rightly think Elvis would have been a radical influence on your folks. Most likely, I'd say romantic." He wrapped his arms around me. "So reincarnation was an early thought of yours?"

"Uh-huh." I pushed away from his chest so that I could look into his eyes. They were sparkling with blue light. "Is that upsetting for you? 'Cause it was upsetting for my folks."

"Well now, Miss Dina." Smiling, he winked at me. "I wouldn't say 'upsetting' is the right word. It is, however, a bold vision for someone so young."

I spoke firmly, "You see, early on, I realized that life was all about possibilities and believing in them. My idea is that when a person crosses from this world to the next, they rest and study what they learned. Then they come back again with another chance to do it better."

Having spoken my most secret thoughts, I felt drained but wanted to finish. I continued in a soft voice, "And the rest of my idea is that when a person has learned enough, they advance to a higher level. That's when they can help others. That's when they can become an angel."

The rain was gone, and a deep afternoon sun offered its warm light. It seemed to collect in pools and drip off the faded wallpaper. Gil spoke thoughtfully, "Ideas are a wondrous gift, Dina."

"Mm-hmm." I chewed on my lower lip and tingled with the perception of what could be. Facing him, I lifted my head. "But it takes courage to embrace them."

"Yes, it does." He shifted his weight to hold me in a tender embrace. With his fingers under my chin, he tilted my face toward him. "We all have a say in makin' our destiny."

"Yes, I believe that. But to embrace ideas that are out of step, ideas like what I've just told you…" I paused, looking confused. "Can it, I mean, is it…?"

His hands cupped my face. "That's quite a question."

I traced his hands with my fingertips. My voice was breathless. "I'll bet you have quite an answer."

He grinned, "If you believe, then it's so." His lips touched mine with a feathery softness. He continued, "The voyage of a spirit is the essence of life itself."

I cleared my throat. "Well, now that you mention spirit, isn't that similar to having an angel watch over you?" I felt the catch of his breath as he looked at me. The silence around us was suddenly heavy, but I pushed forward. "You come into this world with a spirit guide who helps you cross from heaven to here. Isn't that another word for angel?"

L.L. Nielsen

Gil sounded surprised. "Y'all come up with that at about five years old?"

"Nope." I maintained eye contact. "A lot earlier. It was another one of those things I just knew. And here's the kicker." A smile settled over my face. "We also have a guide who helps us cross back to heaven." Leaning toward him, I whispered softly, "An angel, and I do believe you are mine."

Gil raised his hand to stroke my hair. "You've been a big responsibility, Dina. Kept me on my toes. And just have a look at us now."

"I gave him a sideward glance. "And…"

"You were heaven-sent. An accountability that I cherished." He blinked and gave his head a shake. "But I never anticipated this result."

"Well, Gil, I learned in Sunday school that to love is human, to believe is divine."

His fingers trailed tenderly across my face. "That is a very sensitive thought." His lips moved to my eyebrows, down to my cheek. "I'm honored."

"So am I." I raised my lips to his. "We're sharing a bit of both worlds." Our kiss was sweet with the love we felt. I lowered my head against his shoulder.

He responded thoughtfully, "There is a journey ahead of us that you will never be able to share with those you leave behind. Can you accept that?"

"I can tell them that I'm going to a beautiful place."

"Yes, that you can say." His strong arms enveloped me. "This is your life, Dina. This very moment is yours. What will you do with it?"

"I think I'll lay with it awhile." My eyes felt weary, and I let them shut. "It's powerful, you know? To express so much

216

and then contemplate it." My body was tired, but in a comfortable way. I let serenity form a shield around me as I felt the years gradually resolve into harmony then melt into the universe. My voice was barely audible as I whispered, "It's an awakening. There are heights I never imagined."

"I know." His strength gathered around me lovingly, and I knew it was time to leave the old ranch and head home.

As we crossed through the kitchen, I noticed that the bouquet of wildflowers had scattered more petals across the Formica surface, forming a swirl of completed patterns.

Gil's voice broke into my thoughts. "Carrots for sweet Mary and Joe?" He shut the refrigerator door and held out several bunches with leafy, green tops. "I say carrots in so much as they've already had their apples."

I couldn't help but chuckle as I replied, "Only if you have Wipe-Ups so I can clean my hands." He snorted indignantly as he opened the door.

The leaves of fall had been blown away, leaving the tallest of treetops with bare branches. Gil closed the kitchen door of the old ranch. It was a final gesture.

We moved across the porch toward the weathered steps. Off to the side, the glider was still. We paused, and Gil spoke, "Seems like it's waitin' for someone." I looked at the rusty chains, wondering if they would support our weight. "Care to swing with me, Miss Dina?" He looked so silly holding the carrots that I had to laugh as I settled into the glider seat next to him.

He replied casually, "The cushions were taken in some time ago, but still in all, it has a nice feel. Don'cha think?" He pushed the heels of his boots into the old floorboards. The chain creaked, and we began to swing.

Dampness seeped through my jeans from the aged wooden frame as we gently moved to and fro. "I always liked it here," I murmured.

I touched Gil's fingers. The leafy greens tickled my palm, and I giggled.

He squeezed my hand. "Me too."

A reflection lay gently in my mind that, at some level throughout the years, I had always been aware of his presence. I let the memory float through the fresh air.

Leaving the porch swing, gently rocking to its own melody, we walked toward the corral. Sweet Mary saw us first. Exhaling loudly, she pushed her head toward me, encouraging me to stroke her velvety nose until she saw the carrots. We laughed as she munched aggressively, making a mess of the food and my hand. Joe, smelling of damp hay, nudged me next, and I gave him his share of goodies. Gil got in the act, and we fed each horse until our supply was gone. I lingered for a moment as memories of a little girl and then a distraught teen whisked through my mind.

"Hey, Dina. Y'all ready for a, what'd ya call it? A wash-up?"

"Wipe-Up."

"Sounds the same to me." Smiling, he motioned me toward the rusty pump. "We gotta do somethin' to get all that nasty horse slobber off your dainty little hands." His arm muscles flexed under his shirt as he began to push the handle.

Within minutes, I was holding my hands under icy water. "Whoa! Just as cold as I remember it." I felt my finger grow numb and quickly shook my hands free of the water. "Here, let me pump for you."

He stuck his hands under the stream of chilly water. "Hey!" Pulling them back, he looked at me suspiciously.

"Can't pump all day." I motioned for him to finish up.

Taking a deep breath, he plunged his hands under the pump's spigot and replied wryly, "Next time I go and get drool on me, I'll remember this little exercise."

Laughing, we dried our hands across our jeans, and Gil reached for my stiff fingers. "I had no idea you little girls were so tough."

"Live and learn."

There was a pause in the air. His lips were slightly open as he studied me. His eyes held mine, and the moment lasted until he spoke softly, "Ain't that the truth." He brought my fingers to his lips and blew warm air across my hands until I felt the cold leave my joints and a cozy heat return.

I glanced back at the porch. Butch was curled on the glider seat, tucked into a ball and swinging gently as the old ranch prepared to meet another winter's season. Its gray frame, no longer sheltered by greenery, reached upward through the empty trees, seeking the glow of afternoon's sun. I smiled gently. Words weren't necessary as we headed back toward the old gate.

"I need to work on my duffle bag." A silent moment held my thoughts captive. When I continued, my voice was weary but carried the strength of my convictions. "I've started sorting through things. I'll need to finish up; then I can do the packing."

Gil pushed the brim of his cowboy hat back. "You made that decision?"

"Yes, I did."

"I'll be there for you. You know that." He reached for my hand, letting his fingers intertwine with mine.

"My life feels as if it's quivering behind me, about to disappear." I stopped, looking calmly into his eyes. "I want to keep a fragment of it preserved. I want to keep this day. I want to put it in my duffle bag. Can I do that?"

"A recognized sensation that you'll feel again?"

I paused. "Is that what you call it?"

"I call it love." The gate lay ahead of us. He lifted me off the ground and swung me in a circle. "The scenery of life holds infinite variety, and it goes round and round, sweet Dina." I felt airborne as we spun across the earth path.

Gently he released me, and I asked, "Will I have wings?"

"We all have wings." He smiled and said, "They're folded till we need 'em."

"And we know when we need them?"

"Absolutely, Miss Dina." Gil winked mischievously. "Same as when the geese know to fly south."

"Hmm. You know that story too?"

"Yes, ma'am." He leaned closer. "You told it real nice to Rachel. She needed to hear it, and you needed to tell it."

"So I did." I began to smooth my shirt. "Let's get back to real life for a moment."

Gil raised his eyebrows. "Is that a pun?"

I laughed. "I've got to go. I'd better be back in that hammock when Rachel comes looking for me." Pausing, I felt a wry half-smile take over. "It's hard to live in this world and be so close to the next world at the same time. A person can only truly be in one place." I looked happily into his eyes. "And right now I need a little more space here. I have a date with destiny, you know, and I want time to enjoy it." Catching my breath, I paused. "The family photo albums. Have I told you about them?"

"Please do." His movements were unhurried. A boyish smile eased across his face, creating slowness in time.

I smiled. "Jillian was the photo keeper. She took the pictures, put them in books, and labeled them. Then Rachel and I thought we'd lost all the albums and boy, were we in big trouble. But they're really somewhere in the garage." My brows knit in frustration. "I know we can find them."

Gil drew me close. "It's nice to collect visual impressions."

"Labeled visual impressions," I corrected him. "We're talking about my older sister. Dad always said that Jillian was a born recorder of events. She used to drive us wild with her camera, but it was really okay because we all loved to look at our history."

He replied softly, "A memory trail."

"Yes, that's it. A reflection of what we did with the years." Touching my heart, I looked back at Gil. "The most beautiful day ever is right here."

He looked tall and broad against the autumn foliage, and I thought of the ancient elms I had long admired. He spoke softly, "We gather impressions like leaves in the wind, and when it's time, sweet Dina, we release what we don't need."

I touched his face, feeling the roughness of his beginning beard. He held me tightly as time dripped slowly around us. I felt wrapped in the ancient patina of his love. "Will I see you soon?"

His warm breath caressed my neck. "What y'all got in mind?"

My eyes were pools of liquid blue as I gazed into the sky. "A moonlight ride?"

Chapter 11

The walk home was easy. I felt wings at my feet carry me along the country lane and looked down to see if it was so. I laughed at my sloppy socks and old sneakers. How had I managed to dance at all in tennis shoes? Then I thought, *Wait a minute, I was with my angel. Lots of stuff can happen when you're with an angel.* Clouds of dusty earth scattered with each step, and I wondered why things were so dry after the rain. The past hours of the afternoon seemed to hide themselves away in the private essence of my heart.

I went directly to the hammock and picked up the blanket that had fallen on the ground. I fluffed the pillow and put it behind my head. It felt good to lie down after my walk. I allowed my eyes to shut. A quick snooze would feel good.

"Dina, you look radiant," Rachel said as she stood over me. "A little rest will do wonders for you."

"If only you knew." I wiggled my eyebrows in jest.

"Is that so?" Rachel helped me up and said, "Close your eyes. I have a surprise for you."

"It's been a day filled with surprises," I replied pleasantly.

"Really?"

"Sure has, and all good ones." I winked. "However, if you want me to close my eyes now, it means you'll have to be careful with me. I wouldn't want to walk into anything and break."

She looked concerned.

"Joke! Rachel, it's a joke."

"Oh. Okay." She let it pass with a sigh. "Shut your eyes and no peeking."

"Done." I held my hands in front of me. "So where are you taking me?"

"Remember how you've been asking about the old photo albums?" She guided me carefully toward the house. I heard a door open, and she led me inside. "Well, ta-da! You can open your eyes!"

Spread across the table were several books holding family pictures. Rachel's voice held a triumphant note. "I found them in the garage, behind the old boxes of dishes. We must have put them there when we cleaned up. Let's see, that would be—"

"Several years ago," I murmured. Moving toward the first album, I smiled. "This is great." I touched it tenderly. "Really great."

"Are you feeling well enough to do this now?" Rachel looked at me anxiously. "If you're still sleepy, this can wait."

I flapped my hand across her shoulder. "There, there, caretaker. I believe you just told me that I looked radiant. I've already slept, and now I'm calm and awake and I'm not going to wander off."

"I'm sorry about the new pill, but you've been so full of, hmm, unusual ideas that I wanted to, gosh, I guess calm you down."

"And you did." I grinned, feeling peaceful deep inside.

Waiting for the teapot to boil, Rachel hummed softly then fluffed the cushions, indicating she wanted me to sit down. I followed her instructions as I carried a photo album to the family room, where I plopped into the freshly puffed chair.

The first picture I saw was taken the day Rachel came home from the hospital. "You marked this one for me to see. Didn't you?"

"Never."

With a snort, I turned my attention back to the picture. Jillian and I were sitting on the sofa with Mother, who was holding the new baby. It was titled "My Girls." I motioned to Rachel. "Come here and have a look."

Leaving the teapot, she moved toward my chair. Peering over my shoulder, she commented, "Yeah. That's me."

I placed my finger on the photograph. "I was only two but excited and happy about the arrival of a baby sister. Somehow it seemed like a good idea."

"Glad you felt that way." Rachel sat on the arm of the chair. "Sort of a light approach. I appreciated that, in so much as Jillian was far more serious about the event."

"I know." I patted her hand. "For years, Jillian continued to point out that with each new sister, her responsibilities grew more profound."

Rachel replied with a contemptuous half-smile, "As we grew older, we were forever impressed with Jillian's escalating vocabulary. 'Profound' was another of her notable words. I use it often."

I thought about her remark. "Really?"

"Sure."

I looked at Rachel. "Often?"

She shrugged. "Whenever it's necessary."

I looked at the picture again and smiled. Right from the start, Rachel was golden curls and creamy skin. "Hey, you were bright and cute from day one."

Rachel bobbed her blonde head in my direction. "But of course."

Christmas pictures flew by as dolls and toys danced across the pages. There was the photo of Jillian putting the star on top of the tree. Rachel pointed at it, and we exchanged a nod. She replied, "You do know that our elder sister claimed that honor ever since we could remember."

"Yup." I replied. "Bet she still does it."

"Don't you wonder how she explained that to Tony?" Rachel mused, "I mean the part about how she was the only one capable of placing the star in the center of the tree."

"Well..." I thought about it. "It could be considered a skill. You know, center placement?"

Rachel shook her head. "I think not. At any time, I could have taken over the star-placing job."

"Really?" I nodded, impressed.

"Sure. It was a no-brainer, in my opinion."

"Wait a minute." A new respect for Rachel was forming in my mind. "Are you saying our older, wiser sister made a big deal out of a no-brainer?"

Rachel raised her eyebrows. Smiling at me, she turned the page and commented, "Oh look. Here's Daddy carving the turkey. Gosh, it was roasted to a golden brown and wonderfully moist. Mom sure knew how to cook."

"Mmm." I sniffed the air. "I can almost smell the scrumptious aromas wafting from the oven." Looking at Rachel, I shrugged. "Too bad we didn't learn the skill of baking a perfect turkey."

"Yes. At least one of us should have done that. You know, taken an interest in the kitchen."

"You're good in the kitchen."

"I never did master the Thanksgiving turkey," she explained with a sigh. "I guess I thought Mom would always be around."

I held her hand. "It's a common mistake we all make." I squeezed her fingers. "You need to let it go."

Flipping through the book, I quickly settled on pictures of my fifth birthday. The wooden rod, with all the extensions, that my mother had used to hang the wash on was decorated in pastel crepe paper, with long streamers for each guest to hold as they wound around the maypole. I smiled and wondered where Gil had been. Maybe angels didn't show up in photographs. I made a mental note to ask him.

Rachel pointed at the picture. "See how Jillian labeled your party, 'Such a lucky girl, being born in the spring.'"

I nodded. "It was true. My parties were always filled with butterflies and soft breezes." Pointing to a corner of the photo, I smiled. "See who's there?"

"Gosh." Rachel bent in front of me to study the print. "Is that the big, old, white cat?" Her voice took on an astonishing tone. "With a pink bow around his neck?"

"Yup. That was Vinnie."

"I don't remember him hanging around birthday parties. He was always busy supervising the activities of the barn, like chasing mice and doing challenging stuff."

"So true. But he put up with this disturbance because it was important to me." I looked up at Rachel, grinning. "Plus I promised him ice cream when I tied the pink bow around his neck. Look." I pointed. "You can see by his expression how annoyed he was, but still he put up with my childish exuberance." I smiled happily. "And he did get ice cream along with a taste of cake." I nodded to myself, thinking this was a memory to pack.

"Wait a minute." Rachel sat back. "I remember now. His white face was stained with lavender for days. You had lilac frosting on your cake. Yucky lilac frosting."

"It wasn't yucky." I looked at her with a raised eyebrow. "Your fingers were stained purple too." I settled back to continue my trip through the photo books and added, "Plus it was my favorite color." I paused. "At that time."

We looked at faded photos of Rachel holding a stuffed bear while I sat on Grandma Nana's lap and of Jillian playing the piano while we all watched her recital. There were county fair photos of me with baby pigs, Rachel in a ballet costume, and dozens of school pictures where we appeared clean and often toothless, depending on our age; all were good memories to be packed in my duffle bag.

Rachel pointed at a picture where both her front teeth were missing and commented, "Why did Jillian always have teeth for her school photos and we didn't?"

"Good question." I paused in thought.

"Could it have been better genes?"

"I think not." Leaning toward Rachel, I replied in sisterly confidence, "I've always been of the opinion that her teeth were afraid to fall out before a school picture."

"Hmm." Rachel nodded. "I never thought of that."

Cuddled up in the chair, I continued to turn the pages, and we laughed about our dated clothes and hair ribbons. We watched as we grew from little girls into teenagers. I smiled and frowned, feeling happiness with some pictures and acute embarrassment with others.

"See." I pointed emphatically to a picture of myself in a flouncy, blue frock. "It was the world's ugliest dress."

Rachel commented dryly, "You called that one right."

"Of course, it didn't help that I was chubby and my date was the gangly son of our parents' best friends." I shifted positions, settling more comfortably against the cushions. "Kyle wasn't to blame. Nor was I, for that matter. It was all Theodore Wilson's fault."

"Yes," Rachel agreed. "I remember the story. Wasn't he another love of your life? And he invited—"

"Marla Packer to be his date for the graduation dance. Oh, never mind that we were all ninth graders, while Kyle, my date,"—I thumped my chest—"was tall and skinny, and only in eighth grade."

Rachel sat straighter. "I thought he was mature."

"Sure you did," I explained patiently. "That's because you were in seventh grade."

Sighing, Rachel commiserated with me. "That last year in middle school was tough for you."

"Yes, everything was a crushing blow to my ego, and it accumulated when Theodore didn't invite me to the big dance." I shook my head. "All I'd wanted to do was stay home and lick my wounds." Pursing my lips, I looked at my sister. "Seemed like a reasonable request to me."

"I agree. I was appalled when our parents would have none of your attitude." Rachel tipped her head in thought. "I remember Mother arranging your date with Kyle."

I laughed. "It was embarrassing for both of us." I pointed at the photo again. Looking at the blue dress of numerous flounces, I shook my head. The flowers pinned on the shoulder had made me sneeze, and all the starchy ruffles had rubbed my underarms raw. Kyle, standing next to me, looked acutely self-conscious in a suit that didn't fit. I added, "Then there was Kyle's little 'perspiration problem'…"

"His deodorant failed him." Rachel quipped. "Even I knew that."

"He was just nervous."

Rachel pointed at the picture. "Well, I can understand that. You looked uneasy in all those ruffles."

"Twitchy and itchy." I replied. We both snickered.

"In the end, we made the best of a bad situation. Because when the dance ended, and that was none too soon,"—I rolled my eyes and went on—"all the graceful couples were squired away by their parents to attend that late-night supper, the one sponsored by the school.

"Kyle and I had been picked up by his older brother, Jack." I tipped my head in Rachel's direction. "Do you remember how Jack had driven home from college with Jillian for that weekend?"

"Wasn't he one of her many admirers?"

Nodding, I continued. "Well, Kyle and I convinced Jack that we wanted pizza more than a school dinner, and because Jack was secretly in love with Jillian, he'd wanted to please me so that I'd carry a good report to my older sister."

Rachel was affirmative. "And you did."

"Of course. It was the least I could do for Jack. He surrendered to our pleas and took us to Papa Geno's, where Kyle and I stuffed our faces with pepperoni and cheese pizza while drinking numerous Cokes and laughing about the dance." I snickered again. "Unfortunately, neither of us had given a thought about money to pay for the pizza, so Jack graciously paid the tab."

Good-naturedly, Rachel responded, "Even then, being in love with Jillian was a complicated affair."

"Oh. So true," I agreed. "But once she found out that we'd stuck Jack with our bill, she called Kyle and asked him to come to the house. When he arrived, Jillian invited him into the parlor, the serious room in the house. She had a sour expression on her face and appeared hostile."

"That's right!" Rachel exclaimed. "She was just beginning her early lawyer mode then."

"Courtroom posture, she called it. She stood very straight and began to pace. After she had our complete attention, she started reviewing what we'd done and then telling us that we had to pay back every penny that Jack had spent." I laughed, shaking my head. "Kyle was actually scared of her."

"I can appreciate that." Rachel nodded. "She was tall and formidable. And I'm not saying that just because I was the shortest one in the family."

Sitting back in the chair, I closed my eyes in thought. *Yes, the journey across my life was definitely interesting.*

Perhaps not earth-shaking, but certainly filled with enter-taining memories.

Rachel and I stared off into space for several minutes. Finally she replied, "The last time I saw Kyle he had grown quite nicely into his lean frame. He was fine-looking and muscular, confident in wearing the summer whites of a naval officer."

I nodded. "Definitely a changed man."

The teapot whistled, and Rachel got up.

More pages flew past until the caption "Ah, the picture of rejection?" made me smile. The question mark was put in by Jillian deliberately. I remembered my dismay at not making the final tryouts for the cheerleading squad in my senior year. I'd come home and plunked down on the back porch step, feeling very sorry for myself.

"Look," Rachel exclaimed happily as she placed a cup of tea in front of me. "I took that one!"

"You sure did." I faked a harsh tone. "Didn't you see how bummed out I was?"

"It was my fifteenth birthday," she spoke defensively. "I had a new camera, and I wanted to take pictures of everyone. I remember the day clearly. Jillian was home from college for the weekend. She'd given me the camera."

"Yes, and she convinced me to be patient and pose for you. You took a couple of shots then ran off to photograph birds and bugs and anything else that moved."

"I was filled with energy as a child."

"Yes, you were, and in your zest to photograph every living thing, you almost tipped over the special Jillian drink."

We exchanged a look and started laughing again. Rachel said, "I remember the special drink. Jillian would make tall glasses of lemonade, which she'd garnish with an orange slice and a maraschino cherry. She called it her 'bouncy punch.'"

I explained, "She'd given one to me to brighten my mood while I'd poured out my woes about how the cheerleaders were the most popular girls in school and the best liked and invited everywhere. When I was done complaining, our wise, older sister told me that the best-liked girls in school were the ones who were sincere, the ones who helped people, the ones who cared." I paused, thinking back. "She had also carefully avoided saying that cheerleaders, by nature, had some athletic ability and tended to be tall and thin. Or short and petite." I glanced at Rachel and finished my reflection. "None of those categories described me."

We retired to our private thoughts. I remembered that it had taken a few days for all that Jillian had told me to sink in, but once it registered, it had changed my life. Instead of trying to be what I wasn't, I'd concentrated on being what I was. My fingertips brushed the photo gently. I smiled, thinking that life revealed itself in private meaning when you least expected it. Here was another moment to pack.

Rachel twisted a finger through her hair. "I never made cheerleader either." We exchanged a sisterly nod before she replied, "It wasn't that important." She shrugged. "Not really. Not in the great scheme of things."

We cruised through the books until we came to the picture of me in my red cap and gown. I was smiling at the camera; it was graduation day.

"High school was behind me," I replied. "My motto was 'Look out, college, here I come.'" I faced Rachel.

"It was catchy," she replied as she got up to prepare dinner. "And I got your room all to myself. I really spread out. It was great."

It was also the day my Grandma Nana had given me the pretty little diamond heart. No one had ever received such a present, but Nana had told me that I was special.

My older sister always got things first, as was right. My baby sister got the cutest dolls, as was her due. However, being the middle child was also unique, and therefore I was given the wondrous necklace that had been a gift to Grandma Nana from Granddaddy so many years ago.

I adored the necklace and had always planned to give it to my own daughter someday. After all, that was how family traditions were born. Of course, back then as I passed through adolescence on the road to becoming a woman, I'd thought life was forever.

Closing the book, I paused. Rachel called out from the kitchen. "I really did miss you when you went away to college. Suddenly I was all alone. No one to talk to. That's why I called so often."

"I know. I missed you too and loved all the dumb things you used to say."

"Know what else I did?" Rachel came around the corner. "I even called Jillian, and she talked to me almost every time."

I got up, deciding to stretch my legs. "Me too. I called Jillian because I didn't have a clue what to do in college. She talked me through a lot of stuff."

"She's our older sister. She's always cared."

I walked down the hall toward my bedroom. Once there, I opened the drawer that contained my treasures. I looked for the golden Godiva box that served as keeper of my jewelry. I removed the tiny diamond necklace, wrapping it carefully in a piece of tissue. In my top drawer, I found some pink ribbon and tied it around the package, ending with a small bow on top.

Writing a note to Rachel, I reminded her how the necklace had belonged to Grandma Nana and how I hoped that she would give the pretty diamond to her first daughter.

I collected my notes labeled "Fragments of a Simpler Life" and put them with the other items in the envelope marked with Jillian's name. *I'll bet she does it,* I thought. *And here's my contribution.* After all, I too had seen some great stuff through the wavy glass.

I checked the rest of the contents in Jillian's envelope, making sure the note attached to the package of lemonade was securely stuck on. It read, "Thanks for the good advice." I'd drawn a cherry and orange on a corner of the note and added, "Here's to bouncy punch." I took two ten-dollar bills from my wallet and labeled them, "Keep buying pumpkins."

I opened my bottom drawer and removed the white linen napkin I had folded into the shape of flower petals. The hand-printed instructions and a detailed diagram were placed on top. I slipped it carefully into the snowy white gift bag and signed the wedding card for Rachel and Carl. I hoped they'd be pleasantly surprised.

In the bottom drawer, I found the blue egg that Jillian had painted in a summer craft class. She'd given one to me and the other to Rachel, telling us that one day they would be treasures. It was time to pass that treasure on, and Mrs. Kopeck came to mind. I scribbled a note to her, expressing my deep belief in her business philosophy, and wished her continued success. A part of me wanted to leave her an insulated thermos, but that wasn't going to happen, I told myself, because I'd flat run out of time.

Joking that I had saved a bundle on lawyer's fees by taking care of distributing my wealth on my own, I walked back to the kitchen, where the fragrance of chamomile tea filled the room.

Rachel had placed the last few albums on the table next to the chair. She had opened one book to a shot of Phil and me in ballroom competition. "You two were really good," she exclaimed with enthusiasm. "You had the moves, and he had the flair. What a team!"

"We were good." I smiled secretively. "But the cowboy is better."

Rachel paused, treating my comment lightly. "If you say so."

I knew that it was time to release the old memory of dancing with Phil. Nothing had been as wonderful as the waltz this afternoon. The sorting was getting easier. This was good, as I was feeling tired.

As I neared the end of my memory trail, I saw the photo of the white-water rafting trip with Amy and Sue. "Gosh, we had a fantastic time!" I remarked.

"I remember all the preparations you made." Rachel smiled. "I was still in high school, but I swore I'd go rafting someday." We studied the photograph for a few minutes before she asked, "What happened to them?"

"Well, Amy kept in touch for several years after college. We were always going to get together and go rafting again." I paused, thinking back. "Guess time got lost." I wondered briefly where lost time went, but the question was too deep to pursue. "And the last I heard, Sue was living in France with her boyfriend." I smiled, wishing them all happiness.

Turning to Rachel, I asked, "Why don't you ask Carl to take you rafting?"

"Perhaps I will." She added with a grin, "I think he's very athletic."

"Do you?" I asked, trying to look sincere.

"You've never seen him toss a Frisbee for his dog." Rachel huffed. "He has a very good throwing arm."

"Really? Well then, this is a great idea." I tossed my hands in the air. "And maybe, just maybe, he'd bring the big, hairy pooch on a rafting trip. You know the dog I'm talking about, right? The one in the photograph that's on his desk?" I nodded happily. "Dogs love water."

"No." Rachel was emphatic. "Fido doesn't like water." She smiled mischievously. "We'd be on our own."

"You don't say."

"Now you're sounding like Mother."

I grinned, turning my attention back to the photographs. "Hey look. Tony and Jillian. This was taken in the parlor when they announced their engagement."

"You mean Jillian announced their engagement." Rachel smiled.

"Yes," I agreed. "It was a beautifully prepared speech. Took almost five minutes to read, and then you and I applauded."

"I merely followed your lead," Rachel added in her own defense, "being the youngest."

"Oh, please," I quipped. "You were old enough to know better."

"Maybe. But as I recall, Jillian gave us a curt nod, and that stopped the applause right in the middle of a vigorous clap!"

"Good thing she did that. I was about to let loose with one of my ear-piercing whistles, followed by a thumbs-up sign."

"That would have rocked her world." Rachel's straight line caused me to burst out in laughter. She joined me as we giggled together.

After a few minutes, she looked at me wide-eyed. "I still say, with all kidding aside, that Tony looked surprised at the announcement of their engagement."

We exchanged another smirk, and I replied with my standard line, "He was delighted to marry Jillian."

"Yes! Because she told him he was!" We chuckled, again at our routine, both of us knowing that Tony's look of surprise had come not from the way Jillian had made the announcement but from our outlandish behavior in an attempt to embarrass our older sister. I thought how wonderful it was to be a family.

I flipped through the pages until the time my illness was diagnosed. Some things I didn't have to relive. The best part was that the albums had been found and the family photographs would be preserved.

I fluffed my sister's hair and said, "Life, sweet Rachel, is grand. And should be recorded." I grinned. "Did I really say that?"

"Yes, you did, and I'm going to tell Jillian." She added pleasantly, "You know how much she enjoys being right."

Rachel collected our teacups and announced it was time for dinner. I sat in silence with the photo albums surrounding me. It was life played out in a roller coaster of pictures, and I had enjoyed the ride.

A late dinner was set before me. I pushed the watermelon Jell-O across my plate as I studied the night sky. Its liquid darkness held a clear quality that I found refreshing.

As we were washing the dishes, Carl phoned, and Rachel stumbled with her words, which encouraged me to poke fun at them. She introduced the subject of a white-water adventure, and it seemed to go over well.

As the night lengthened, I felt weariness settle over my bones, and I napped under the afghan that my mother had made. Dreams of a land drenched in orange blossoms and silver light held my thoughts in a comforting embrace. The taste of honey slipped through my mind. I could sense Gil's essence as he drifted calmly through my dreams.

When I woke, the television offered the evening news. The yellow glow of Rachel's reading light collected in soft pools against her cheeks. I knew instinctively that my younger sister would read many books to her children. I chided her, "You need more light than that." Sitting up, I peeked at Rachel's book. "Oh!" I let out my breath in a whoosh. "Love poems?" I spoke louder, "Love poems? Rachel!"

"A small gift from Carl." Looking over her reading glasses, she smiled sweetly and asked, "Are you done making fun?"

"Yes, actually I am. And on that note, I'm off to bed." Standing, I felt wobbly as I leaned over to touch my lips to Rachel's blonde hair. "You're really a terrific sister. Even when you were little and sticky, I still loved you."

"That's not what you said then."

"I know." As I walked down the hallway, the night felt silent and wise.

Chapter 12

The seizure struck as I moved toward the bathroom. Lightheadedness grabbed me in a savage attack, forcing me to double over. Dizziness swept through me, and I staggered, reaching for something to hold on to. Waves of nausea followed while the cancer and my body raged in final battle. A part of me realized that it was happening too fast, and a horrid death was spinning around me. I grasped at the towel bar, but my strength failed as I sank to the tile floor. My muscles tensed as if caught in a vice, and I began to jerk uncontrollably. Fresh pain stabbed my body, engulfing me in hot waves as I thrashed on the bathroom floor, until unconsciousness cut off my torment.

From a far distance, I heard my sister's voice filled with anxiety. "Dina, can you hear me?" My upper lids pulled my eyes open. With hazy vision I saw that Rachel stood over my bed. I wanted to speak to her, but the words didn't form. Forcing my eyes to focus, I saw that Carl stood at her side. I breathed a sigh of relief. Looking at my sister, I saw that her blonde curls fell forward, and all of her freckles were in place. I thought I smiled.

She cried softly. "Dina, baby, please talk to me."

"She needs to be in the hospital." Carl bent forward, a worried look creasing his brow as he reached for my wrist. "Her pulse is erratic." Turning to Rachel, he spoke firmly, "I think we should move her as quickly as possible."

"No! She hates the hospital." Rachel's voice had reached the breaking point. Holding her hands over her mouth, she continued to breathe with shaky gasps of air. Looking at Carl, she pleaded, "Let her be. Please let her stay in her own bed."

"Rachel, as her doctor—"

"Stop." Her eyes brimmed with tears. "Tell me as her friend, Carl, not as her doctor."

His sigh came from deep within, torn between professional responsibility and his feelings of love for my sister. I heard the grief carved within his words and felt sorry for both of them. They had tried so hard. All of them had—the nurses, my family, my friends—everyone, but now the disease was almost over. The cancer was no longer sneaking around, picking which bones or organs to attack next. I could feel its pressure throughout my body. And in the middle of this deathly battle, all I wanted was to have Gil at my side, but I couldn't express this to anyone.

Blinking slowly, I forced myself to a conscious state and whispered, "Hi." My voice was limp, fragile with fear. "Guess I lost it, huh?"

Rachel gathered my emaciated body in her arms as she said, "Hi, baby." She struggled not to cry. "How are you feeling now? Carl gave you something to stop the seizure."

The darkness was pierced only by the bedside lamp, leaving the shadows free to quiver in the weak light. Sadness permeated my small bedroom, and I feared that hospice would be my final destination.

As waves of conscientious floated around me, I became aware of the effect the drug had on my body. A feeling of lightness stretched down my legs, and I thought that I rose one foot several inches in an attempt to check my ability of control. My head swam in a vacuum of recessed pain. It was far enough away so that I didn't care. "That was some injection, Doc." I smiled weakly, thinking that it wasn't so bad if all I felt was the idea of the pain, not the reality.

Rachel fussed with my blankets. She told me she had found my favorite nightgown and helped me pull it over my head. When she asked what she could do to make me feel better, I looked toward the fireplace. She shook her head, and I knew the answer was no. She still worried that a fire would not be good for my breathing. Why did the living pride themselves on knowing so much about the dying? I should have insisted on having a fire when I could still make decisions. A part of me said that my ability to decide what was right had come and gone.

Nothing could take away the pain, but mentally the richness of glowing flames was a comforting image that I wanted to enjoy one more time. I knew that it would warm the cold in my body and give me a feeling soft with forgetfulness.

Rachel left the room to bring back a glass of water that I wouldn't drink. Carl stepped toward the bed. "Okay." Reaching out for my hand, he spoke quietly, "I'll build the fire."

"Whoa." I tried to moisten my parched lips. "I must be going fast."

His voice held tears. "Ahh, Dina." Carefully, he applied a lip balm for me then brushed the tangles of thinning hair from my face.

I pushed my lips together and murmured, "Mmm, that's better." I took a moment for myself then looked at him. "You know it's my time to go?"

He nodded sadly.

Feeling myself begin to drift, I asked, "Will you be there for her?"

His voice was filled with compassion. "You know I will." He reached for my hand again and squeezed my fingers, the same way that I had squeezed Rachel's fingers earlier that evening. "Do you also know that I love your sister and will always take care of her?"

A thought surfaced in my fuzzy mind. "Do you have a personal scheduling book?" Carl shook his head in confusion, causing me to smile. "That makes me happy." My words were slurred. "Jillian and Tony have to schedule time together. They have a very busy life."

He nodded. "So I've been told."

My voice was faint. "Rachel will be really good at bedtime stories. Your children will be lucky."

"Yes." He paused, reflecting on the love he felt for Rachel. "They will be very lucky." He blinked rapidly, and I could see the moisture in his eyes. I also understood that his emotions were close to the surface, and I tried to direct a change in our conversation.

"Hey, I left you a wedding present." My words felt heavy, but I wanted to finish my thought. I took another deep breath. "Oh, I know you haven't asked her yet, but you will." I tried to wiggle my finger to emphasize my next point, but I couldn't make it work, so I continued without the hand gesture. "You may not get the full meaning of my present right away, but Rachel will explain it all to you." Still feeling fuzzy, I went on, "It's about napkins and flowers and Grandma Nana." I flinched as a needle of pain shot across my chest, taking my breath away.

Carl leaned forward. "Where is the pain, Dina? I can make it go away."

Taking a moment, I mentally explored my body, wondering where it would attack next. "It's okay now. I sort of feel strong. Oh, not like I want to run a mile, but not so weak." Squinting at him, I saw that he was filling a needle from a small bottle. "Am I making any sense?" I shifted on the pillow, and a burst of raw throbbing exploded down my back. "It's strong," I whispered as Carl gave me the injection.

Within moments, the agony was pushed farther into the blackness of the medication. I sought Carl's eyes, smiling weakly. "You give good drugs, Doc." I managed a soft laugh. "I feel like I'm cushioned in a cloud. Will you help me to the chair by the fireplace?"

"Give the meds a chance to work."

"Gotcha." I released my breath, allowing myself to enter a semiconscious state.

When Rachel entered my room, I knew that she spoke with Carl in hushed tones. I opened my eyes and immediately felt that the fire had quickly heated my bedroom. It burned brightly against the darkness, encouraging the scent of pine resin to float toward me. I yawned and stretched, feeling spacey but comfortable.

Carl helped me to the chair that had been placed close to the old, stone fireplace. I noticed the glass of water on the small table next to me and smiled at my sister.

We gathered together in front of the screen that kept the burning logs from sending sparks into the room. Gently we talked, laughing softly, sharing the last moments. Carl injected another painkiller into a vein on my ankle. It took effect immediately, offering relief from the raging torment that slid in and out of my body. I felt drowsy and peaceful. Rachel kissed my forehead while Carl added another log to the fire. I was tired, and they promised to check on me later.

My sister left the room first, but I was aware that Carl lingered a moment longer. I wondered if he felt the peace that encircled me. He had told Rachel that it was often like that when people were in transition. Even in cold hospital rooms, he had often sensed the love and warmth that materialized from out of nowhere. I hoped he could feel it now and would share it with my sisters when the time was right. He took a deep breath, and I felt his prayer settle around me. He knew that Rachel would need him. I knew that he wanted to be there for her.

There was a companionship of sound as the fire crackled and spit. Gently, Carl closed the door to my bedroom. I let my eyes shut, feeling the grace of the moment.

When I woke, the fire had burned down to glowing embers. My body felt warm. I was stiff but rested, and the pain remained smothered under the medication, allowing me time to think about any other memories I wanted to pack. Letting my mind dance among my warmest thoughts, I chose only the secret essence of myself, mentally folding and placing it in the duffle bag. Then I began to wait.

A sudden noise at the glass caught my attention. I tossed the blanket to the floor and surprised myself at my ability to move quickly. I reached the door that opened to the terrace and flung it wide. "Oh, Gil! Oh, wow! Hi!" I beamed with joy.

Moonlight bonded with his cowboy hat, like a wafting halo. I tumbled into his hug, feeling the brisk, night air that clung to his long drover's coat. "See, it's still there. Your halo. You probably dust if off for official events."

He held me firmly and whispered in my ear, "Dina, you say the dangdest stuff."

"Is it true? Can you do that?"

He paused, considering my question carefully. "I've never thought about it as such, but"—he looked up—"if it's there, it's where it's supposed to be."

"How did you know I wanted you?" My voice was breathy. "Needed you now?"

"That's an easy one. I'm your number one guy. I'm your angel and I know things." His lips brushed my forehead. "Besides, y'all said a moonlight ride. I assumed you wanted me to come to you. It's kinda hard to walk that old country lane late at night." He held me at arm's length. "'Course I could have sashayed myself 'round to the front door and announced my arrival proper-like."

"Ohh…" I smiled as I thought of the amazed look that would have been on Rachel's face. "Probably not a good idea. My sister has been through a lot already. And even though the doc is a great guy, he'd never be able to comprehend you or why you had come calling." I shook my head. "Never mind. It's best that you came directly here."

Gil removed his cowboy hat, letting his fingers travel the outer brim. "I realize that comin' to your bedroom door is a might forward on my part…"

"'A might forward.'" I laughed. "Are you kidding? Did you say a might forward?"

"Yes, ma'am, I did."

"After the things we've done, I don't think coming to my bedroom door is at all forward."

He looked down at his boots then slowly raised his head; a mischievous smile crossed his face. "Tell y'all a secret." He winked. "I was just makin' a funny. Wanted to see if you were on top of the game."

"Is that so?" I softly kissed the hollow of his neck. "And how did I do?"

He grinned at me. "You're with it."

I laughed. "A 'good-old-boy' angel with a sense of humor. I like that."

"Is that how y'all think of me?" he replied in an astonished tone. He replaced his hat and reached into his long coat. "I brought you a little present, in spite of the fact that I am the subject of your jest. But now I'm not so sure if I'm of a mind to give it to you."

"Let me see it." I reached toward his coat, but he stepped away. "Come on, Gil, what did you bring me?"

"Well, seeing as you put it so nicely, sayin' please and all."

"Please."

"Now, how could I possibly say no to sugar sweetness like that?" His eyes reflected knowledge as he reached into a deep pocket. Then seconds slowed to a softer pace as he handed me a lovely white rose. I felt myself stand straighter. Tightness formed in my throat. I gasped in a mouthful of air. My eyes filled with tears.

Time stood quietly in wait as I reached for the flower. Holding the stem, I found myself breathing deeply with an even rhythm as tranquility mixed with wisdom. I held the velvet petals against my cheek, letting them brush away the last of my tears.

Gil opened his arms. "There's no reason for sorrow."

My voice was only a whisper. "I know."

His coat flew wide, and I stepped inside. The coarse flannel of his shirt was scratchy against my cotton nightgown, but soon the comforting warmth from his chest filtered through my body as he shared the force of his strength with me. I held Vinnie's rose tenderly against my heart.

Slowly, I realized that I had many things to tell Gil. "Oh, gosh," I said as I stepped back. "It's been quite a night."

"Has it now?" He touched my face with a gentle caress. "Been sittin' by the fire? You got yourself some rosy cheeks, girl."

"Yeah." I took a deep breath that turned into a shaky laugh. "I guess I do."

He reached out to me with strong hands. I laid the rose on my bed and placed my fingertips gently against his palms. I felt his gaze linger on my face as I slipped into his sapphire eyes. "I've packed my duffle." I slung the imaginary bag over my shoulder and settled it into a comfortable position. "See?"

"Ya need help with it?"

"No." I smiled. "Oh." I placed my hand over my mouth and continued, "Where or where are those pesky manners of mine?"

Gil raised his eyebrow as I replied, "I mean it was sweet of you to ask, sir, but no thank you."

"Are you a'pokin' fun at me again?"

I offered a charming smile. "Certainly not."

Tipping his head, he grinned, and I noticed how tall and rugged he looked standing in my small bedroom. It occurred to me that he was the only man who had ever been in that room, and I let myself enjoy the view.

Finally, clearing my throat, I focused on what I wanted to share with him. "So here's what I've packed—a combination of delightful moments."

"Sounds good, Miss Dina. Would y'all like to elaborate some?"

I nodded. "I've included some corners, a few colors, a breeze or two." I smiled. "Memories, photos, and lots of sunshine. And lessons to study so that I know more next time around."

"My now." He stood with his legs apart. His fingers pulled the brim of his hat lower. "That does sound like a duffle bag filled with mighty fine items."

"Oh, I'm not done. You see, as I went over my list, I found that yesterday is everywhere in today. And the past and the present walk together." A frown wrinkled my forehead. "But you already knew that. Didn't you?"

"Sweet Dina." He stepped forward, letting his fingers caress my cheek. "Life walks with a measured pace."

His cowboy hat sat low over his forehead. I reached up to tilt it back. "It's time for our moonlight ride to the top of the ridge." I turned toward the chair, reaching for my blanket. "And I'm ready to go. But first I need to leave something for Rachel." I picked up Vinnie's rose and brought it to my lips, enjoying the delicate scent that lingered just under my nose. Placing it tenderly on the table next to the water glass, I smiled at its perfect form, a tiny cloud of white against the dimness of my bedroom.

Slowly I turned and walked toward Gil. He gathered me in his arms, lifting me from the floor as he carried me toward the doors of my terrace. His great coat flapped across his legs as a blast of cold wind invaded my room. It bore an edge of frost that promised sleet. I smelled the night and thought, *Snow is coming.*

His warm breath nuzzled my skin as he whispered, "Not for another month. Then wind-born flakes of white will cover the earth once more."

"You're doing it again, but it's actually kind of nice. Saves on words." I nuzzled closer. "Besides, I'm getting used to it."

"That's good," he responded with a grin. "Communication is a fine thing to share."

"Uh-huh." I nodded at his words. As he turned to pull the door shut, I glanced at the dying embers of my warming fire and felt that my final good-bye lingered in the room, held within its moment of silence and dignity. It was as I had wanted it to be.

Cuddling close to his chest, I asked, "Where are the horses? Did you ride through the valley? You didn't ride up the drive, did you?"

"I'm not slow witted, if that's what you're askin'."

"No, of course you wouldn't have used the drive." I sat up. "I can walk, you know. Lots of painkillers give a person a false sense of security." I paused in thought, grinned, and said, "At least I can walk for a short distance."

"Whew. That's a lot of questions for a little gal." Gently he released me until my feet touched the cold, damp pavement. Letting his hands travel across my body in a feathery touch, he replied pleasantly, "I want y'all to stand on this wall while I get Joey." His hands went around my waist, and he lifted me effortlessly up to the top of the retaining wall that bordered my bedroom. He paused for a moment as his dover's coat billowed about him in the night winds. "My now. Look in the glass of your bedroom window. Aren't you pretty just standin' there."

Reflected in the wavy glass of the darkened windows, I saw myself awash in moon-splashed light. My favorite nightgown was frayed at the hem, but it was long, giving an illusion of floating that diffused my feet. The blanket, draped across my shoulders, offered warmth as it swayed with the slight breeze. I studied the vision curiously until I heard Joey approach then turned toward the sound.

Gil reached for me in a fluid movement, lifting me onto his saddle, settling me into his arms. I snuggled closer as his hand stroked my hair, gently pushing it behind my ear. Pure contentment filled me, leaving me with a feeling of strength and peace.

The horse carried us up the narrow path where the ridge line nestled among a thousand stars. I felt time gliding past me. As the temperature began to drop, Gil pulled me further into the warmness of his long coat. I inhaled deeply the smells of leather and soap as they mixed with the pine scent of the clear night air.

I felt giddy with joy, and my need to talk surfaced. "I thought angels were different, you know? I didn't think you could cook or eat or dance or—"

"Really?" He seemed surprised and muttered, "Hmm."

"Well, Gil." I wanted to be honest with him. "I just didn't think you could do ordinary stuff."

"That so?" He seemed amused with my comment. "Did y'all think I could make it rain?"

"I wasn't sure." Twisting in his arms, I smiled up at him. "It's a wondrous talent. I'm still in awe." Snuggling closer, I murmured, "You soar above others. I'll bet your classroom was something to behold."

"That it was." He pulled the blanket up and tucked it securely around my neck. "A real heaven high."

I smiled. "Like graduating top of your class?"

"Somethin' like that." He tilted my chin with his free hand, reaching down to brush my lips with his mouth. "Y'all cozy enough?"

"That's nice," I murmured. His breath was warm against my cheek. "And lightning…that's in your job description too. Right?"

Kissing the top of my head, he replied, "I'm might proud of that ability. Took to it right off. Liked the flash."

"Flash and streaks—I was truly impressed."

"Real glad, Miss Dina, that you enjoyed the show."

The wind kicked up a notch, and I commented dryly, "That brother of yours is everywhere."

"So he is. Tell ya what." He shifted me in the saddle, moving me closer to the warmth of his body. "This is better." I felt his love as it infused the space between us.

Resting for a moment in the aura of heat that he had created, I laid my head on his chest. "You know, Gil, now that I think about it, I was surprised that you could make love." I looked at him. "Well, it's just that it's very personal. It's so…" I stumbled for the right words. "Well, it's really hands-on, and you were quite good at it."

"My word, Miss Dina, you are direct." He held me protectively. "Fortunately, I have become accustomed to this charming characteristic that you so lovingly possess."

"Are you going to get into trouble about the physical contact?"

"I'd like to think not. As I recall, makin' love was most natural with you."

"Is that going to be your story?"

"Ya." He took a deep breath. I looked into his eyes and could see that they danced with amusement. "That's it."

"So you're allowed some latitude in how you call a situation?"

Lowering his head, he kissed my temple. "You are not a situation. You, Miss Dina, are a state of mind, a right fine state of mind." He made a clicking sound to Joey as we rounded a bend. "And most important of all," he whispered in my ear, "and I plan to hang my hat on this one, angels are love; they come from it, they live with it, and they offer it. I think I'll add in various forms."

"Seems like you've been rehearsing that one?"

" How's it sound to you?"

"Well, it's a convincing argument. I think it will carry you far." I smiled. "Besides, I'll be right there for you."

"That so?" He drew his coat around me, sealing in the heat. "Just don't help me out, 'less I need it." I sensed his smile as he murmured into my hair, "Heck of a way to start off."

I pushed my back into the broad expanse of his chest. "You do have quite a sense of humor."

"It's been evolvin'."

Timelessness filled the night as sugar-coated stars swam above the treetops. The winds of winter pushed at the horse's pace, muting the sounds of hoofs along the path. As we neared the top, the trees fell away from our sight, and the sky exploded with light like a burst of music.

"It's so lovely," I whispered.

He held me firmly, taking care that the blanket covered my frail body. "That it is." He reached down, and his warm breath nuzzled my ear. "I've had the time of my life, Dina. I wouldn't have missed it for the world."

Looking deeply into the sky, I murmured, "I believe I once said that to you."

"So you did."

I smiled happily as I replied, "The pleasure was mine."

I sensed him reach up and touch the brim of his cowboy hat. Then his lips brushed my cheek as he spoke, "Words given from the heart."

Sitting up abruptly, I faced him. "Wait a minute." I raised my eyebrows. "Can we say things like that?"

"'Course we can." He shrugged. "Long as it's the truth."

I heaved a deep sigh. "I have so many new things to learn."

"Not to worry none. We'll take it nice and slow." Giving Joey a nudge, he spoke quietly, placing a kiss behind my ear. "Say when, sweet Dina. Tell me when you want to fly." Joey gingerly stepped along the narrow path.

Glittering stars filled my vision, but one stood out among the others. The wishing star shimmered high in the heavens. I held it in my vision, letting a feeling of peace float over me as we continued our climb.

Reaching the top of the ridge, I put my hand on the saddle horn, pulling myself up straight. I could feel a shining light deep within myself. Leaving the security of Gil's coat, I let my blanket fall from my shoulders and the radiance soared. Cold air encircled me. The land lay at my feet, tiny dots of moonlit pastures and twinkling lights from farmhouses. This had been my life, and it was beautiful. Breathing in, I nodded at Gil.

The splendor of my wings began to unfold. They shimmered with iridescent light as the moon's glow passed through them, and I felt the tickling flutter of their movement. My senses quickened as a tangle of clouds reached out to me. Gil nudged Joey forward, and the smells of the earth became a part of my past. Wrapped in the soft deepness of night, we flew into the sky, where a lacy trail of stars welcomed me home.